Tara Sue Me wrote her first novel at the age of twelve. It would be twenty years before she picked up her pen to write the second.

After completing several traditional romances, she decided to try her hand at something spicier and started work on *The Submissive*. What began as a writing exercise quickly took on a life of its own, and sequels *The Dominant* and *The Training* soon followed. Originally published online, the trilogy was a huge hit with readers around the world. Each of the books has now been read and reread more than a million times.

Tara kept her identity and her writing life secret, not even telling her husband what she was working on. To this day, only a handful of people know the truth (though she has told her husband). They live together in the southeastern United States with their two children.

Find out more about Tara by visiting her website www.tarasueme. com, or visit her on Facebook www.facebook.com/TaraSueMeBooks and on Twitter @tarasueme.

Praise for Tara Sue Me's breathtakingly sensual Submissive series:

'I HIGHLY recommend *The Submissive* by Tara Sue Me. It's so worth it. This book crackles with sexual lightning right from the beginning . . . It has heart and the characters are majorly flawed in a beautiful way. They aren't perfect, but they may be perfect together. Step into Tara Sue Me's world of dominance and submission. It's erotic, thrilling, and will leave you panting for more' *Martini Reviews*

'For those *Fifty Shades* fans pining for a little more spice on their e-reader . . . the *Guardian* recommends Tara Sue Me's Submissive Trilogy, starring handsome CEO Nathaniel West, a man on the prowl for a new submissive, and the librarian Abby, who is yearning for some

D0130721

More praise for Tara Sue Me:

'Unbelievably fantastic! . . . Nathaniel is something special, and he has that . . . something "more" that makes him who he is and makes me love him more than all the others. Beneath the cold and detached surface there is a sweet and loving man, and I adored how Abby managed to crack his armour a tiny bit at a time . . . I can't wait to continue this beautiful story' *Mind Reader*

'A blazing hot BDSM story between a billionaire and someone who's admired him from afar. I really enjoyed this smoking tale and recommend it to erotic romance readers' *Night Owl Reviews*

'Tara Sue Me's *The Submissive* was a story unlike anything I'd ever read, and it completely captivated me . . . It's an emotional, compelling story about two people who work to make their relationship exactly what they need it to be, and how they're BOTH stronger for it' *Books Make Me Happy*

'I am awed by Tara Sue Me . . . a very powerful book written with grace and style. The characters were brought to life with a love story that will leave you wanting for more' *Guilty Pleasures Book Reviews*

'Very passionate . . . The characters are very easy to relate to and there is a depth to their feelings that is intriguing and engaging . . . intense and very, VERY H-O-T' *Harlequin Junkie*

'This is the kind of erotic writing that makes the genre amazing' *Debbie's Book Bag*

TARA SUE ME

THE Collar

HEADLINE PUBLISHING GROUP
An Hachette UK Company
Carmelite House
50 Victoria Embankment
London EC4Y 0DZ

www.headlineeternal.com
www.headline.co.uk
www.hachette.co.uk

headline
ETERNAL

Copyright © 2015 Tara Sue Me

The right of Tara Sue Me to be identified as the Author of
the Work has been asserted by her in accordance with the
Copyright, Designs and Patents Act 1988.

Published by arrangement with NAL,
A member of Penguin Group (USA) LLC,
A Penguin Random House Company

First published in Great Britain in 2015
by HEADLINE ETERNAL
An imprint of HEADLINE PUBLISHING GROUP

1

Apart from any use permitted under UK copyright law, this publication
may only be reproduced, stored, or transmitted, in any form, or by any means,
with prior permission in writing of the publishers or, in the case of
reprographic production, in accordance with the terms of licences issued
by the Copyright Licensing Agency.

All characters in this publication are fictitious and any resemblance
to real persons, living or dead, is purely coincidental.

Cataloguing in Publication Data is available from the British Library

ISBN 978 1 4722 2652 5

Offset in Perpetua by Avon DataSet Ltd, Bidford-on-Avon, Warwickshire

Printed and bound by CPI Group (UK) Ltd, Croydon, CR0 4YY

MIX
Paper from
responsible sources
FSC
www.fsc.org   FSC® C104740

Headline's polic... ...lable
products and n... ...her
controlled sourc... ...ed to
conform to

Coventry City Council	
TIL*	
3 8002 02250 276 1	
Askews & Holts	Dec-2015
	£7.99

For those who wait with full hearts and empty arms.

Acknowledgments

Writing a book is largely a solitary occupation, but I don't see how it's possible for anyone to do completely alone. I knew when I first wrote Jeff and Dena together in *Seduced By Fire* that their story would hurt my heart. Fortunately, I had many people with me on the journey who gave of their time and talent.

First of all, for everyone who has waited patiently for this story, thank you. It always humbled me to have you read my words. You're my favorite.

Raechel, thank you for taking the time to listen to my ideas and answering all my questions. You make me keep it real; I just wish we lived closer together. I wish all good things for you.

Elle Mason, there were times I feared this book would never see the light of day, and you were always there to offer encouragement or listen to me rant. You have been indispensable, and I hope to one day return the favor.

Cyndy Aleo, I think you read my first three chapters 4083 times. I don't know if that's enough to qualify you for sainthood, but it should be. This was the book that gave me the courage to trust my voice, and you were a big part of that. Thank you for never letting me get by with mere words on a page.

Rebecca Grace Allen, I treasure the time we spent working out the wrinkles in this one and thank you for not letting me take the easy way out. Remember, if anyone asks, I'm just that awesome. The truth is our secret!

Tonya and Lauren, the final version is so very different from what you first saw. You don't know how much I appreciate your thoughts and insights.

Eden Barber, your comments made Jeff and Dena better. I'm so very thankful you were there and willing to help.

Claire Zion, thank you for believing in this story. I know I say it about every book, but THIS one's my favorite. I really mean it this time.

Steve Axelrod, thank you will never be enough. I wouldn't be here without you.

Mr. Sue Me, one day we'll be reunited with our own two angels. If you get there before me, tell them I love them and never forgot. I'll do the same for you.

THE
Collar

Prologue

Abby
New York City

I stood in front of the large picture windows in our New York City penthouse bedroom and gazed outside. It was eleven at night and the outside lights illuminated the room. From behind the glass, everything appeared so peaceful and calm.

Footsteps echoed in the hallway, and I turned to watch Nathaniel come in. I'd left him talking on the phone earlier. *Probably that Charlene woman again.*

I was trying to trust my husband with his choice of employee, but it proved difficult when that employee clearly wanted a different sort of relationship. My fingers drifted to my neck, and I traced the platinum collar I wore. I smirked. Charlene could never even begin to imagine the type of relationship Nathaniel needed.

Nathaniel cleared his throat and inclined his head slightly toward the center of the rug.

Shit. I scurried to the middle of the floor and knelt.

"You left," he said. His voice held no judgment and he wasn't angry, but I thought I heard a trace of disappointment in his words.

"I wanted to give you privacy, Master."

"The call concerned you, so I would have preferred for you to remain. Next time you will wait for my dismissal before leaving."

The call concerned me? That meant it probably hadn't been Charlene after all. "I'm sorry, Master."

"Nothing to apologize for. I didn't give you any instruction regarding your behavior while I was on the phone."

I waited for him to explain how the call concerned me. Instead, he walked to me and held out his hand. Surprised, I let him help me to my feet and we went to sit on the bench at the foot of the bed.

"It was Jeff on the phone," he said.

"Jeff Parks?" I asked. From Delaware? I wondered. Why would he be calling?

"When we were in Delaware, you had a talk with Daniel's submissive, Julie."

"Yes." We'd actually talked twice: the night I met her at the cocktail party and days later, when I interviewed her for my blog, The Secret Life of a Submissive Wife. I'd typed up the interview notes a few days ago. I couldn't imagine anything we chatted about being interesting enough for her Dom to ask Jeff to call mine.

"Julie told Daniel that she wished their BDSM group had long-term couples like us."

"Ah." Yes, I remembered that. I stroked his cheek, the skin

scruffy under my fingertips. "She said we gave her hope for her relationship."

His eyes grew dark with longing and he leaned in close. "I would like nothing more than for us to be an example of a committed, long-term Dominant and submissive couple. Beating the odds. Staying together."

I tried to bring his head down so I could kiss him, but he didn't budge.

"Wait," he whispered.

I swallowed my sigh, trying not to show how impatient I was for him, but he saw right through me anyway.

"In a minute," he said. "Jeff wanted to invite us to their next group meeting and play party. He thought we could lead a discussion and do a demo scene."

We had just started meeting again with our own group, but that didn't preclude us from meeting with another.

He ran his fingers through my hair, and his lips brushed against my cheek, sparking my arousal. "Is that something you're interested in?"

"Yes," I said, not even needing to think about it. "I really liked Julie and Daniel and Jeff. And you know I like doing demos."

He starting working on my buttons, undoing them one at a time until my shirt hung off my shoulders. "I'll call him back and tell him we'll be there." He pushed the material of my bra aside, exposing a nipple, and I groaned as he gave it a slight pinch. "Later, though. Much, much later."

Chapter One

Present day

Jeff Parks knew it was taking all of Dena's willpower not to look his way. And since he had once had that willpower bend to his command, he was well aware of the strength involved. On any other given night, he'd be using his own willpower not to stare, but in light of his recent decision—

"Have you been listening to anything I've said in the last five minutes?" his friend and fellow Dom, Daniel, asked.

Jeff looked back to the man standing at his side. It was late on a Thursday night and their local BDSM group meeting had just ended. No one was in a hurry to leave, though. Everyone wanted to stay around and talk with Nathaniel and Abby. At the moment, Nathaniel stood beside Daniel, grinning. The guest Dominant had led a discussion about keeping D/s relationships from getting stale. Considering the two scenes Jeff had participated in a few months ago with the married couple, staleness wasn't an issue between Nathaniel and Abby.

"Sorry. What?" Jeff asked Daniel.

"Nothing important. Just going over plans for the play party tomorrow night."

"Your house at ten."

"At least you remember that part," Daniel said in his not-quite-teasing voice.

"I've got a lot on my mind." He might as well go ahead and tell Daniel everything. He'd find out eventually and the two of them had been friends for long enough that he deserved to hear the news from Jeff himself. "I'm moving."

"You're what?" Daniel asked in shock.

"Why?" Nathaniel asked at the same time.

Jeff's gaze automatically found Dena again. She was talking with Abby and Julie. Daniel's submissive must have said something funny, because Dena snorted with laughter, shaking her head. Her long blond hair swayed with the movement.

"Ah," Daniel said.

"It's not what you think."

Daniel cocked an eyebrow and crossed his arms. "Julie told me about watching you two play."

Jeff had imagined as much; in fact, he would have been more surprised if Julie had not told Daniel. That night, months ago, he and Dena had played for Julie while she was trying to decide if she could accept her submissive nature. Though that night had helped Daniel and Julie, for Jeff it'd served only as a catalyst for his decision to move. He gave a nod in reply.

Daniel watched the two women. "It slips my mind some-times. Your history with her."

"Nothing slips your mind."

Daniel tipped his head. "Does her work within the group bother you?"

Dena was the most experienced submissive within their local group. As such, she was often called upon to participate in demonstrations. She also worked with Daniel and other senior Dominants when they had mentees.

Jeff had uncollared her years ago, and he knew he no longer had the right or authority to dictate what she did and did not do with other Doms. He told everyone it didn't bother him. The truth was, though, it did.

But that was what he wanted, wasn't it? Wasn't that why he'd worked so hard to keep distance between them?

"No," he said in answer to Daniel's question. "That's not it. Her work here doesn't bother me."

Jeff really didn't want to talk about it. Months later and he still couldn't forget that night. Having Dena kneel before him again, for her to offer herself for their mutual pleasure. To have her back in his house and arms. He wasn't sure he could shake it off.

Dena finally looked his way, saw him watching, and dropped her eyes. It hadn't done her any good, either; odds were she was still dealing with her own memories of the night.

Daniel, of course, noticed Dena's slight response when she caught Jeff's gaze. "How many times have you played since you two broke up?" Daniel asked.

"Once. That time Julie watched."

"I see."

"Moving really doesn't have anything to do with Dena." He wondered if the lie sounded as wooden to Daniel as it did to him.

"Of course it doesn't."

Daniel didn't say anything further, but instead kept his gaze on Jeff as if expecting him to confess everything. Had Jeff not used the same tactic himself numerous times before, it might have worked.

"It doesn't," Jeff stated again. "We split up years ago. We weren't right for each other. She's high society and I'm a high school dropout, a loser."

"Bullshit," Daniel said. "You're a successful man with your own business. And you're my friend."

"And mine," Nathaniel echoed. "In fact, if you tried to tell me we couldn't be friends because of something you did when you were sixteen, I'd kick your ass."

"It's different. Besides, I'm moving to Colorado—at least for a while," Jeff said. "I need to go help Dad with his business. He needs to retire, and he's been asking me to help get everything in order."

Daniel's laughter drew the attention of several group members. "Insurance? You?"

Jeff's father ran an insurance company he'd taken over from his own father. That Jeff wanted nothing to do with it had always been the bane of his dad's existence. Jeff had opened his own business, a security service, eight years ago. It was a two-man operation, small, but profitable enough. They offered personal protection and also security services for other businesses.

"It won't be forever, just a few months. Tom said he could handle the business here." His partner had actually been less than thrilled, but he'd realized he didn't have a choice.

"Hell, you're serious," Nathaniel said.

Jeff just nodded once.

"Have you told Dena?" Daniel finally asked.

He resisted the urge to look at her. "No."

"I heard her father's on the short list for vice president."

Dena's father was a senator with career aspirations that reached to the White House. That, paired with Jeff's past, had been part of what made him decide to break things off with Dena three years ago. He forced himself not to think of the other reasons.

"From what I know of Senator Jenkins, he'll get it." Jeff wasn't surprised at the bitterness in his voice.

The two men looked at him sharply but seemed to sense his unwillingness to discuss the man in question. Jeff had come to terms with the senator a long time ago, but that didn't mean he liked him or wanted to talk about him.

"You're still on to be dungeon monitor tomorrow night?" Daniel asked, changing the subject.

"Yes. I'll be there." His last play party with the group. He wondered if Dena would be attending with anyone. Would his last sight of her be watching as she offered her submission to another? Maybe it would be better that way. If he knew she had someone to look after her, perhaps then he could somehow find the strength to leave her once and for all.

Julie laughed at something Abby West said. Dena hadn't been listening to the lively brunette submissive whose husband, and Dominant, had just finished leading a group discussion. Dena's attention had been on the tiny piece of paper on the floor, because if she looked at it just so, she could see Jeff out of the corner of her eye. He was talking to Daniel and, from all appearances, trying very hard not to look her way.

"So, Dena," Abby said, making her abandon the paper on the floor. "What do you do?"

"I'm a criminal prosecutor for the State of Delaware."

Most of the time when she told people what she did for a living, they looked surprised. Abby simply nodded as if that's what she expected her to say.

"That sounds like a challenge," she replied.

"It is, but I love it and can't imagine doing anything else."

Dena couldn't help but notice that the entire time they talked, Abby was totally engaged in their conversation yet still fully aware of her Master on the other side of the room. Ready to move at either his command or perceived need.

Dena had once served Jeff in a similar manner, and watching Abby was an almost painful reminder of what she had lost.

"They're looking over here again," Julie said, leaning close to Dena. "Daniel not so much, but Jeff can't keep his eyes off you."

"Stop," Dena said, glancing at Abby, but once more the other woman appeared completely unsurprised.

"I'm serious. He hasn't stopped looking this way since the meeting ended."

"Probably because *you* keep looking at *him*." Dena couldn't help but smile at Julie's liveliness. Her friend, the newly collared submissive of one of the group's most senior Dominants, had certainly flourished following her collaring ceremony. If she was honest, most of the time Dena was happy for her, but sometimes it hurt her heart. It was all too easy to remember the heady feeling of belonging to the one you loved.

"Jeff doesn't even know I'm standing here. He's too wrapped up in you."

"Let's change the subject," she said, not wanting to talk about things better left in the past. But a movement behind her caught her attention—was Jeff leaving?—and she couldn't think of anything to change the subject to.

"How are things with you and Daniel?" Abby asked Julie, apparently picking up on Dena's inability to think about anything other than Jeff. "Not that I really need to ask. You both look blissfully in love."

As always, a smile lit up Julie's expression at the mention of her Dom. "He's asked me to move in with him."

That tidbit of information from Julie was enough to capture Dena's attention. "Are you?"

"I don't know. Probably. I'm at his house eighty percent of the time anyway."

"Do I hear a 'but' in there somewhere?" Abby asked.

Julie's gaze drifted to where the men were talking. "It's just a big step, you know? Selling my house. And I've never lived with anyone before." Her hand drifted to her throat. Traced her collar. "But then I think how much I'd like being with him all the time. . . . I know you don't like talking about your past, but with Jeff? Did you?"

Dena suppressed her sigh. So much for changing the subject. "I didn't live with him at first, but I eventually moved in with him. I'd already moved out before he took his collar back, though."

Julie's eyes danced with numerous questions. Friend that she was, she didn't voice them.

"That's all I'm saying about it, other than no, I never once regretted moving in together." She did regret moving out. Maybe if she had stayed, they'd still be together.

Julie nodded. "The commute to the shop would be longer."

"That's something to take into consideration."

"But I don't think it'll really matter all that much. Not when compared to all the positives."

Dena didn't tell her that she'd walk to work, uphill both ways, if it meant she could wear Jeff's collar again and live in his cabin once more.

You just need to get over him, she told herself. *It's never going to be the way it was.*

Dena forced her gaze away from Jeff. "You'll make the right decision. For you and Daniel both."

"Sorry, girls," Abby said, interrupting. "Master just signaled that he's ready to leave. I'll see you both tomorrow."

Dena and Julie said their good-byes and then watched as Abby joined Nathaniel. The tall, dark Dominant watched his wife with a look of masculine appreciation laced with red-blooded lust.

"I really like her," Julie said. Across the room, Nathaniel whispered something in Abby's ear and then ran his hand down her back. "But Nathaniel seems so intense. He's harder to read."

"Jeff's intense. Intense can be good."

Julie didn't look convinced.

"You'll see what I mean at their demo tomorrow night," Dena said.

"We're also doing a demo at the party tomorrow." There was a combination of excitement and nerves in Julie's voice.

"I remember. How do you feel about it?" It would be her first time playing in public. Dena made a mental note to call her before the party so she could walk her through any-last minute jitters.

"I'm looking forward to it, but at the same time, I'm not quite ready for it to be tomorrow yet."

Dena laughed. "I understand completely."

"More than anything, I'm excited about showing Master—"

"Showing me what?" the man in question asked, coming up behind Julie and wrapping his arms around her.

Daniel was almost the polar opposite of Jeff. Not just physically, although Jeff had dark hair and eyes compared to Daniel's dirty-blond hair and blue eyes. The men's personalities differed, too. Yet even with Daniel's easygoing and friendly ways, Dena had always been drawn to the more introverted Jeff.

"We're talking about tomorrow night," Dena said, looking over Daniel's shoulder to see if she could find Jeff. He didn't appear to be in the room anymore.

"He just left," Daniel said.

"Oh, I wasn't . . ." she started, but then stopped at Daniel's expression and rolled her eyes. "All right, I was looking for him."

He gave a self-satisfied nod before dipping his head and whispering into Julie's ear. Julie whispered back, lifting an arm to wrap around his neck.

"Okay, you two," Dena said. "That's it. I have to leave. You guys are so sweet my teeth hurt."

And she was hoping, more than just a tiny bit, that she would run into Jeff in the parking lot. She walked quickly, but not so fast that it would be obvious she was rushing, down the hallway and out the community center's main door to the parking lot. Just in time to watch the taillights of Jeff's truck pulling out.

"You wouldn't have done or said anything anyway," she said out loud in the darkness. What was left to say?

She replayed the evening in her head as she drove to her apartment. In her mind she tried to see if Julie had been right about Jeff watching her most of the evening. She'd felt the heavy weight of his stare numerous times, but she'd acted as if she didn't.

A foolish game, she realized. They weren't in grade school. The next time he stared at her, she'd call him on it and insist on knowing what his problem was. She smiled at her decision. She'd done it in the past. He really should know better.

He'd be at the party the following night, but acting as dungeon monitor. Since it'd be his responsibility to ensure order and safety, he really wouldn't be free to pay her any attention. It would be the same as always, each of them pretending there was nothing between them. No past, no present, and sure as hell no future.

The thought made her feel empty inside.

She parked her car and made her way to her apartment, the empty feeling growing with each step. She was in her thirties, unmarried, lived alone, and didn't even date seriously. Sure, she loved her job, but she knew that wasn't enough to keep her satisfied in the long term. And though reminiscing about the past served no purpose, she imagined briefly what life could have been like if she'd made different choices.

"Waste of time," she muttered to herself. "Does no good living backward."

She unlocked her door and bent down to pick up the delivery menu some food joint had shoved under her door. Maybe it'd be something new. She was always on the lookout for new take-out places.

But instead of a menu, it was a handwritten note, and she felt faint when she read the words printed with red ink.

Better watch out, bitch.

Her body shook, but she composed herself enough to close and dead bolt the door. She glanced around her apartment. The lamp in the living room gave off enough light for her to see that nothing looked out of place.

Her cat, Bentley, was curled up on the couch. He stretched, then hopped down to welcome her home by weaving in between her legs. The apartment was secure. No one could have gotten in, but she picked Bentley up and checked all the rooms anyway.

When she finished her perusal, she went back to the note. Her first thought was to call the police, but she quickly decided that was not the best thing to do. With her father being who he was, word would get out, and before she knew it, she'd have around-the-clock security. While that could be a good thing, she'd worked too hard to get out from under her father's scrutiny to throw away her freedom.

She sank down onto the couch. She had to do something, though. Things were starting to escalate. At first there were the phone calls she didn't think much about. They could easily be written off as crank calls. But then they started happening in the middle of the night, and she knew it was more than a wrong number.

When she answered, no one ever spoke on the line. Whoever was calling simply breathed into the receiver. Now, unless it was a number she recognized, she let it go to voice mail. But that was akin to ignoring the problem in the hopes it'd go away. And problems never went away on their own.

She couldn't prove the person who'd been calling her was the same person who left the note, but nothing else made sense. Harassing by phone she could sweep to the side. A note slid under her door, she could not. The note could be from anyone: a criminal she put away, an enemy of her father's, or simply an attention seeker who wanted fifteen minutes of fame. There were too many variables, and the only thing she knew for sure was she couldn't ignore it. Whoever it was knew where she lived, and while she was reluctant to go to the authorities, she wasn't stupid.

She needed someone knowledgeable and discreet. Someone she could trust not to run to the police or the media. But someone experienced in personal protection.

There was only one person she knew like that. With a resolute sigh, she admitted the inevitable. She needed Jeff.

Jeff was in the middle of packing up his kitchen when his cell phone rang. With a huff he placed the half-filled box on the countertop and glanced at the caller ID.

"Daniel?" he answered.

"Jeff, hey," his friend replied. "I need your help."

He leaned a hip against the counter. "Sure. What can I do?"

"Julie's been up all night, throwing up."

"Sorry to hear that. Hope she gets better soon."

"I'll tell her, but listen, about tonight."

"The play party?"

"Yes, would you mind taking over? Since it's at my guest-house, I'll serve as dungeon monitor, but I need someone to do the demo."

Daniel wouldn't play with anyone except Julie now that he'd collared her, so Jeff wasn't surprised he was looking for someone to take over. He just wasn't sure he was in the mood to be that person.

"I thought Nathaniel and Abby were doing the demo?"

"They are, but they're doing a more advanced session. Julie and I were going to do something less intense." His friend sighed. "Didn't you hear anything at the meeting?"

Jeff decided not to answer the question. Hell no, he hadn't been paying attention at the meeting. He'd been watching Dena. "You sure Julie's really sick and it's not just nerves at playing in public for the first time?"

"I should be offended you even asked me that, but I suppose it's a reasonable question. Yes, I'm sure she's sick. I was with her all night, holding her hair back for her."

With Daniel's words, a memory threatened to wash over him, and he grabbed onto the counter to steady himself.

She was on her knees on the bathroom floor, rocking back and forth. Between bouts of vomiting, she held her lower abdomen. She hurt and there wasn't a damn thing he could do. She wasn't even happy he stayed in the bathroom with her. He'd never felt so helpless in his life.

"This isn't normal," he said as another spasm hit her. "You need to call the doctor."

"I'm fine. It affects everyone differently."

"Not like this. Either you call or I will."

She mumbled something that may have been in agreement with him, but then a particularly hard wave of nausea overwhelmed her and, no matter what her wishes, he moved behind her. Gently, he pulled her hair back while she emptied what was left in her stomach. Afterward, she col-

lapsed into his arms and he silently cursed himself for being useless. It wasn't something he was used to, and he hated that he couldn't take her pain away. So instead he held her, stroked her hair, and whispered that everything was going to be okay.

But when she moved, there was blood between her legs and they both knew things would never be okay again.

"Jeff?"

He shook his head. "Huh? Sorry. What?"

"This is starting to become a bad habit. I was giving you a rundown of what I'd planned to demo. Did you hear any of it?"

"No."

Daniel sighed. "Maybe we should just cancel the whole thing."

"No. It'll be fine. Repeat what you were saying."

"We were just going to do a light flogging scene. I thought we should offer something more basic, especially with the increased interest in the lifestyle."

"Yes, that's fine. Who have you lined up to sub?" The silence from the other end of the phone made him suspicious. "Daniel?"

"I haven't called any subs yet. I wanted to discuss it with you first."

"I'll call. Who's on the list?" He wasn't all that happy to potentially be playing with someone new. But it'd be a light scene, and as long as they were able to talk some beforehand, it'd be okay. Besides, once he found out who was free, he could probably pick someone he knew.

"Well, funny thing." Daniel cleared his throat, and Jeff had a feeling what he said next wouldn't be funny at all. "There's only one sub available, and it's only because she had a business conference fall through at the last second."

"Lucky for us. Who is it?"

"Dena."

Jeff arrived early at the party the next night. His demo with Dena was scheduled after Nathaniel and Abby's. Since they were using the same room, he couldn't set up yet. To pass the time, he found a seat and settled in to watch the couple he'd met in Delaware.

He'd seen Abby three times. The first time, she'd been drunk at a nightclub and found herself in trouble. Jeff had been the one to help her and get her home to Nathaniel. And hadn't that been a surprise? He happened to be in New York only because of a meeting he had scheduled with Nathaniel West.

When Nathaniel found out he was a Dominant, he'd invited Jeff to participate in two scenes he had planned. One was just the three of them, but the second involved two other men.

In the far corner of the room, Nathaniel was setting up for his demo. Tonight the scene would involve the two of them only. Though the two scenes he'd been in with the couple hadn't involved much participation on his part.

He still smiled remembering how Nathaniel had made clear in no uncertain terms exactly what he was allowed to do with Abby and what he was not. Jeff respected that. It was a Dom's responsibility to ensure his submissive was treated appropriately. For Abby, that meant he'd been invited to watch and there would be no sexual touching. He'd heard Nathaniel West was a hard businessman to deal with, but he had the feeling that was nothing compared to Dominant Nathaniel.

Right now he had Abby bound with her arms above her head, held in place by chains bolted to the ceiling. They had their eyes locked on each other and he spoke softly to her. Abby nodded at whatever he said, but a noticeable shiver shook her body. Nathaniel kissed her briefly and then blindfolded her. It wasn't until he slipped earplugs into her ears that Jeff understood the shiver. Sensory deprivation could be intense, especially in a strange place.

Nathaniel ran his hands over her body a few times to ground her and then addressed the growing crowd. "As you can see, I've used both a blindfold and earplugs on my submissive. By taking away her ability to see and hear, I've put her in a very vulnerable position. And she's bound, which further intensifies that vulnerability."

Jeff glanced around the room. Nathaniel had certainly drawn a crowd. In addition to Daniel, who was overseeing the demo, there were about ten people in the room watching from an appropriate distance. A fairly high number for this early in the evening. Dena, he noted, wasn't present.

"What are some things I need to keep in mind as the scene continues?" Nathaniel asked the crowd. Several people replied back, and he acknowledged each person's answer. Yet even though he spoke effortlessly with the group gathered, he remained by Abby's side, completely aware, it seemed, of her every move, no matter how slight.

"I haven't gagged her for two reasons," he continued. "One, she needs the ability to safeword, though I could have given her a bell to drop. And the second reason is I want to hear her, because my Abigail makes the most delightful sounds when I have her like this."

Jeff noticed additional people had entered the room. He stood up and walked toward the back in case Daniel needed help.

"With her sight and hearing gone," Nathaniel said, stepping behind her, "her sense of touch is heightened. Keep in mind, she hasn't heard any of what I've been saying." Then, to prove his point, he addressed her. "Abigail, if you can hear me, say, 'Yes, Master.'"

There was silence from the bound woman.

"When you have your submissive in a position like this, you need to remember that sensory deprivation can be very scary. Of course, it's up to you if you choose to alleviate that fear or ramp it up."

There were chuckles from the Dominants watching and mumbled protests from the submissives.

Nathaniel grinned. "I'm not opposed to a good mind fuck, but Abigail has been a good girl this week." He cocked his head. "Mostly. So I won't be too mean. Regardless, she always yelps the first time I touch her when she's like this."

As if proving his point, he ran one finger down the inside of her arm, and there was a faint murmur from the crowd when Abby squeaked in surprise.

"So deep inside her mind," Nathaniel said, continuing to run his hands up and down her body. "She expects my touch, but isn't sure when or where it's coming from. Every move I make is so much more intense because it's the only thing she has to focus on."

He had captured the attention of the entire group. No one moved as they watched him stroke the beautifully bound submissive. He moved his hands against her in a slow and sensual manner, eliciting a low moan from Abby.

"One downside of removing your submissive's hearing is the inability to talk with her. She can't hear your questions. It seems obvious, but you'd be surprised at how many Dominants forget this in the middle of a scene." He placed a kiss on the nape of Abby's neck and she sighed. Nathaniel continued speaking with a smile. "She won't be able to hear you give permission for her release. Again, play that any way you want. I told Abigail before we started that she could come whenever she wished. She replied that she didn't think she'd be able to come at all. I'm taking that as a challenge."

Jeff shook his head. From what he knew of Nathaniel, the man wouldn't stop until he'd made her come.

Nathaniel slipped the fingers of one hand inside her while remaining pressed against her back. While he worked her body, it seemed as if he closed out the crowd around them, focusing all his attention on his wife. Though Jeff had watched many scenes in the past, the one before him seemed somehow more intimate than the others. Nathaniel and Abby appeared to breathe in unison, they were so connected.

"Oh, fuck!" Abby panted.

"Give me what I want, baby," Nathaniel murmured, obviously knowing she couldn't hear.

Abby rose to her toes and started babbling German. Jeff chuckled, remembering it was her way of delaying orgasm.

"None of that now." Nathaniel shifted his fingers. "You're going to come for me."

She was obviously fighting it for some reason, but Nathaniel was undeterred, rocking his hips against her backside while still working his fingers.

"You're going to come, and you're going to come now." His mouth was at her neck as he spoke; then he nipped her shoulder.

"Holy fucking shit!" she shouted, the German forgotten as her husband obviously then did something new with his hand. "I can't . . . FUCK."

Her body stiffened briefly, and then she babbled as her climax rippled through her. A satisfied hum fell over the crowd, and Nathaniel kissed her shoulder and pulled out the earplugs.

"That's my girl," he said before unbuckling her and removing the blindfold. He looked around the room, searching, and his gaze fell on Jeff's.

A room, Jeff thought. He'd want a private room to take her to.

He pushed back from the wall, found Daniel, and mouthed, "Blue bedroom." Daniel nodded in agreement. The blue bedroom was used exclusively for aftercare at parties. Jeff waited until Nathaniel had Abby gathered in his arms before leading him down the hall to the bedroom.

He checked the room to make sure it had an adequate stock of blankets and water; then he closed the door behind him, giving the couple the privacy they needed. Jeff was sure people would have questions for the visiting pair, but it was understood those would have to wait.

Out in the hallway, he looked again for Dena but didn't see her. He'd go set up the room for their demo and then check again for her.

She still hadn't made it to the party when he finished setting up for their demo. Impatient and worried, he waited for her outside on one of the guesthouse's private porches. The possibility she wouldn't show existed, he decided, recalling the conversation he had with her when he'd called her about the demo.

"Julie's sick? But I spoke to her last night and she was fine."

"I'm just telling you what Daniel told me."

"I swear, if I didn't know her better . . ."

"Yes?"

"Nothing."

"Listen, Dena, if you're not up to it or don't want to—"

"No. It's fine. I'll be there."

Jeff saw the headlights of her car approaching and slung his bag over his shoulder. As he watched, she parked and got out of the car. Wrapping her coat tightly around her body, she glanced over her shoulder before walking toward him.

She nodded at his bag. "I thought you said basics? You pack your entire playroom?"

God, he loved her wit. In the years since their split, he'd been with enough women to know he'd never find her equal. Aside from her physical beauty, she had a lively intellect and a carefree attitude. And though she was a brilliant attorney who could command an entire courtroom, it was when she submitted herself to his control that she fully came alive.

"Don't ask a question you don't want the answer to," he said. Half the fun of play was getting inside her mind, and he'd always enjoyed catching her off guard.

As expected, his words sobered her up. "You're right, Sir. I apologize."

"You were almost late," he said.

"But I wasn't."

He nodded. "We're going to be in the sitting room off the kitchen. I want you in position in twenty minutes. Proper position this time. None of that sloppy business like the last time, unless you want to see exactly what I have in my bag in long and excruciating detail. Understood?"

Her chin lifted. "Completely, Sir."

Seventeen minutes later he walked into the sitting room and frowned. Dena was nowhere to be seen. She had three minutes left, but it wasn't like her not to be at least five minutes early. After Nathaniel's demo, he'd positioned a padded table in the room. Daniel had planned only to demonstrate a flogging, but Jeff had decided to add a bondage element as well.

He glanced over the people moving through the guesthouse. The crowd had grown since the earlier demo, mostly new people, though he did recognize quite a few of those present. His gaze fell on a large clock. One minute left. Was she baiting him?

Five minutes after the demo was supposed to start, he looked across the room to Daniel and raised an eyebrow. Daniel looked out into the hallway and shook his head.

Jeff sighed. *Well, fuck.*

"Sorry to disappoint everyone, but it looks like we're not going to be having the scheduled demo," Jeff said to the crowd.

There was murmuring as the crowd broke up. Nathaniel had been standing near the back with his arms around Abby, but as the crowd left, he took her hand and led her to where Jeff stood.

"What's happening?" Nathaniel asked.

"Missing a submissive," Jeff said. "I know she's here. I spoke to her when she arrived. Gave her plenty of time to get ready."

Abby whispered something to Nathaniel. At his nod, she spoke. "Is it Dena, Sir?"

"Yes. Have you seen her?"

"Our paths crossed in the bathroom. I was walking out, and she was walking in. I only remember because she was on the phone and I thought that odd."

Jeff glanced at Nathaniel. "Do you mind if Abby goes to see if she's still there and if everything's okay?"

"Of course not." He turned to his wife. "Abigail?"

"Be right back, Master," she said, spinning to walk out the door.

"Has she done this before?" Nathaniel asked.

"Never. She's always on time. Early even." Jeff looked up as Daniel came back into the room. "Is she ever late for a mentor session?"

"No. She's always early," Daniel said.

So what was her problem tonight? Jeff wondered. He had a sinking suspicion it was him. He was the reason she hadn't shown up. Hell, she hadn't sounded like she wanted to do the demo in the first place. That much had been obvious when he'd called her.

"You probably should have asked another Dom to run the demo with her," he told Daniel.

"No," he answered. "She should have spoken up if she had an issue with it. She's experienced enough to know better."

"Where is everyone?"

The three men turned toward the door. Dena stood there with her hands on her hips. She was still wearing her party outfit, which was against the rules for a submissive in a demo.

"And she should know better than *that*," Daniel added with a pat on Jeff's shoulders. "You were the Dom in the demo; I'll let you handle her."

"Thanks," Jeff muttered. He'd been looking forward to the demo with Dena; this coming confrontation he was not looking forward to.

"Dena." Nathaniel nodded to her on his way out.

"Sirs," she said as he and Daniel walked by her.

The two men closed the door behind them, leaving Jeff and Dena alone.

"Where did everyone go?" Dena asked. "I thought we were going to do a demo? Why—"

Jeff snapped his fingers, and she stopped talking. "On your knees. Now. No talking unless I ask you a question."

She huffed but knelt down where she was.

"The demo was scheduled to start twenty minutes ago. You didn't show up, so I canceled it."

"I was just running a little late—"

"Did I ask a question?" He wasn't sure what had gotten into her tonight. She was never this disrespectful or belligerent.

"No, Sir."

"Then you are not to speak."

She exhaled deeply.

"I'm extremely disappointed in your behavior tonight. I had a scene planned and prepared. I came early to set up. You didn't even have the decency to show up on time. That was your only job tonight—to show up on time—and you didn't do it. Then, when you did decide to stroll in, you showed up in your clothes."

He kept her in his sight while he talked. She was shaking a bit. Probably afraid of what he was going to do. "What do you have to say for yourself?"

"I lost track of time, Sir."

"Lost track of time? I've known you for years and you have never been late. Are you okay? Is there something going on?" Because her behavior was so out of character, he had to be sure.

"No, Sir. I'm fine."

He walked to where she knelt. "Look at me." When she lifted her head, he continued. "I'm not fine. I'm the opposite of fine. It's your fault, and you're going to deal with the consequences."

Chapter Two

Seven years ago

Dena took a deep breath and knocked on the door to the large two-story house that stood just on the outskirts of Wilmington, Delaware. Though she'd been a sexual submissive for four years, she always felt slightly apprehensive when showing up at her first function with a new group.

She'd recently taken a job in the district attorney's office and had moved to Wilmington a few weeks ago. Being somewhat settled in her new apartment and job, she'd searched for a local BDSM group. The day before, she'd attended a group meeting and filled out paperwork so that she could join the play party tonight.

The group's dynamics had impressed her. They were structured, without being overly so. The guidelines were simple, fair, and in place to provide safety and confidentiality. She felt comfort in knowing her previous Dominant would have never been accepted.

"The asshole," she mumbled while waiting for the door to open. Then she shook her head; she wasn't going to think about him tonight. This was a new start, and she was ready to meet new people.

The front door opened and a guy with a shaved head and a friendly smile greeted her with a warm "Hello."

She shook his hand and noted he wore a green bracelet, a switch, according to the group's color system. As a submissive, Dena's bracelet was red. A Dom or Domme would have a black one.

"Hi," she said. "Dena J."

The guy looked over his clipboard, and a frown came over his face. "I don't see your name, Dena J."

"My first meeting was yesterday. I filled out the papers there."

"Your name should still be here." He looked up. "I'm sorry. I can't let you in."

She squared her shoulders and tried not to show how disappointed she was. "I filled out and turned in all the paperwork yesterday. I'm all dressed up." She had bought a new corset specifically for the party. It was a deep blue and black lace piece that gave her slim figure curves. "Isn't there something you can do? Please."

His frown deepened. "I really can't, but——" He turned and looked over his shoulder, speaking to someone behind him. "Master Parks, I need your help, Sir." He turned back to Dena and said, "Stay here for a minute."

A few people looked her way in curiosity and she sighed. There went her hope of blending in unnoticed. Maybe she should leave, try again next month, or try a new group altogether.

"Is there a problem?"

The voice was low and deep, and something about it made her heart pound. She looked up and met the eyes of the voice's owner. He was tall and well built, with short dark hair and dark eyes that were somber and serious. There was something in the way he moved, though, the way his long legs covered the distance to her, that exuded sexual confidence. He came to a stop right in front of her, crossed his arms, and frowned. Her gaze slid from his face to his muscular biceps and then to the floor. The entire time, her heart continued its racing beat.

"This is Dena J," the guy who opened the door said. "She went to the meeting yesterday and filled out paperwork, but her name's not on the list."

"I wasn't there," Master Parks said. "I can't say one way or another."

There was a long silence while Dena kept looking at the floor, but she felt his eyes on her so she knew he was still considering what to do with her. It took almost all of her self-discipline and years of experience as a submissive to remain still under his scrutiny.

"Look at me," he finally said, and she knew he wasn't talking to the greeter.

Her gaze met his once more, and his dark eyes searched hers. It was so intense, it was as if he could somehow peel away the mask she always wore and little by little expose her soul. She felt more naked than she'd ever been in her entire life.

"Dena," he said.

Her reply was a whisper. "Yes, Sir?"

"I understand you were at the meeting yesterday and somehow your paperwork got lost?"

Maybe he had some blank forms with him. She'd just fill them out again. "Yes, Sir."

But he didn't move to get papers or anything. He just kept staring at her. "I'll vouch for her," he finally said, not once looking at the greeter.

"Thank you, Master Parks," the man said.

He simply nodded in reply and motioned for Dena to follow him. "Come with me. I'll show you where you can put your coat."

When he turned and walked toward a hallway, she shivered. Partly because of his scrutiny, but even more so because as she'd looked into his eyes, she'd observed his own secrets. He, too, wore a mask. She had the overwhelming urge to see what was under it.

For the moment, though, she followed behind him as he wove in and out of the small groups of other people in the house. He nodded to a few, spoke a greeting to one or two. There were a variety of people in attendance. A few couples appeared to be paired up, but they passed a group of four women who all watched as Master Parks walked by.

At the end of the hallway, he pushed open a door to a small bedroom. A pile of coats covered the twin bed in the middle of the room.

"You can leave your coat in here."

She unbuckled the belt of her raincoat and shrugged out of it. "Thank you, Sir."

She'd expected him to leave, but instead he watched as she put her coat on top of the pile. Quite on purpose, she stretched out as she laid it down, knowing that by doing so, she'd be showing off her toned legs. She mentally patted herself on the back for selecting the miniskirt to wear with the corset instead of the long, flowing one.

Makes getting up at five a.m. to jog worth it.

"How long have you been a submissive?" he asked.

"Four years, Sir."

"You've played in public?"

"Yes, Sir."

She turned around to find he was, in fact, watching her and with a look that clearly said he knew exactly what she'd been up to. A faint smile touched his lips. Just barely noticeable. But there. A surge of victory shot through her.

"Four years," he repeated. "The assumption would be that because of your experience, you don't need a detailed rundown of protocol." Before she could respond, he continued. "I've learned, however, that assumptions typically come back to kick your ass, so I'll give you a rundown anyway."

"Thank you, Sir." She was relieved. She'd read the paperwork, but not everything had been spelled out as clearly as she preferred. Out of habit, she shifted her gaze to the floor.

"Look at me, Dena." He spoke softly and waited until she lifted her head. "I can't speak for other Dominants in the group, but I want your eyes on me when we talk unless I tell you differently."

"Thank you, Sir," she replied. Something about the gruffness of his voice made her hyperaware of how long it'd been since she'd played with anyone. She wondered if his touch would match the roughness of his voice.

He nodded. "The group safe word is 'red.' Say it and the scene stops immediately. You'll probably also have a few members come by to make sure you're okay. Dungeon monitors have a yellow armband on. If you have questions or need anything, see one of them. As you've already noticed, no one is allowed inside who hasn't been approved. But if someone comes up to you and you have any questions about their character or intent before you play, feel free to ask me."

She wondered if he was at the party with anyone. He was extremely good-looking in a rough and rustic kind of way. She'd always been attracted to his type, probably because it was so different from her father.

Stop thinking about your father!

"The two rooms upstairs are for demos," Master Parks continued. "Basement is free space to play—just make sure everything's clean before you leave. Most Dominants bring their own toys, since we're rather attached to our favorites. Kitchen is neutral; no play allowed. Only certain members are allowed to play with doors closed. Again, if you have any questions, ask a DM or me."

She nodded.

"I think that's all. Do you have any questions?"

"Just one, Sir."

His forehead wrinkled as if he were trying to decide what he left out. "Yes?"

"What's your favorite?"

"Favorite what?"

"Toy." Her mind swam with images of him holding a flogger, smacking her backside with a crop, blindfolding her. "You said most Dominants had a favorite. I was wondering if you did."

His eyes darkened and his lips parted just a tiny bit. He had really full, kissable lips. She bet he had nice teeth, too. Probably amazing what he could do with those lips and teeth.

"Actually," he said, taking a step closer to her. There was very little space between them now; her belly tightened at how close he was. "I'm more of a bondage guy." He captured her wrist, and his hands were warm and strong. Softly, he whispered in her ear, "How about you, Dena? What's your favorite?"

She licked her lips. When had her mouth gotten so dry? And could he see how hard she was breathing? Probably, she decided. But instead of feeling shame at how much he turned her on, she squared her shoulders and answered, "All of it, Sir. I like all of it."

Jeff Parks had taken one look at the beautiful blonde while she stood in the foyer and had known immediately she was out of his league. As a man who'd been raised in the lower middle class, it didn't take much for him to recognize the look of someone with a completely different upbringing. Everything about her screamed upper class, from her perfect makeup and meticulously styled hair right down to the neatly painted red toenails peeking out of her ridiculously high heels.

She reminded him of an angel, she was so perfectly put together. And though she was at a BDSM play party, he knew he wasn't anywhere near angelic enough to be in her world. He'd faltered briefly when she'd said she had four years' experience and then again when she'd asked what his favorite toy was, all the while looking at him with the bluest eyes he'd ever seen.

Even now, standing in the kitchen, watching her move around the house, he wondered if he'd made a huge mistake in not asking if she wanted to play. If he closed his eyes, he could still smell the faint scent of jasmine that he'd first noticed when he'd taken her wrist.

"You plan on asking her to play, or are you going to sit here and stare at her all night?"

He turned at the sound of Daniel's voice. "I don't know what you're talking about."

"Don't even deny it." Daniel nodded toward Dena. "The new blonde. I was thinking of asking her, but from the looks of it, you'll pound anyone who approaches her into the ground."

Jeff's body tensed as a relatively new Dom walked up to her. She turned and smiled at the guy but peeked toward Jeff out of the corner of her eye. The tension left him when she sweetly shook her head.

"Looks like someone's waiting for you," Daniel said as the guy walked off.

"Shut the fuck up."

"Or maybe she was looking at me." Daniel pushed off from the counter. "Wonder if she looks as good with that corset off? Only one way to find out."

Damned if he was going to let Daniel have her. Though he probably should. They were both so much alike: blond good looks, wealthy, full of life.

"Sit down," he said to his friend, surprised at how rough his voice sounded.

Daniel smiled in victory and sat on a nearby barstool. "About damn time."

Jeff pretended not to hear him as he walked toward Dena.

She sat in the living room, a plate of cheese balanced on her knees and an open bottle of water on the floor by her feet.

"Mind if I sit down?" he asked.

"Master Parks," she said, shifting the plate to one hand and attempting to stand up. "Please, have a seat."

He motioned for her to sit back down and took a seat beside her.

"How's your evening going?" he asked.

She glanced at the floor briefly, but he was pleased to note she looked up and met his eyes without being told. "Very nice, Sir. Everyone's so friendly."

"And yet you're sitting here by yourself."

"Not anymore," she said with a seductive grin.

His cock hardened at her words, and he recalled what Daniel had said. Had she been waiting for him?

"You're an attractive woman," he said. "I'm sure you could play with just about any Dominant you wanted."

She was a woman who knew exactly how desirable she was. She didn't blush or brush off his compliment. Instead, she simply tipped her head in agreement. "I've never been one to play with just *any* Dominant, Sir."

He decided to see if Daniel had been right after all. They were in the living room, where light play was allowed. "Take your shoes off and tell me how long you've lived in Wilmington."

If she had no interest in him or playing, he knew she'd refuse. He braced himself for that possibility.

Ever so smoothly, she put her plate aside and unbuckled her heels, slid her feet out of them. "I moved into the area four weeks ago. I just took a new job."

"Are you wearing anything under the skirt?"

Her eyes darkened. "Yes, Sir."

"Good, because I didn't ask why you moved here. Stand up and take the skirt off."

She didn't hesitate at all. Moving quickly, she stood up, slid the skirt over her hips and down her legs, stepped out of it, and handed it to him. "I'm sorry for not following directions, Sir."

Fuck, he wanted her. She was gorgeous and an experienced submissive. She moved with the self-confidence of a person unafraid to admit her needs and wants. And, quite possibly, she wanted him, too.

Still, he wasn't one to jump into a scene without knowing a bit more about his partner. He fisted his hands against his thighs, forcing himself to take it slow and easy.

"Tell me about your worst experience as a submissive," he continued.

For just a second, he thought she wouldn't do it. He'd asked her something she wasn't prepared for, and it unsettled her. She had a poker face a lot of the time, but every so often he could see hints of the woman underneath. A desire to seduce that woman and claim the submissive inside was growing within him quickly.

"My worst experience," she said, "was the day I left my old Master. It was more than knowing I'd disappointed him. I actually *felt* his disappointment. It was like it burned me and weighted me down and picked me apart all at the same time. He was my Master, had been for almost a year. I'd lived to serve and please him. To knowingly do something he didn't agree with? It killed a part of me."

There was something more to the story, he could tell. Even if he couldn't sense it from her expression, what he knew of her in the little time they'd spoken told she wouldn't have left her Dominant without cause.

He had a feeling she'd tell him what it was if he asked, but he decided to leave that conversation for another day.

"Thank you for sharing that with me. I know it wasn't easy," he said. "Now tell me about your best experience as a submissive."

She gave him a seductive smile. "My best experience was the day I left my old Master."

He covered his shock, or at least, he hoped he did. "How so?"

"I was new in the lifestyle when I agreed to wear his collar. I didn't know my own limits and, more important, my worth. He was never physically abusive, but mentally, he wore me down. After a time, I discovered he didn't respect me, didn't value what I brought to the relationship." She shrugged. "I'm a submissive, not a doormat. I deserved more, and I left him so I could find it."

With every word she spoke, she impressed him more and more. He required honesty from anyone he played with, and she obviously understood its importance.

She crossed her legs and swung her foot. Once again, he was struck by her beauty. The outward aspects of it were obvious, but he had a feeling her inner beauty was even more stunning.

He realized she hadn't taken a bite of anything since he'd sat down. He wouldn't think she'd be waiting for him to give her permission to eat, but he should probably make sure. "Don't let me keep you from eating."

She took a block of cheddar from the plate and popped it in

her mouth. His gaze was drawn to her red lips, and he watched as she chewed and swallowed. It was damn near the most erotic thing he'd ever seen in his life.

There was no use denying it: he wanted her. Badly.

But interestingly enough, he wanted to get to know her better just as much. He shouldn't, though. He wasn't meant for her kind. She was too beautiful, too wealthy, too *much*.

He didn't care.

He scooted closer to her. "I see this going one of two ways. One, I take you down to the basement and put my ropes to good use. Or two, we call it a night, I take you to dinner tomorrow, and we see where we go from there."

She leaned in to him. "Honestly, Sir, I'm a greedy submissive and I want them both."

His cock stirred. Oh, yes, she was going to be a delight to master. He traced her lips. "But think of how much better it'll be when I finally take you after you've been thinking about it all night."

She kissed his finger. "Very well, Sir. Tomorrow night it is."

"And just to make sure you stay in the right frame of mind, no playing with yourself or coming until I grant permission." He leaned even closer and whispered in her ear, "And believe me when I say, you don't want to disobey me. My punishments are a bitch."

Jeff picked her up at her apartment the next evening at five. The elegant building was surrounded by pristine landscape and expensive cars, the whole scene just confirming his suspicion about her being a wealthy woman. He felt out of place pulling through the gated entrance to the apartment complex in his truck.

Fuck it, he told himself. It's just dinner.

She opened the door at his knock and smiled. "Hello, Sir."

She looked different than she had the night before. Her makeup was softer, more natural, and her long hair flowed freely around her shoulders. She wore a simple blue dress and looked just as stunning in it as she had in the corset.

"You can call me Jeff."

She closed the door behind her and locked it. "Thanks, but if you don't mind, I prefer *Sir*."

She wanted to keep the lines clear, and while he understood that, part of him rebelled. "*Sir* is fine," he said instead.

They walked in silence to the truck, and he opened the passenger-side door for her.

"Italian okay with you?" he asked once he'd pulled out of the apartment complex.

"It's one of my favorites."

Her words from the previous evening came back to him, and he smiled. "Is that so?"

Her eyebrows crinkled in concentration. "Italian? Yes."

He dropped his voice. "I thought you said you didn't have a favorite. That you liked all of it."

Her laugh was soft and seductive. "How very remiss of me to forget. I did say that, didn't I?"

"You did. I hope you didn't forget what else we discussed."

"No, Sir." Her breathing had changed, becoming ragged.

He'd given a lot of thought to how he wanted the evening to

go. They'd have dinner, get to know each other a little better; then, depending on how things went, he'd see if she wanted to play together. They could exchange checklists and get together in a few days.

He had a simple playroom at his home, but he wouldn't assume she'd be willing to go to an almost perfect stranger's house. The submissives he knew had safety calls set up, and while he could appreciate that, he wanted anyone he played with to feel secure even without a safety call.

Still, even though nothing would happen tonight, they could have fun.

"Remind me what my command was," he ordered.

"I'm not allowed to play with myself or come until you give permission."

"Did you play with yourself or come?"

"No, Sir."

He believed her, but still asked, "And why should I take you at your word?"

"Because I want our first experience together to be pleasurable. Because I want to please you. And because you said your punishments were a bitch."

He glanced at her. Her hands were fisted on her knees. "That's a lot of becauses," he said.

"I had to keep coming up with them."

"Why?"

"Because I really wanted to come last night."

She didn't have to say more. He knew exactly what she meant. In fact, he understood so well, he almost changed his mind about not playing after dinner.

"I found your paperwork," he said, changing the subject. "It was misplaced. I'm sorry for the confusion."

He'd found it tucked away in a stack of uncompleted forms, and to say he'd read through it would be an understatement. He'd pored over it, committing to memory every scrap of information about her. She'd even had the foresight to include a checklist, and he'd gone to bed with images that kept him awake long into the night.

The restaurant he'd picked was a small, locally owned place he went to often. Part of him knew he was introducing her to his world by taking her to one of his favorite places. Subtly showing her the differences between the two of them. What he wasn't sure about was whether he was pointing out those differences so she could accept them or so she would leave.

The hostess greeted them warmly and led them to a secluded booth in the back corner of the restaurant. As they walked, Jeff kept his hand on the small of Dena's back, subtly guiding her and noting how she responded to his touch. She swayed her hips slightly, playing into his hand.

Once they were seated, she sipped her water and handed him the menu. "I'll have whatever you suggest."

He looked at her warily. "You should know I'm not interested in a Master/slave relationship. I'd much rather you order for yourself."

"Trust me. This isn't something I do on a regular basis. And I have my reasons."

So she was testing him? Interesting. But in light of the little he knew about her previous relationship, maybe it made sense.

"And if I order you bread and water?" he asked.

"Then I know everything I need to know."

"Any food allergies or anything you absolutely hate?"

"No."

"Anything you particularly love?"

Joy and possibly relief flooded her expression. He tilted his head.

Did you expect anything less? he silently asked.

She upturned her palm on the table. "I love tomatoes."

When the waitress came by, he ordered them both a side salad with house dressing, extra tomatoes for her, and spaghetti with meatballs.

Dena's hand was still on the table. He placed his over it. "Did I pass?"

"So far." She laced their fingers together.

Her skin was soft and warm, and her hand felt delicate under his. He stroked her palm with his thumb and saw her body shiver in response. He couldn't wait to make her shiver in other ways.

"Tell me how you knew you were a submissive."

She captured her bottom lip between her teeth.

"The truth, Dena," he warned. "I'll know if you're being dishonest."

"That's the thing about good Dominants. You guys see everything."

He narrowed his eyes, partly teasing, partly being serious. "Are you avoiding the question?"

"Busted," she said under her breath.

He didn't say anything else, waiting instead for her to continue. She tried to pull her hand back, but he wouldn't let it go.

"I did it first as an act of defiance."

That was probably the last response he expected. She didn't come across as the rebellious sort, much less the type to act out in such a drastic way. He raised an eyebrow at her.

"I had an ultraconservative upbringing," she said. "Talk a certain way, walk a certain way, look a certain way. I was told who I could be friends with and which boys I could date. Midway through law school, I kinda went wild."

He was still holding her hand, and she'd ceased trying to get away. Law school? Her paperwork didn't list her job. "Interesting."

"I went to a local BDSM party one weekend. I thought it would be the exact opposite of my childhood, something wild and dangerous."

She could have been hurt walking into something new like that. "Risky."

"Yes, but I did my research before I went. Checked it out."

He stroked the base of her palm again. "Always so practical?"

"That, and I wanted to be sure it was safe. Even knowing that, I still felt it'd drive my dad crazy if he found out."

"Did you tell him?"

She laughed and shook her head. "Tell him that not only do I let men tie me up and flog me, but that I *like* it? No way. Just knowing how he would react was enough."

Was enough. Past tense. "Obviously now it's more than rebelling against your father. No one can be a submissive for four years out of spite."

The waiter delivered their salads, and she didn't say anything until he left. Jeff reluctantly let go of her hand so she could eat.

She popped a tomato in her mouth and chewed with a look of

complete bliss. "I found out after a while that being a submissive completed me. It's hard for me to explain to those not in the life- style, but I'm sure you know what I mean."

"Yes, I do know. For myself, I'm not sure I'm even able to separate the man in me from the Dominant. It's just who I am." He had accepted it years ago and no longer felt the need to ex- plain or excuse it.

"I want to get to that point. I still think I'd feel the need to explain myself to people."

"Society's double standard? It's okay for a man to be dom- inant, but a 'real' woman would never consent to being sub- missive."

She nodded. "Yes, exactly."

He leaned across the table and was pleased to note she did the same. She was so close, he could smell her jasmine perfume. "I think," he said, "that it takes more strength to admit what you want. Anyone can sit back and let society tell them what's ex- pected. True courage is saying, 'Screw you. I need this and I'm going to take it.'"

As he spoke, the truth of his words hit him. According to so- ciety, he shouldn't be with a woman like her. She had probably been attending law school when he got his GED. But he wasn't going to listen to society. He wanted her and, if she wanted him, he'd take her.

They finished their salads in silence, and once their pastas were delivered, Dena twirled a bite of spaghetti on her fork.

"Tell me what you do," she asked.

"I recently resigned from the Wilmington Police Depart- ment." He started cutting his spaghetti; he'd never been able to twirl it without making a mess. "I've opened up my own security business."

Her forehead wrinkled. "What does that involve?"

"I do a lot of consulting, working with businesses on improving and streamlining security systems. We do personal protection, too."

"Physical security or online?"

"I mostly do physical, but I have a partner who specializes in network security."

The table fell silent as they ate, and Jeff found he enjoyed sitting with her in companionable quiet. Around them the chatter of other diners filled the room, but it didn't feel odd. If he had to pick one word to describe the atmosphere, he'd go with "friendly."

Dena wiped her mouth. "I bet you have a lot of stories you could tell about your job."

"I've seen my fair share of crazy."

"Has anyone asked you to be their bodyguard? Do you do that type of work?"

"I haven't had that request come up yet. I'd have to think about it before I'd agree to do something like that. It'd be tough being around someone all the time in that kind of capacity. Always having to be on guard."

She twirled more pasta. "It's not fun for the person being guarded either."

"Oh?" That was interesting. It sounded like she spoke from experience.

"I mean"—she shrugged—"I've heard that."

He had a feeling she wasn't telling him the whole story, but before he could ask her more, she shifted in her seat and the movement caused her foot to brush against his under the table. She jerked it back and locked eyes with him at the same time.

One day I'll know your secrets.

And what a delight it would be to discover them all. Already she was tempting him to change his plans for the evening. Dena was unlike any woman he'd ever met. She was intelligent and strong and there was a fierceness that lit her eyes. He wanted to harness that strength and control it, until her fierceness consumed them both.

Dena peeked across the table at Jeff. He was such a curious combination of blue-collar worker and philosophical Dominant. He sent out a protective, nurturing vibe at times, but she could see underneath the signs of an all-powerful Dom.

"If you don't mind me asking, Sir, how many submissives have you collared? I've had only the one Master."

He pushed a bite of pasta onto his fork. "I've never collared a submissive."

Her water glass stopped halfway up to her lips. "Never?"

"Never. I can be hard and abrasive and I recognize I'm not the easiest Dominant to serve. I'm also a bit of a loner, and many women find the combination a turnoff."

It was almost as if he was giving her a warning, trying to tell her not to get close. She didn't care. He was interesting and devilishly handsome. It was going to take a lot more than hearing he was a loner to scare her off.

She took a sip of water. "I'm definitely not a loner—that's for sure. And you may be hard and abrasive in the playroom, but it's already clear to me that you're not a cruel man."

"You don't know me well enough to make that call."

"I'd beg to differ."

There was a flash of desire in his eyes that sent a spark of longing throughout her body, especially when he whispered, "When I have you beg, it won't be about that."

She forced herself to meet his gaze. "I look forward to it, Sir."

The rest of their dinner was charged. Every move he made seemed somehow sexual: from the way he held his fork, to the way his lips parted. It was the most absurd thing when she tried to rationalize it. He was only eating spaghetti. Yet with every bite, every sip, every swallow, his body called to her.

She shifted in her seat as they waited for the bill, hoping to alleviate the dull ache between her legs that screamed for his touch. He'd said she wasn't to come without his permission, but he'd made no mention of playing tonight. She watched him sign the receipt, the entire time imagining his hands on her, holding her, claiming her.

A bead of sweat trickled between her breasts, and she squirmed again.

"You okay?" he asked.

"Fine," she said, forcing her body to be still.

"Another pesky thing about me is that I require absolute honesty at all times." He cocked an eyebrow. "Are you okay?"

"Damn it," she mumbled. She was willing to bet he knew exactly what her problem was and he was going to force her to say it.

"Not answering a direct question? *And* swearing? *Tsk, tsk, tsk.* You're compiling quite a list of infractions. Should make for a memorable night in my playroom."

His expression was serious, but she felt certain there was a trace of humor lingering behind his eyes. She couldn't tell if he was joking or not. She didn't want him to be joking—she thought.

"I looked over your checklist," he said. "I know your limits. If you'd like to come to my house and for us to pick up where we left off last night, say 'Yes, Sir.' If not, say 'No, Sir,' and I'll either take you back to your apartment or we can go for a walk and get to know each other better. The choice is yours and yours alone."

She'd played with a few Doms after leaving her old Master, but none of them had near the intensity Jeff had. He practically oozed control and dominance, and she wanted to experience what he was offering. She had alerted her safety call earlier in the evening; she'd just follow up with her again on the way to Jeff's.

The words left her mouth as soon as she decided. "Yes, Sir."

Victory and possibly relief flashed across his expression. "Let's leave."

They walked together through the crowded restaurant, this time with Jeff leading the way. She was fine with that since walking behind him meant she could check out his ass again.

"Hey, Jeff," the man at the hostess station said, coming out from behind the table and blocking their way. "I didn't know you were here tonight. How've you been?"

"Doing well, Ike," Jeff said, his voice tighter than normal. "Excellent food as always. We enjoyed everything."

At Jeff's use of the word "we" Ike looked her way, and his eyes widened in recognition.

Damn it, no!

But she couldn't do anything but smile and nod as the pudgy man spoke to her. "Hello, Ms. Jenkins. We're honored you dined with us tonight. I trust everything was to your liking."

She risked a peek at Jeff. He was looking at Ike as if the man had grown horns and pointy ears.

"Everything was superb; thank you for asking," she said with her well-practiced fake smile.

"You two know each other?" Jeff asked.

Ike shook his head. "I've never had the pleasure before tonight of talking with Ms. Jenkins, but I've been a supporter of her dad for years."

Clearly it had taken less than a second for Jeff to make the connection in his head. He looked at her, and dread filled her stomach. Damn it. She wasn't ready to tell him. She wanted to wait until later. Much later.

"If you'll excuse us," Jeff said, his voice flat. "I need to be getting Ms. *Jenkins* home."

He didn't speak as they made their way to his truck. He was silent as he opened her door and helped her inside. She was so on edge, she jumped when he closed it. All the sexual tension that had been so prevalent during dinner had evaporated, and all she felt was cold.

It wasn't until he pulled out of the parking lot and turned in the direction of her apartment complex that he spoke. "Dena J. Dena Jenkins. You're Senator Jenkins's daughter."

"Yes."

"Fuck."

"It really doesn't change anything," she said, trying to make her voice sound as normal as possible.

"No, Ms. Jenkins. It changes everything."

Chapter Three

Present day

Twenty minutes ago, being late for the demo hadn't seemed like such a bad idea. The phone call from the stranger had caught her off guard. She'd answered the phone because she was expecting a work call and thought the unknown number might have been it.

Whoever it was laughed when she said hello and then he'd hung up.

It took ten minutes in the bathroom to stop shaking, and she knew she was horribly late to the demo. At the time, playing the forgetful submissive seemed like a good idea. And if he'd already canceled the demo and punished her, well, it would still be more than what she normally got from him.

"Undress," he said. "Then go get the leather strap from my bag and I want you over my knees."

Damn the man. She stood up and slowly undressed, taking

her time. Naked, she jerked the strap from his bag. A spanking was one thing, but she hated the strap. Which, of course, he knew.

She knelt before him and held out the strap.

"Thank you, Dena. Is there something you'd like to say?"

He was falling back into their old punishment ritual. Next she was supposed to thank him for caring enough about her to correct her when she messed up. She grew furious. He never called, they rarely talked, and he expected her to happily fall into place like she still wore his collar?

"Yes, Sir. I have something to say."

He nodded. "Go ahead."

"Fuck you, Sir."

Damn him even more. He didn't even look angry. He simply smiled. "You just added ten strokes."

"Fuck you. Fuck you. *Fuck. You.*"

"Your ass is going to give out long before my hand does. As it stands now, you'll be lucky if you don't have trouble sitting down for a week."

She opened her mouth, but shut it immediately when he snapped his fingers.

"The next thing out of that bratty mouth better be, 'Please, Sir, punish my ass for my lack of respect.'"

She pressed her lips together.

"Say it. Now."

Her heart pounded, but she felt a spark of arousal at his take-charge manner. The Doms in training she was used to didn't have the ability to do that to her. "Please, Sir, punish my ass for my lack of respect."

He patted his lap. "Since you asked so nicely."

Rarely had anyone put her over his knees since her split with Jeff. She'd forgotten how humiliating it was to be naked across someone's lap while they were fully clothed. And it was as if Jeff wanted her to remember, because for several long minutes he did nothing.

When he finally spoke, his voice was low and firm. "You disrespected me not only with your mouth, but with your actions. I'm not going to have you count or thank me. You'll simply take what I give. You showed a serious lack of judgment tonight, and that requires serious consequences. Do you understand?"

Would he not get on with it? "Yes, Sir. I understand."

He kept one hand on her lower back and started slapping her butt with the other. His spanking was just as methodical as she remembered. Each stroke meticulously planned and delivered.

Fuck. She'd forgotten how much it hurt.

She tried to take them silently, but it was too much and she found she couldn't. A knock on the door followed the fifth stroke, and the door opened before Jeff could answer.

"Everything okay in here?" Daniel asked, showing only mild shock at finding them in such a position.

"Answer Master Covington honestly."

Damn the man. He wasn't even breathing heavily.

"Yes, Sir. Everything's fine. Master Parks is showing me the consequences of disrespect."

"If she's scaring people, I can gag her," Jeff said. "But I won't stop. She asked for this."

"No gag needed," Daniel said. "Disrespect is a serious infraction. Continue."

She gritted her teeth as Jeff started again. Somewhere around twelve she lost count and simply took it, relaxing into him as much as possible. He slipped a hand between her legs and murmured about how naughty she was when he found her wet. She took the brief pause to wipe her eyes.

"Five more."

Knowing what was expected, she lifted her ass up. The last five were the hardest, and she cried out when the last one came. He kept her on his lap when it was over, rubbing her back, telling her she took it well.

"I'm sorry, Sir," she finally said.

"Sorry for what?"

"For disrespecting you, Sir."

"Come here."

She scurried from his lap and threw her arms around him, desperate to hold on to him, her anchor in the midst of her emotional turmoil, sobbing gently into his neck. He wrapped her in his strong embrace and whispered that it was over and forgotten. For the longest time, she allowed herself to enjoy being in his arms, listening to his gentle whispers, and she wondered if part of why she goaded him in the first place was to get him to spank her so she could end up in his arms like this.

But being in his arms, hearing him say it was over and forgotten made her feel guilty. He thought she'd been disrespectful and late; she hadn't told him the truth. How could it truly be over and forgotten when he didn't know the entire story?

"You're tensing up," Jeff said, and his arms loosened around her. "Are you uncomfortable being in my lap?"

Damn. Now he thought she had an issue with *him*. She buried her head in his chest and took a deep breath. "Not for the reason you think."

"What?"

She pulled back. "I'm uncomfortable because I didn't tell you the real reason I was late."

His lips tightened into a thin line. "I had a feeling there might be something you weren't telling me. Let me take care of your backside and get you a robe. Then we'll talk." He shifted her slightly. "I need you on your stomach on the couch."

She stood gingerly. Each slight motion of her body caused her backside to scream with pain, but she situated herself the way he asked. His footsteps approached the couch, and he draped the discarded blanket across the upper part of her body. Then he placed a cushion under her head. There was silence as he rubbed ointment onto her aching flesh.

By the time he finished, she was warm and relaxed. If she didn't have to have the upcoming conversation, she'd probably have gone to sleep. In fact, she felt so good, she thought about keeping to her original plan and telling him on Monday.

But he wasn't going to let her forget. When he finished, he lightly brushed her back. "Sit up and slip this robe on. Then you can tell me what's going on."

She pulled herself up and slid her arms into the robe. Jeff sat down beside her, waiting.

She sighed. "I was going to tell you Monday. I was going to come to your office."

"My office? Why? I can count on one hand the number of times you've been to my office."

"When I got home last night, there was a note slipped under my apartment door."

He raised an eyebrow.

"It was threatening," she added.

He looked like she'd slapped him. Or hit him in the gut. "Threatening how?"

She shook her head. "It said, 'Better watch out, bitch.'"

He clenched his fists so tightly the knuckles turned white. "You called the police."

"No."

"Damn it, Dena. You need to call the police."

"It's too close to the election, and Dad's short-listed for vice president. Someone just wants attention."

"Or some criminal you put away is coming after you."

"Which is why I was going to hire you on Monday."

"What?"

"You're into security. I was going to hire you to keep me safe. I need someone I can trust to keep this out of the press. And I need someone good." Her eyes darted around the room, and she bit her bottom lip. He was going to flip out when she told him the rest.

"What else?"

She blinked and tried to look innocent. "What else what?"

"What else aren't you telling me?" he asked, and when she opened her mouth to protest, he cut her off. "Think real good and hard before you say 'nothing.'"

She almost defied him, but then thought better of it. He'd already punished her once tonight. "I've been getting harassing phone calls for the last few months. The last one came tonight."

"Is that why you . . . ? Fuck." He shot to his feet and paced.

"What are you doing?" she asked after several minutes.

"Calming down before I do something I'll regret." He stopped in front of her and crossed his arms. "I'll find the fucking bastard and kill him."

"Sit down," she said. "And think about it. Then you'll see it's probably nothing."

He didn't sit down. "That's why you were late. You were frightened. Why didn't you tell me this then?"

"I didn't want to miss the demo. I honestly didn't know how late it was until I got here and you'd sent everyone away."

"Forget the demo." He sat down beside her. "What about your safety?"

"That's why I was going to come to you Monday. But I wanted tonight. I wanted to do the scene. Maybe tonight was just another demo for you, but it wasn't for me. You used to tell me you demanded complete honesty. Well, I'm giving it to you. I'd have done damn near anything to feel your hands on me again."

"And did you enjoy my hands on you just now? Was it worth it?"

It wasn't what she would have picked, but if she had to choose between nothing from him or a spanking, she'd pick the spanking.

"I'll take what I can get, Sir."

"Dena."

"Let me make it up to you, Sir." She slid carefully from the couch because her backside hurt like the devil, pushed his knees apart, and knelt between them. She waited for him to say or do something. Anything to signal his approval. Finally, he gave a quick nod of his head. His gaze never left her as she unzipped his pants and pulled out his cock.

He sighed when she kissed the tip of it and moaned when she engulfed his length in her mouth.

"So good, Dena. You feel so good."

Then take me back, she wanted to say, but didn't. She'd told him when he'd taken his collar back that she'd return when he begged, and she'd meant it.

But she spoke it with her mouth, her tongue, her touch.

For years Jeff had been the center of her sexual universe, and she'd devoted herself to learning his body. At times she'd felt she knew it better than her own. Serving him had been the source of her greatest pleasure, and though she'd served many Doms in the three years since they'd split, none had come close in comparison.

"Look at me," he whispered in command.

From her place on the floor, she looked up and met his gaze. As she took him, he reached out and stroked her cheek. His touch was soft and gentle. Nothing like the harshness he'd shown minutes before.

She moved up and down on his cock, taking him deep, swirling her tongue around his underside. The entire time he kept his eyes locked on hers, with his fingers lightly brushing her cheek.

He could hold off his climax for damn near forever, but it seemed he wasn't in the mood to delay anything tonight. Though it'd been years since she'd had him in her mouth, she recognized his imminent release by the way he twitched. Because she knew how much he liked it, she relaxed and took his final thrust deep in her throat.

"Fuck," he said, slipping his hand behind her head and holding her in place as he came.

Her eyes filled with tears at the effort it took to swallow everything. It'd been a long time since she'd deep throated, and she hadn't realized how out of practice she was.

After calming her breathing, she kissed the tip of his cock, tucked him back inside his pants, zipped them up, and waited.

"Dena?"

She was no longer his Angel. She squeezed her eyes closed for the briefest of seconds before answering. "Yes?"

He stood and placed a hand on her shoulder. "I'm going to go get you some juice, and after you rest, we're going to talk about this note and the phone calls. Wait here for me."

She nodded and watched him leave the room. Suddenly, the day's events caught up with her and she curled up on the couch. She didn't even try to keep her heavy eyelids from shutting.

"Wake up, Dena," Jeff said softly sometime later. "I need you to drink some before you rest."

"Don't want any."

"Don't care."

He knelt beside her head and held up a glass with a straw. She lifted herself enough to take a few sips so he'd be satisfied but discovered she was thirstier than she'd thought. He chuckled when she drained the glass.

Feeling sated, she closed her eyes and snuggled into the warm blanket he placed over her.

A callused finger brushed her forehead. "Rest well. I'll keep you safe."

Chapter Four

Seven years ago

Dena drummed her fingers on the table. She was at Master Covington's house, waiting for the monthly group meeting to start. Normally, she looked forward to group meetings. But normally, they weren't round-table discussions led by Jeff Parks.

It'd been a month since their disastrous first—and last—date. In that month, Jeff had ignored her when possible. If circumstance required him to speak to her, he was short though always polite.

It shouldn't bother her. She knew she should just tell him to fuck off and go on about her life. Yet for some reason she couldn't. She wanted him. So much so, she'd been unable to work up the excitement to play with anyone else. Several Dominants had approached her, but so far she'd turned them all down.

The room around her quieted as the man in question entered. He had on worn jeans and a black T-shirt and looked deliciously scruffy, almost as if he'd forgotten to shave. He glanced around the room and didn't acknowledge her existence when his gaze passed her.

Forget him. He's not interested.

Except he had been, and she couldn't believe that desire had changed simply because he found out she was a senator's daughter. She vowed to herself to find out what his real problem was.

"I thought we'd spend some time today discussing common stereotypes within the community," Jeff said, starting the meeting.

Dena swallowed a snort, but couldn't stop the "Seriously?" that slipped out under her breath. *Oh, yeah. This should be fun.* How did he get picked to lead this discussion?

Fortunately, her snide comment went unnoticed by Jeff because he continued. "Someone name a common misconception people have."

The bald switch who'd worked the door the night of her first party replied, saying, "If you're a man, you're a Dominant, and if you're female, you're a sub."

Jeff nodded. "Good one. And how often do we make judgments on someone's role before we get to know them?" No one said anything. "Come on, you know you do it. You see a woman like Kelly, dressed as she is now, and what do you think?"

He motioned toward the group's lone Domme, who was wearing a pink sweater and winter-white wool pants. With her red hair falling in soft waves around her shoulders, it would be hard to picture her as she'd be dressed tomorrow: skintight leather dress, knee-high black boots, and fishnet stockings.

Kelly was an officer at the Wilmington Police Department,

and Dena had worked with her on a professional basis. They'd had lunch a few times, and Dena was looking forward to getting to know her better.

"I know what I'd think," Evan Martin said. "I'd think 'Redheads shouldn't wear pink.'"

Jeff shot him a look, but Evan ignored him. "Isn't that in the Redhead Rulebook? Don't wear pink. It'll clash with your hair."

Kelly pressed her lips together and didn't say anything. Knowing her the way she did, Dena guessed she really wanted to rip Evan a new one.

"That's quite enough," Jeff said. "But since you're so interested in talking, you can give us another stereotype."

Evan seemed completely caught off guard and started and stopped several times before finally blurting out, "All kink players are deviants."

Mumbled agreements came from around the table. Obviously, a lot of people had felt they would be looked down upon or thought less of if they admitted their sexual needs. Hell, Dena understood that one. No way did she want the general public knowing about her private life, even though in a perfect world it wouldn't matter.

Daniel asked if Jeff thought there was anything to do to overcome the perception, and for the next ten minutes there was a heated discussion surrounding what one could to. The room was divided between those who didn't care who knew and those who kept it private.

During a lull in the conversation, she raised her hand. Jeff ignored her. She waved her arm. He narrowed his eyes.

"Yes, Dena."

"We've touched on the typical stereotypes, but what about the less common ones?"

"Such as?" He raised an eyebrow. *Watch it,* he seemed to say.

"Such as ethnicity or class distinction." She met his eyebrow raise with one of her own. *Yes, I went there.* "For example, do you think there's a higher number of interracial couples in the community as opposed to society as a whole? Do you think, Sir, that those of us in the lifestyle are more prepared to say to society, 'Screw you. I know what I want and I'm taking it'?"

His face didn't give her a clue that he recognized his own words from that night or if he was angry she brought them up. All he said was, "I wouldn't know. I'm not an expert in such things." He turned away from her. "Any more questions?" he asked the group at large.

If he knew her at all, he would have known it took more than that to shut her down. "I wasn't asking for your expert opinion, Sir. I was asking you personally, as a Dominant with a good number of years of experience."

"Let me be clearer: I don't know."

"Guess."

"No."

The silence in the room hit her then. Not that people had been talking among themselves, but at the moment no one was *moving.* It was as if the entire room was holding its breath, watching their exchange.

Master Covington coughed and stood up. "I think that's a good place to end the discussion. Thank you, Master Parks."

Jeff nodded in reply and little by little the room came to life.

Side conversations were started, and around her people made plans for the next night's play party.

That hadn't gone well.

Jeff spoke quietly to Master Covington and left. Fury rose in her, and she decided to get to the bottom of Jeff's problem once and for all. Ignoring the pointed stares and whispers that followed, she shoved her chair back and went after him.

She found him in the house's kitchen. His back was to her as he stood looking out a window.

"What *exactly* is your problem?"

He turned slowly. "You."

"I kinda figured that part out."

"You graduated summa cum laude from Harvard Law."

She swallowed her shock at this confession that he'd looked her up online. "So?"

"You admitted your interest in submission started as an act of rebellion against your father. Who happens to be a senator."

"And you said no one could be a submissive for four years out of spite."

He walked toward her slowly. So slowly she could see the gradual change from irritation to desire. "You'll have to excuse me," he said when he was steps from her, "if I have a hard time picturing a spoiled little rich girl who went on to be a supersuccessful Harvard lawyer on her knees as a submissive."

She put her hands on her hips. "Damn, are you serious? And after that entire discussion on stereotypes, too."

"Can I say you're showing a perfect example of submission at the moment?" he asked, his voice heavy with sarcasm.

"I'm submissive for either my Master or the man topping me in a scene. Right now you're just a judgmental asshole."

His jaw tightened.

"Tell me," she continued. "What bothers you the most, the fact that I'm rich or that I graduated from Harvard?"

"Both. They both bother me. This isn't a game for me. It's my life. I was being honest when I told you the reasons why I've never collared a submissive."

"I'm insulted you think I see this as a game."

He shrugged. "Good thing we never made it to my playroom."

"I'll make you a deal."

"Not interested."

She ignored his comment. "Give me an hour and a half in your playroom, and if I'm not the best damn submissive you've ever been with, I'll leave the group."

The look he gave her should have made her drop to her knees, but she forced herself to remain upright.

His voice was husky when he replied. "I appreciate the gesture, Ms. Jenkins, but I can't make that sort of deal. I will, however, agree to forty-five minutes at the party tomorrow night. And if you aren't the best, you and I agree to stay the hell away from each other from now on."

The next night, Jeff waited for Dena in the living room of Daniel's guesthouse. It would serve him right if she didn't show up. He couldn't deny he'd acted like an ass toward her. He'd been shocked when he'd found out she was Senator Jenkins's daughter. Who wouldn't have been?

He'd gone home after seeing her safely inside her apartment and searched for her online. He'd learned she was a Harvard Law School graduate who'd surprised her family by turning down a position at a prestigious firm to work for the State of Delaware. When you paired that with what he knew about her reasons for initially joining the local community, he had a pretty good idea of how she was wired.

She was a fighter who took what she wanted even when those around her thought she should do otherwise. But how was she as a submissive? Would she try to top from the bottom? The more he learned about her, the more he wanted to find out.

But he wanted her to decide he was what she wanted. The downside of his strategy was that he'd pissed her off in the process.

"Master Parks?"

He looked up to find she'd entered the room. She looked even more stunning than she had at the first play party. Tonight she wore a white corset and a short white, clingy skirt, with her blond hair falling to her shoulders in soft curls. The effect was breathtaking.

"Dena." He stood.

He meant to say something. To invite her to sit beside him. Ask how her day had been. Anything. Instead, he watched dumbstruck as she hesitantly moved toward him. When she made it to his side, she gracefully slid to her knees, kneeling before him.

He couldn't stop his hand from reaching out to settle on the top of her head. Her hair was soft and silky. He stroked it and heard her sigh in pleasure.

"Look at me," he whispered.

Clear blue eyes met his. She looked at him with need, want, and just a slight hint of lingering anger.

"Thank you for suggesting this," he said. He'd planned to talk with her before they played, but seeing her on her knees made him change his mind. He had a copy of her checklist, and she'd agreed to be his for forty-five minutes tonight. Talking could wait.

"My pleasure, Sir."

"There's a spare room to the right of the kitchen. Let's go. You can walk in front of me."

She led the way and he followed. As they passed Daniel in the kitchen, he gave Jeff a self-satisfied nod.

Jeff tilted his head toward the room. "Make sure we're not interrupted too much."

Because they were at a party, he knew a senior member would look in on them at least once. He accepted that; he just didn't want their scene interrupted numerous times.

He closed the door behind him. He'd set everything up earlier in the evening. A St. Andrew's Cross stood at the back of the room, with his toy bag and ropes beside it. Dena would see the giant wooden "X" and infer he had a bondage scene planned.

Dena knelt in the middle of the room. Her butt rested on her feet and her knees were pressed together. If they played together again, he'd instruct her in the way he preferred his submissives to wait, but for tonight she was fine.

He stood before her and pictured how they would look to an outsider: Dena, dressed in white, with her pale skin and blond hair. He would look like her opposite with his dark hair and black jeans and T-shirt. Likely as not, they had nothing in common

except their lifestyle. Fortunately, for the next forty-five minutes, that was all they needed.

"What's your safe word, Dena?"

"Red, Sir."

"Anytime you feel like you need to stop, use it and we can talk."

"Thank you, Sir."

"Stand up and take off that corset and skirt. They're too pristine for what I have planned for tonight."

She obeyed quickly, standing up and slipping the skirt down
over her hips, putting it to the side. But then she hesitated.

"Is there a problem already?" he asked.

"I can't get the corset off by myself, Sir."

He eyed the white contraption, noting the laces and ties were
in the back. "How did you get it on?"

"One of the other submissives helped." She was contorting her
body this way and that in a vain attempt to reach the top hook.
Though it probably wasn't her intent, the movement was doing
magnificent things to her figure. At one point, one of her breasts
threatened to pop out.

"Enough," he finally said, putting an end to her wiggly dance.
"As enjoyable as this is, I have no intention of watching you try
to undress for the rest of our time together. You have two minutes to get out of that corset. If I have to help, you'll be naked
the rest of the night." He looked at his watch. "Time starts now."

Though she'd marked exhibitionism as "likes a lot," she apparently wasn't in the mood to spend the remainder of her time
at the play party naked. Her movements intensified as she strug-
gled to undo the corset. With thirty seconds remaining, she let
out a satisfied "Aha," and the garment fell to the ground.

She stood before him breathing heavily, a look of triumph on her face.

"Very nice, Dena," he said. "Now take off the panties and come here."

When she was naked except for her white heels, she walked over to the cross where he stood. Fuck, she was even more gorgeous naked. Every inch of her was perfect.

"I want your back to the cross," he instructed her.

Taking a length of red rope and a length of black, he bound her to the cross, spread-eagle. He worked slowly, taking his time, running his fingertips along her skin before he decorated it. Done correctly, bondage was an art form, and for the night, he had the most beautiful canvas imaginable.

He secured her legs and went to work on her arms. As he bound her, he made sure to touch and tease her. She impressed him by remaining still. He stepped back and saw she had her eyes closed and had fallen into a deep, rhythmic breathing pattern.

"Are you okay?" he asked.

"Yes, Sir."

"Nothing too tight or uncomfortable?"

"No, Sir."

"I'm getting ready to be a little evil."

"I look forward to it, Sir."

Ever so slowly he trailed another rope along her torso before wrapping it around her chest, making something that resembled a bra. He purposely left her nipples exposed, and he circled them with his fingers, pulling slightly. She rewarded him with a gasp.

Next he draped a thin red rope over her right shoulder so the ends trailed on either side of her body. She sucked in a breath as he slowly worked his hands down her torso. He took the ends of the rope and tied a knot, placing it on the right side of her clit. He repeated the same thing on her left side.

When finished, he stepped back to admire his work. "You're completely at my mercy now. I can do anything I want to that fuckable body."

Tied and bound as she was, every slight movement, every breath, would cause the ropes to tease her clit. She knew this, of course, and she was trying her best to stay completely still. Which was why he needed to incentivize her to do differently.

He picked a lightweight flogger out of his bag. "I gave you a command a little more than a month ago. Do you remember?"

The shocked expression she gave him told him she did but was hoping he hadn't. "Yes, Sir, but since——"

"'Yes, Sir' is enough. I didn't ask for commentary. How many times have you come in the last month?"

"I don't remember, Sir."

He flicked the flogger against her upper thighs. "Try."

"Umm, four?"

"Are you asking me?"

"Probably eleven, Sir."

"That's a bit different from four."

She took a deep breath and shivered as the ropes moved. "Nineteen, Sir."

"Nineteen?" He picked up a flogger with heavier tails. "Is that your last number?"

"Yes, Sir. That's my best guess."

He glanced at his watch. "We have a little more than twenty minutes left, so as punishment, I'm going to flog you for nineteen minutes."

Her eyes grew dark. "Please, Sir."

He gave her a sadistic smile and then started. First he used the lighter-weight flogger softly across her body to make her nerve endings come alive. He followed with the heavier one, but only on her upper thighs, making sure some of the tails landed between her legs.

The heavy flogger left faint pink marks on her thighs, and he alternated occasionally with the lighter one. It kept her off guard, but judging by her soft moans and intakes of breath, it was turning her on. He could probably use heavier strokes, but he was hesitant to on their first scene. *First scene.* He'd make damn sure there was a second.

She whimpered. "Please, Sir, let me come."

"No." He moved to her breasts, landing just on the tips of her nipples.

Her body jerked. "Fuck."

"Okay to continue?" He thought it was but felt the need to check in more frequently.

"Yes, please. Please don't stop, Sir."

It was the affirmation he'd been waiting for. With a flogger in each hand, he rained stroke after stroke on her, alternating implement and intensity until her moans of pleasure filled the room. Her sweet cries fueled him, and he brought her closer and closer to the edge.

He flicked the tails of one flogger across her clit. "Need to come?"

"Yes. Please. Sir."

"I'm going to flog your pussy nineteen times. You can't come until I've finished. Count."

She whimpered but counted each stroke. After the nineteenth one, he put the floggers aside and walked close to her. She still looked like an angel, but damn it all, he never knew an angel could look so seductive and absolutely fuckable.

"Very nice, Dena." He slipped a hand between her legs, easily pushed two fingers inside, and thumbed her clit. "Come for me now, you naughty girl. Come on my fingers."

With a yelp, she finally let loose, and a massive orgasm rocked her as she pulled against the restraints.

"That's my girl. So good." Leaning against her, he whispered in her ear, "The next time you come, it'll be with my cock pushed inside that hot pussy."

He trailed kisses from her ear, across her cheek, and down to her mouth. Though he wanted to spend time kissing her, he knew he needed to untie her first.

He untied her faster than he'd tied her, promising himself that if she was agreeable, he'd soon have her bound for a much longer, more intense session. He started at her legs and moved up, running his lips along the skin he exposed. When he unbound her arms, she swayed into him.

"You okay?" he asked, gathering her in his arms.

"Incredible, Sir."

He half carried, half walked her to a nearby love seat and sat her on his lap. She shivered a bit, so he wrapped a blanket around her. For several minutes he kept her like that, enjoying the feel of her and inhaling her delicate jasmine scent. He stroked her hair and murmured how impressed he was with her.

At one point, she pulled back and looked at him. "What's your verdict, Sir?"

"You very well might be the best I've ever played with."

Her forehead wrinkled. "Might be?"

He shifted his seat, and the movement caused his erection to brush against her. "I need another session to ensure a thorough evaluation."

She looked down and wrapped the blanket around her tighter. "Why would you want to play with me again, Sir?"

"I was an ass, and I'm asking you to forgive me. I want very much to play with you again."

"On one condition."

"Name it."

"You let me take care of that massive erection I'm sitting on."

He swallowed a laugh. That was what he'd been expecting. "Our forty-five minutes are up."

She ran a hand down his chest and gave a mock sigh. "Too bad. I was looking forward to showing off my oral skills."

His erection grew harder, and he shifted her off his lap. "Don't let me stop you. I've been dreaming about having that hot, sassy mouth around my dick."

The next Friday night, Dena pulled up to Jeff's house shortly after six. She stepped out of her car and admired the rustic but modern cabin. It looked exactly like the house she'd have pictured Jeff in. Set back in the woods and with no neighbor in sight, the house looked like it was deep in the wilderness rather than so near a large city.

He was actually smiling when he opened the door. Smiling. She rarely saw him with anything other than a neutral expression, and her breath caught at how handsome he was when he was happy.

"Dena," he said, holding the door open for her. "So glad you could make it."

Earlier in the week, he'd asked her to come to his house for dinner tonight. Even though it'd been Monday, the memory of their time at the party was fresh in her mind. And while they'd spent the rest of the evening together, he didn't take her. When she'd questioned him about it, he'd told her their first time wasn't going to be at his friend's house where the potential existed for them to be interrupted.

She hoped that meant there was more on the menu at his house tonight than just food.

"I've been looking forward to this all week," she said, stepping inside. "Your house is amazing."

The inside boasted exposed-beam ceilings and wide-planked wooden floors. There was an overall feel of warmth and comfort and *home* that on the surface appeared at odds with the cool demeanor Jeff portrayed. Such a mystery he was.

"Thanks. I had it built a few years ago." There was a touch of pride in his voice. "I wanted something different, but homey and comfortable."

"You found it."

"Come on into the kitchen with me. I was just getting ready to pull the fish out of the oven."

He led her to the kitchen, and as they drew near, the mouth-watering smell of citrus and teriyaki greeted her. "Something smells good."

"It's a marinade my grandma taught me. Really easy."

"I'll take your word for it. I don't cook."

But she certainly enjoyed watching him in the kitchen. The way his shirt stretched over his muscles, the power in his thighs when he knelt down to find a pan in a low cabinet.

He stood up and faced her once he'd taken the fish out. "Do you have a safety call?"

"No." Her heart started pounding. He wouldn't have asked if he didn't have something planned after dinner, would he? "I trust you."

"Thank you," he said, then turned his attention back to getting everything ready for dinner.

He didn't bring up anything remotely connected to play while they ate. Instead they chatted about simpler matters. He asked what her favorite movie was and when she said *Gone With the Wind*, they debated whether the book or the movie was better.

"I'm so glad you see things my way," Dena joked. "I'm not sure I've ever seen a movie I thought was better than the book." She took her last bite of fish and smiled.

He didn't reply, and silence fell across the table. Her heart started to beat in her throat as she met his piercing stare, and all thoughts of movies and books fled her mind. All that remained was Jeff.

"You have a decision to make," he finally said. "We can go outside and walk and then maybe watch a movie, or we can pick up where we left off at the party. The decision's yours alone, but you should know that if you pick the latter, it'll be more than my fingers fucking you."

Finally, he was going to give her what she wanted. He sat

across the table from her, leaning back casually in his chair, his fingers playing with his wineglass as he waited for her answer.

"Will you show me where your bathroom is, Sir?" she asked.

A momentary look of confusion crossed his face, but he nodded and pushed back from the table. He led her down a short hallway, past what looked to be a makeshift playroom and, across from that, a bedroom. The bathroom was at the far end of the hall.

"I'll be in the kitchen cleaning up," he said.

Once inside, she closed the door and looked at herself in the mirror. She checked her makeup and finger combed her hair. Then she slowly undressed completely, placing her discarded clothing in a neat pile on the countertop.

When she stepped out of the bathroom, she made her way directly to the kitchen. Jeff stood at the sink with his back to her. Moving as quietly as she could, she went to the middle of the room, knelt down, and dropped her gaze to the wooden floor.

In her mind, she tried to picture what Jeff was doing by listening as he finished up the dishes. The water was running, so he was rinsing them. Then that turned off and the soft clinking indicated he was probably putting them in a drying rack.

He's turned around now, she thought, and held her breath.

"Dena," he whispered in a low, rough voice.

"I picked the second option, Sir."

He walked three steps forward, and his feet came into view. "Look at me."

She lifted her head and met his dark eyes. They were veiled, and she couldn't make out what he was thinking. The urge to jump to her feet threatened to overwhelm her, but she forced her body to remain still.

"You're sure this is what you want?" he asked.

"Yes, Sir."

"Just to be clear, for the rest of our time together tonight, until I say otherwise, your body is mine." His voice still had the gravelly undertone to it.

"Yes, Sir. That's what I want."

He nodded once. "I'll meet you in the bedroom in five minutes. Second door on the left. On your back in the middle of the bed."

So he wasn't taking her to the playroom. She rose to her feet silently. He hadn't given her permission to speak, and until he did or asked her a direct question, she would remain quiet. Without a word, she walked to the bedroom, conscious the entire time of the heat of his eyes as he watched her go.

He entered the room only seconds after she got into position in the middle of the bed. Though he knew she was naked, he still had all his clothes on.

He climbed onto the bed to her left, his eyes sweeping over her body in an appreciative manner. Ever so slowly his lips curved into a sultry smile. "Damn, you're beautiful. Makes me so hard seeing you on my bed like this. Offering your body to me, knowing I'll make it good for you."

It was a promise he gave her. A promise of pleasure. Her belly tightened just thinking about it.

"What's your safe word, Dena?"

Her mouth was dry when she answered. "Red, Sir."

"I want to be inside you too badly to do anything too intense, but use your safe word if you feel the need."

She nodded. *Fuck, yes.* She wanted him inside her, too.

"Lift your hands above your head and hold on to the bars on the headboard."

Her hands slipped up and wrapped around the vertical bars on the wooden headboard. The position lifted her chest to him.

"Fucking gorgeous," he said, leaning over her. With one hand, he cupped her face and then brushed his lips against hers. "Keep your hands there and I'll fuck you and let you come. Move them once and all you get is my release on your belly."

She gulped. He meant every word. Her grip on the bars tightened.

He trailed kisses down her body, his hands following behind. Though he wasn't rough, he wasn't gentle either. And just like she'd thought months ago, he could do wonderful things with his mouth. Within a matter of seconds, need, desire, and lust pounded throughout her body, and she lifted her hips, craving his touch there.

"Not yet," he said, thumbs flicking her nipples and giving them the occasional pinch.

She moaned, but dropped her butt back onto the bed.

"Know what I'm doing?" he asked.

"Yes, Sir. You're trying to drive me fucking insane with the need to have you inside me."

He laughed, obviously not expecting her answer. "Yes, well, other than that."

"No. That's all I have."

A fingertip ran down her arm, swirling in the crook of her elbow and then traveling down to sweep across her wrist. "I'm learning your body because one night with you isn't going to be enough. I want to know all I can about you. What places are ticklish? Where do you like it rough? And where can I touch you that will drive you fucking insane with the need to have me inside you?"

His repetition of her words made her whimper. *Now*, she wanted to say. *Take me now.*

But he was thorough in his exploration of her body and took his time. He caressed her all over and kissed most of her body. Between his fingers, his mouth, and his tongue, she was a quivering ball of unrequited lust by the time he shifted off her and started removing his clothes.

"What did I tell you in the kitchen would happen if you went with option two?" he asked, slipping out of his shirt and tossing it to the floor.

"That you would fuck me with more than your fingers."

Please. Please. Please.

He unbuckled his jeans and pushed them down. "You had me in your mouth a few nights ago, and as good as it felt to be there, tonight I'm going to fill another part of you." He slipped a finger between her legs. "Part your knees and show me how much you want it."

She didn't even hesitate before she let her knees fall to either side.

"Damn, you're beautiful," he said, looking over her offered body.

He was beautiful, too. She'd yet to see him naked, and as he stood at the edge of the bed, removing the last of his clothes, she allowed her gaze to travel across his body.

He was exquisitely made, all hewed and lean muscle. She tightened her fingers around the headboard so she wouldn't be tempted to reach out and touch him. Her gaze drifted lower, and she couldn't hold back a gasp of appreciation when she spied his erection.

He gave her a sultry half smile that told her he knew exactly what she was thinking and lowered himself onto the bed. He stroked her knee and placed a gentle kiss on it. Dena shivered.

"One day soon I'm going to spend hours doing nothing but kissing every inch of you." He nipped the skin on the side of her kneecap, and she yelped. "But not today. Today I want you too damn bad."

She sucked in a breath as his finger made a path from her knee up across her thigh and inched closer and closer to that empty, aching spot.

"Look at this," he said, skimming her entrance. "How wet you are." He brought his finger to her mouth. "Clean it."

She parted her lips and took his finger inside, tasting herself, and she bit the tip of it just because it was there and she could.

"Like it rough?" he asked.

"Is there any other way, Sir?"

He chuckled before lowering his head to hers and taking her lips in a kiss. She'd had her share of first kisses. Most of them were tentative and awkward. Not so with Jeff. The way his mouth claimed hers while his hands explored her body left no doubt he was not giving anything. He was taking.

For a second she despaired that he'd told her to keep her hands still. She'd love to run her fingers through his hair and down his back. But she wanted even more to please him and knew there'd be time for her to learn his body soon enough. So she relaxed into his touch and simply let herself feel.

Jeff seemed to pick up on her surrender because he ended the kiss and rose to his knees to put on a condom. She kept her eyes on his as he stroked the insides of her thighs.

Was he hesitating? Surely not. *Please,* she almost begged. Instead, she arched her back, thrilled when the movement appeared to break whatever spell he was under. He shifted his hips forward, and her eyes fluttered closed as he pressed inside her.

With a groan, he thrust once and filled her completely, damn near making her eyes roll to the back of her head in pleasure.

"Fuck. Yes," she said, and then sucked in a breath as he started pumping in and out of her.

"Feels so good," he panted, flicking first her right nipple and then her left.

"Yes," she hissed in reply, because everything about him felt good, from his hands on her to the way he moved inside her.

He slowed down, and she nearly whined until he started nibbling on her neck and hit one of her favorite spots. She bucked against him. "More."

"Mmm, like that spot?" he asked, scraping the area gently with his teeth and sending shock waves of pleasure throughout her body.

"Oh, God. Yes, Sir."

"I'm going to learn all your spots," he promised, moving his hips faster. "And I'm going to be very thorough."

She had no doubt of that. "I want to learn your spots, too, Sir." Or that's what she meant to say, but he began stroking hard and deep inside her and it came out sounding like, "Want . . . spot . . . fuck!"

His only reply was a grunt, and there weren't any further

words as he drove them both to climax. She fisted the headboard as hard as she could, trying to hold off her orgasm until she knew it was inevitable.

"Please. Sir."

He didn't slow down but simply said, "Yes," and dropped a hand between them to circle her clit.

With his permission granted, she threw her head back and focused on the feelings he created within her. He thrust deeply and kept moving as she climaxed around him. He slipped his hands up to cover hers, and their fingers entwined while he held still, reaching his own release.

They lay there for a time, holding hands, wrapped up in each other. Jeff kissed her again, but this time it was soft and reverent. She sighed in contentment when he whispered, "Touch me."

Chapter Five

Present day

Two hours later, a much more content Dena sat at Daniel's kitchen table, drinking another glass of juice. Jeff had wanted to give her chocolate milk, but Daniel didn't have any. She'd loved chocolate milk when she lived with him. When she wore his collar, almost every night before they went to bed, he'd pour her a glass and bring it to her. A simple thing to anyone else, but one that never failed to put a smile on her face. Even after her outlandish behavior at the demo, he still wanted to care for her. He hadn't realized until tonight how much he missed not being able to do things for her.

The party was over. For an hour, Jeff had watched Dena while she slept and thought about the note she'd received. In his opinion, there was only one thing to do. He wondered how she'd take his suggestion.

Because she'd worn party clothes under her coat, he'd needed to find her something to wear. Though he loved seeing her in the corset she'd worn to the party, he needed her in something more *practical* for the upcoming discussion. Anything of Julie's was out of the question since she was a petite five feet three. Dena stood close to five eight. Fortunately, he carried extra clothes in his bag.

So while she sat drinking juice at Daniel's table, talking to Abby and Nathaniel, she was wearing one of his T-shirts. It was still impossibly large, but his heart clenched at the sight. Seeing her dressed in his shirt brought back the memory of the many mornings she'd sat at his table wearing one.

"Nice shirt," Daniel said, walking into the kitchen.

Dena glanced down at the large garment. "Thanks. He not only carries arnica cream, but he packs an extra outfit."

He laughed at the look she shot him. "And a good thing, too. You'd be sitting there in a corset if I didn't."

She wrinkled her nose and turned her attention to Daniel. "How's Julie?"

"She kept down the broth I took her. Maybe she'll get some sleep tonight."

Dena yawned. "I know I'm still tired."

"No one will have to rock me to sleep tonight," Abby said, stifling her own yawn. Nathaniel bent down and whispered something in her ear that made her giggle.

Daniel stood with his arms crossed. "I trust your judgment, Jeff, but what exactly happened after Nathaniel and I left?"

Jeff glanced at Dena before answering. "I'm sure she's never been anything other than a perfect submissive with you, but I believe her exact words to me tonight were, 'Fuck you. Fuck you. *Fuck. You.*'"

Abby stared at Dena in disbelief. "You said that?"

Dena nodded and waved in Jeff's direction. "Yes, but he forgot the, 'Fuck you, *Sir*,' I said first."

"Right, 'Fuck you, *Sir.*' That's what earned you ten strokes, wasn't it?" Her ass would still be sore. She really didn't need the reminder, but Jeff needed her to understand he wasn't ready to joke about it just yet.

Dena's back straightened. "Yes, Sir."

"That's not like you. What's going on?" Daniel asked.

She glanced at him, but Jeff shook his head. "Since you remember everything word for word," he said, "you tell him. Besides, I'm interested in whether or not he thinks you need another reminder about being honest."

He wouldn't let Daniel touch her, of course, not tonight. She'd had enough for one day. But the fact was her behavior was unacceptable for someone who'd been a submissive for as long as her. He felt certain he'd made that point clear, but he wanted her to know how serious he took her misbehavior.

She pushed the empty juice glass away. "I had a threatening note slipped under my door last night."

"You did? Shit," Daniel said.

"And she's had harassing phone calls before then, including one tonight. And she didn't call the police. And she didn't tell me about it until after I punished her for being late, dressed, and the multiple 'fuck yous,'" Jeff said before she could continue.

She cut her eyes at him. "I'm sorry, Sir. I thought you wanted me to tell what happened."

Jeff shrugged. "I'm an impatient bastard."

Her mouth opened as if she was going to say something, but at the last minute, she closed it.

"Learned your lesson, I see?"

"I decided I'd prefer flogging, subspace, and screaming orgasms as opposed to just screaming. Sir."

"You're assuming my hands will be on you again in the future."

"I assume nothing." But her eyes had darkened and her nipples grew hard under his shirt.

He fisted his hands, and his cock hardened at the subtle suggestion. He was fighting a losing battle. As long as he stayed in Delaware, he knew it would be only a matter of time before he took her again. Unfortunately, plans had changed in the last few hours.

Daniel cleared his throat. "I'll let you guys stay in the guesthouse tonight so you can work this out privately, but can we go back to the note?"

Dena's head snapped up as if she'd forgotten other people were in the room. "I have a pretrial Monday morning. The only thing I'm working out this weekend is opening arguments." She narrowed her eyes at Jeff. "And I'll do it privately."

He walked to where she sat and looked down at her. "This from the woman who two minutes ago said she assumed nothing."

"That was in regard to you and me."

"As of two hours ago, anything pertaining to you also pertains to me."

"I don't know what you mean."

He turned and spoke to Daniel. "Since Dena doesn't want the police involved and planned on hiring me Monday for security detail, I've decided to respect her wishes. Assuming, of course, she moves in with me until the threat has passed."

Daniel and Dena both spoke at once.

"So you aren't going to—"

"Have you lost—"

Jeff held his hand up and addressed Daniel first. "No, I'm not. I'll be staying for the foreseeable future."

Then he turned to Dena. "I assure you I have full control of my mind. You may not agree, but your apartment is a security nightmare. You don't want to call the police, fine, but you play by my rules, and that means staying with me. I know my place is secure and safe. And the second thing is, you don't tell your father about my involvement."

She crossed her arms. "I hate it when you go all Dom on me outside the playroom. When you act like I can't make my own decisions."

"First of all, you love it when I go all Dom on you *in* the bedroom. And I don't think you would have come to me if you didn't trust me to take control of this situation, too. Say otherwise and I'll make you lift that shirt, spread your legs, and say it again while I prove what a liar you are."

She crossed her legs, and he forced himself not to smile.

"Second, I recognize you're an intelligent woman, fully capable of making your own decisions. But the fact is, when it comes to security, I'm the expert, and if you don't want me to call the police, we'll go about this my way."

"Just a minute," Nathaniel said. "I know it's not any of my business, but why wouldn't you want the police called?"

"Because the media would get involved, and they'd drag my dad into it, making it an even bigger mess." Dena sighed. "I worked my ass off for years to break the association with my father. Or as much as I could anyway."

Nathaniel frowned. He didn't appear to like Dena's answer, but he glanced over to Jeff and his features relaxed. "I'll leave it to you and Jeff, then."

"That's the . . ." Abby started and then stopped.

"That's the what?" Nathaniel asked when it became clear she wasn't going to finish her thought.

Abby's gaze bounced between Jeff and Daniel. "I'll tell you in the car."

Nathaniel gave a curt nod. "We do need to be leaving. We're meeting with the Realtor early tomorrow morning."

They said their good-byes and left after promising to touch base with everyone the next day.

Dena ran her fingers through her hair. "I have a ton of stuff I'll have to pack if I'm going to your house."

"Not a problem," Jeff assured her.

"I have a cat."

"The dogs will look after it."

"I still don't cook."

"I still do."

"I'm scared."

He knew she wasn't just talking about the note. She was worried about moving back in with him. He understood and shared those worries. After all, he was the one who'd planned to move to the other side of the country in an attempt to escape the hold she had on him.

So what kind of fool was he to insist she move in with him?

He wasn't sure he wanted to answer that.

Instead, he looked her straight in the eye and told her the truth. "I'm scared, too."

*   *   *

Daniel sneaked out of the kitchen after Abby and Nathaniel left. He didn't think Jeff and Dena would notice he'd left anytime soon. When they did realize he wasn't in the room, they would show themselves out. They probably wouldn't take him up on his offer to stay in the guest room. If he knew Jeff, he'd have Dena in his house tonight. Humming slightly, he jogged up the stairs, anxious to get to his bedroom. He'd come back downstairs and lock up in a bit.

He didn't bother to knock, but swung the door open and closed it behind him after he stepped inside.

Julie rolled over in bed, propped up on an elbow, and gave him a seductive smile. "Well?"

He pointed to the floor. "Come greet your Master properly, kitten."

She scurried out of bed and dropped to her knees before him. She was naked; the only thing she had on was his collar. He unbuttoned his jeans and kicked them and his boxer briefs off with a few shakes of his legs.

"I've had a hard-on for the last four hours. All I've been thinking about is fucking you." He tapped her chin. "Open up."

He slid inside her offered mouth, sighing in pleasure as her warmth enveloped him. He wasn't going to last long, not after observing others for the last few hours. That paired with the barely contained tension between Jeff and Dena would have him climaxing within minutes.

Fuck.

Especially when Julie did that with her tongue.

Oh well. He'd come quickly this time, cuddle and talk with Julie, and then he'd have her again. Slower.

He fisted his hands in her hair. "Don't miss a drop."

She tightened her grip on his thighs, her nails digging into his skin, and the sharp pain pushed him over the edge.

"Fuck," he said, releasing into her with a grunt.

Sated, he withdrew from her mouth and grinned when she dropped back to her heels and licked her bottom lip. A devilish smile danced on her expression.

"You aren't going to throw up on me, are you?" he asked.

She laughed. "I can't believe we pulled off that lie about me being sick."

He stripped off his shirt and climbed into bed, holding up the sheet so she could scramble in beside him. Once she had her back to his chest, he wrapped his arms around her and kissed the back of her head.

"No one had any reason to doubt me. I was always such an upstanding guy before you."

She snorted. "Sure, blame it on me. The vomiting was your idea."

"Stomach flu can strike anyone at any time. And because it's so nasty and dreaded, no one's going to examine it too closely."

"Dena will kill me if she ever finds out."

"Jeff will kick my ass."

She ran a finger down his arm. "But if it goes the way we plan, they'll be thanking us. All we did was work it out so they had to play together. It's not like we tricked them into getting married or something."

He held her quietly for a few minutes. It never crossed his mind to keep the note from her. He required honesty from her, and it was only fair he gave her the same. She was silent as he told her, but when he finished, she turned in his arms to face him.

"She told me a few weeks ago that she's been getting a lot of prank calls: someone calling and not saying anything or just breathing heavy. I didn't know about the note."

"You knew about the phone calls?"

"Yes, and she made me promise I wouldn't tell. She didn't want it getting back to Jeff." She sighed. "I wish I had told you."

"Me too." But he understood the importance of keeping a friend's confidence. "Jeff's having her stay at his place and has postponed his move."

She was silent for several minutes, thinking. "I probably could have done the demo after all."

"You'll have plenty of opportunities in the future. Though Dena's ass probably wishes you'd done the demo tonight."

"What? Why?"

"She showed up late to the demo tonight. Because of the phone call, but no one knew that at the time. She got mouthy to Jeff. Told him to fuck off."

"She didn't."

"She did."

"Damn."

"Let's just say the consequences were swift and unforgettable."

She giggled. "Ouch."

"They worked it out. They were all but making out when I left them."

"I hope we did the right thing."

He rolled her onto her back. "Too late to worry about that now. We'll just have to see how it plays out."

"Speaking of playing out, I've been lying up here all night

thinking up all the naughty things we could be doing while you were at the guesthouse being dungeon monitor."

He captured both her hands in one of his, pulling them above her head. She stretched under him, her back arching in anticipation.

"Me too," he said. "Why don't I show you a few of them?"

Dena would have squirmed in her seat in Daniel's kitchen if doing so hadn't hurt her backside so much. She'd admitted the day before that she'd walk to work uphill both ways if she could live with Jeff again, so what was her problem? It didn't take a lot of thinking to know:

He was doing it only to protect her.

It wouldn't really mean anything.

She wouldn't be wearing his collar.

But she felt better knowing he had reservations as well about the new arrangement. Somehow knowing the great, unflappable Jeff was scared made her feel less so. Both of them would be going into this situation knowing they were walking into a minefield.

"We need rules," she said. "Expectations. Lines."

Rules, expectations, and lines would create boundaries not only for their lives, but she hoped for her heart as well. Part of her knew it was wishful thinking. When had a heart ever listened to rules? But as unrealistic as it was, she felt she had to say it.

"There's too much history between us," she continued. They'd lived together for more than three years. "Too many memories in that house."

His jaw tightened, and she knew he was struggling to stay in control of his emotions. "You think I don't know that? Hell, I live there, Dena. I *live* there."

She'd never given much thought before to how Jeff had been able to stay in the house they'd shared. He was a man, and she realized she'd assumed the memories didn't bother him. Seeing him now, dragging a hand through his tousled hair, grief etched into the lines on his face, she knew she'd been wrong. She reached for the empty juice glass and spun it slowly in her hands.

"I'm sorry," she whispered. "Of course you know. It's just hard for me to picture myself going back."

She'd imagined returning to him, but it'd never been under circumstances like this.

"I get that, but I won't apologize for doing what's necessary to keep you safe."

"I still think you're overdoing it, but I know you well enough to know you aren't going to change your mind."

He gave her the smallest of smiles. "And I know you well enough to know you had to speak yours. I always appreciated that."

"Appreciation." She nodded. "That certainly explains the sore ass."

He raised an eyebrow. "Before we travel down that road, I think we should go back to what you said earlier about boundaries and expectations."

"Should we write this down?"

"I don't think that's necessary."

"First things first," she said. "I'm going to make a wild guess and assume telling you to fuck off is a definite no-no."

He shook his head. "Damn it, Dena."

"I know. I know. You're not ready to joke about it yet. It just helps me."

He'd been right months ago when he'd told her they were their best inside the playroom. Outside, they just butted heads.

So why did she still want him?

Because part of her loved submitting to him when they were playing together and then giving him hell outside when they weren't. But she had to admit, they'd gotten to the point when they started doing more than butt heads. It'd almost seemed as though they had tried to hurt each other. When it became unhealthy and the hurts could no longer be ignored, he'd taken his collar back.

Which had been the biggest hurt of all.

"Why don't we discuss boundaries when we get back to my cabin?" he suggested.

"Because I'd like to have everything ironed out before walking into your place."

"It's late and we still have to go by your apartment so you can pull your stuff together."

"Then we can stay in Daniel's guesthouse tonight and get my stuff tomorrow." He could push all he wanted. She wasn't going to agree to go to his place until they both knew and accepted what would happen when she got there. Besides, who knew how long she'd be with him. It'd take her longer than ten minutes to pack.

He crossed his arms in his typical stance. He probably thought he looked commanding and unmovable. All she could think about was how hot he looked in the short-sleeved T-shirt with his biceps stretching the sleeves.

Probably she was borderline exhausted and just needed to sleep.

You get punchy when you're too tired, she told herself. *Watch it.*

"We're not staying in the guesthouse. We'll go to my house and you can get your stuff tomorrow," he said. "We can talk in the car."

"I'd rather talk here." And not just so she could stare at his arms. "I want everything worked out before we head to your place."

"Why? Because you might change your mind?"

No, she wouldn't. Even though it wouldn't be the same as when she wore his collar, she'd still be at his house. That was more than she had two days ago. Already they'd spoken more than they had in the last few years put together. If she went she could still hope that, forced to live under the same roof, he might decide he wanted her back.

"No. I'm not going to change my mind. I just want us both in agreement as to what will and will not happen once I'm at your place."

"You keep saying that." He leaned against the countertop. "What are you so worried about?"

"Before, when I was . . ." she began. She lost her nerve, then admonished herself. *Say it. Just say it.* "When I wore your collar, things were different. I was your submissive. I'm not now and I'm not going to act like I am."

He nodded. "Fair enough. That means the playroom is off-limits. You can stay in the guest room and I'll be in the master bedroom."

Her gut twisted. The guest room. Hell, it was going to be nine kinds of odd to be living in Jeff's house and staying in the guest room. She'd shared his room when she lived with him before. The guest room was for guests.

"I have a trial coming up the end of next week. I'm going to need a lot of time and quiet and privacy. I'll be working late almost every night. I don't want you to worry."

"You know how secluded the cabin is. There's no one around for miles. That's part of what makes it so safe. If someone shows up who doesn't belong, I'll know."

Of course she remembered. She remembered everything about his house and the land he'd built it on. Tucked away out of the city, it looked more like a rural hunting lodge than a house just a few miles from one of the state's largest cities.

She never had to worry about anyone unexpectedly showing up at Jeff's. He had no nearby neighbors, and the road near his house didn't lead anywhere else. She remembered all too well how often he'd liked to exploit that fact when she'd worn his collar. The days he'd have her walk around the house naked, including walking out to get the mail once the mailman had left. It'd taken her some time to get used to it, but eventually she'd grown to enjoy it.

Mostly, she'd enjoyed his reaction to her being naked all day long. The way his gaze had followed her wherever she went. The undeniable look of desire, pride, and male satisfaction he had about her. How he'd watch while she went to the mailbox and then take her against the door as soon as she returned.

"Did you hear anything I just said?" he asked.

Shit, no. "Yes."

He looked at her in amusement. "What did I say, then?"

"It's not really fair how you know when I'm lying." She waited for him to say something, but he just stood and watched her. "No. I don't know what you were saying. I was too busy remembering other things."

But he didn't react to her provocation. "I said, you'll have plenty of time and privacy to work. I won't disturb you. I'll be trying to find out who's behind this note. But you're not driving anywhere alone. Either you go with me or you don't go at all."

"Absolutely not. There's no——"

He held a hand up to quiet her. "It's not negotiable. Anyone could follow you while you were driving, and if you're going to be working late, that's even worse. You're hiring me to keep you safe, remember? My rules."

Damn it all. Now she would feel like a prisoner with Jeff following her everywhere she went. It would be like her father all over again. But honestly, she asked herself, what did she expect? "I should have gone to someone else," she grumbled.

"And you know what I would have done if I'd found out."

He'd have gone ape shit if she'd hired another security person to help her. Now that she thought about it, maybe that would have been the thing to do. But no sooner had the thought crossed her mind than she knew she'd never have done it. Watching a jealous Jeff might be entertaining for a few minutes, but it would have been a childish thing to do, and she didn't play childish games.

"Bottom line is I want the best," she said.

"Which is why I'm going to be somewhat of an ass and an overbearing bastard to ensure your safety."

"Well, at least this way you'll have an excuse."

"You came to me, remember? It's either me or your father."

Jeff hated her father. She'd never been able to figure out exactly why. Growing up, her father had been okay. He'd gotten along with most of her high school dates. Even in college when she'd invite boys over for a long break, her father had been cordial. But never had he been that way with Jeff. He'd never even pretended. Neither of them had.

"Okay. Fine," she said. "I'll let you drive me."

"Glad you see things my way. I don't want your father involved either. I'll have enough shit to put up with if your dad ever finds out I knew you were threatened and didn't call the police."

It hit her then why he was willing to take her on.

"You're doing this to spite my father."

He didn't deny it.

"Damn it, Jeff."

"I won't say the thought never crossed my mind, but no, that's not it."

"Then what is it?"

His expression became pained, and she knew whatever he was getting ready to say would cost him. He wasn't a man who often admitted his feelings.

"You know damn well it would kill me if anything happened to you, Dena."

Which was as close to an "I love you" as she was going to get out of him. He'd let it slip the night Daniel collared Julie, but he probably wouldn't say the words again. Especially with her moving in.

Suddenly, she realized how very tired she was.

"Let's go to your place. I'm ready to crash."

Chapter Six

Six years ago

Dena woke to the smell of frying bacon and smiled. She loved lazy Saturday mornings at Jeff's house. Every time she slept over on a Friday night, he'd make her breakfast the next morning.

He hadn't collared her yet, but neither one of them played with anyone else. They'd been together for six months, ever since the night of the play party when he'd given her forty-five minutes and they'd ended up staying in the room until the party ended.

She slowly stretched her arms over her head, reliving the prior night's activities through the slight aches and pains that greeted her. Jeff hadn't been lying when he'd told her on their first date that he knew he could be hard to serve. He was tough and demanding, but when she gave him her best, his rewards were unlike anything she'd ever experienced before.

He wasn't like anyone she'd ever been with. The way he looked at her while they were in his playroom, like he wanted to worship her and ravage her both at the same time, left her wanting to give herself completely to him. He'd made it clear he didn't want a Master/slave relationship, and that was fine with her. She just wanted more than what they had now.

Not that she was complaining. She spent most Friday nights at his house, and they went to the group meetings and parties together. She just wanted more. But she was afraid to say anything for fear of ruining what they had.

Wearing one of Jeff's T-shirts, she walked to the kitchen and stopped for just a second in the doorway to watch him. He had on only a pair of sweatpants, which was fine by her. Situated the way he was, she had a great view of his muscular back. He transferred the bacon from the pan to a serving plate, and she almost sighed at the way such a simple act made his muscles move.

She padded over to him and wrapped her arms around him, placing a kiss right in the middle of his back. "Good morning, handsome."

He turned around and gave her a soft kiss. "Good morning to you. Ready for breakfast?"

She set the table, and within minutes they were settled at his cozy table, eating.

"You don't want any coffee?" he asked, nodding toward her glass of orange juice.

"Not this morning. I decided I like having enamel on my teeth."

He scoffed. "It's not that bad."

"We're going to have to disagree on the whole question of

what constitutes good coffee." She spread jam on a piece of toast. "Or maybe we could spend the night at my apartment for once and I could make you coffee. Why is it we always spend the night here, anyway?"

"Because I'm the one with all the fun toys."

"Right." She perked up. "We could make my spare bedroom a playroom."

He cocked an eyebrow at her. "I'm sure the Homeowners' Association would love that."

"Pesky homeowners."

"You're welcome to make coffee anytime you'd like. Assuming you get up before I do."

Which would never happen on a Saturday morning. It was one of her few chances to sleep in. "I get up at five Monday through Friday to jog. I typically take off on Saturdays, but you never know." She gave a small laugh. "You might wake up to find I'm off running down the street and there's coffee brewing in the kitchen."

It was supposed to be a lighthearted joke, so she was surprised when he didn't smile.

"There's another option," he said. "You could move in with me."

He was asking her to move in? Her heart began to race. "Here?"

"It's actually a two-part request."

There was more? She held her breath and waited. He reached across the table and took her hands.

"I enjoy our time together, Dena, and I'd like more of it. I want more of you." His dark eyes were heavy with emotion. "I'd like to offer you my collar."

She was speechless. She, who Jeff said could talk the bark off a tree, had no words.

"Dena?"

She blinked and realized her eyes were wet. "Jeff," she finally managed to get out. Pushing back from the table, she walked the few steps to him and climbed in his lap. "Yes," she said, wrapping her arms around him. "Yes. Collar me. Make me yours."

The next weekend she arrived to the playroom early, not surprised to find Jeff inside waiting. Lit candles were everywhere: lining the tables and his cabinets, even placed on the room's lone window ledge. They should have given the room a soft, romantic look, but she knew there was probably only one reason he'd have candles out.

He looked particularly handsome waiting for her in his black jeans and T-shirt. *Dark as the devil himself,* her grandmother would say. And Dena had a feeling Jeff would be unusually devilish tonight.

The thought made her smile in spite of her misgivings, and she walked into the room, her nerves at attention just thinking about what he might do to her. His eyes never left her body as she made her way toward him.

He nodded at her, and she dropped to her knees before him, moving quickly into his desired waiting position.

He brushed her cheek. "Why are you here tonight?"

"To become yours, Sir."

When her previous Dom collared her, he'd invited his friends over. Though she wouldn't have minded Jeff collaring her with group members present, she thought it more intimate and personal with just the two of them.

"Will you wear my collar, Dena?"

Her heart thumped with anticipation. "Yes, Sir."

He buckled something around her throat. "It's black leather, so I won't ask you to wear it to work. Instead, you'll wear this." It was a beautiful silver cufflike bracelet. "It has 'Property of Master Jeff' on the inside." He latched it around her right wrist. "What do you think?"

Her entire body somehow perceived the weight of his ownership. She felt protected and cared for. "I love them, Sir."

"You will address me as 'Master' when we're in this room."

"Yes, Master," she said, delighting in the knowledge that she and she alone held that privilege.

"Kiss my feet in thanks."

It wasn't the first time he'd asked her to do that, and she'd discovered it was something she enjoyed. There was something raw about kissing someone's feet. She couldn't explain why, but the entire process turned her on.

She slid to her elbows and lowered her body. "Thank you for collaring me, Master," she whispered before placing a kiss on the top of his foot. "I'm honored to wear the symbol of your dominance," she said before kissing the other.

"I'm honored to have you wear it," he said. "Now crawl to the table and get on your back."

She even liked crawling for him, knowing he couldn't keep his eyes off her. She moved slowly, making sure he got an eyeful, and flipped her hair over her shoulder before getting on the table. She usually wore it down for him. He liked to stroke it and loved to pull it.

He'd laid a sheet across the leather table. Nearby were unlit candles, a fire extinguisher, a lighter, and a bowl of ice cubes. Her belly quivered with both excitement and dread. They'd never done wax play before.

"I thought a night as special as this called for candles," he said, taking a bottle she hadn't noticed and pouring what appeared to be oil into his hands.

"Very appropriate, Master," she said even though she wasn't completely sure.

"Tell me why you're nervous," he commanded softly while he started a sensual massage along her upper body. "Why the fear in your eyes?"

For some reason, it always surprised her when he read her emotions like that. No one else had ever been able to do so.

"I've only done this a few times," she said, her mouth suddenly dry. "It wasn't my favorite."

He talked while carefully rubbing oil into her upper arms. "This isn't a hard limit for you."

"No, Master, and I can already tell this will be different. He didn't use the oil."

His hands moved across her chest, and she wanted to relax under his touch, but memories of the past wouldn't let her.

"The oil makes it easier to get the wax off. Plus, it gives me a reason to touch you all over." He leaned down and whispered in her ear, "As if I need one."

Her heart pounded faster at his words, and she gave him a little smile.

"Here's how this is going to work." He moved down her body to coat her belly with oil. "I'm going to continue, and you're not allowed to think of the past. Anytime a memory tries to enter your mind, you remind yourself that you're mine and that I'm a jealous Master. Understood?" He looked up and waited.

"Yes, Master."

He was at her legs now, massaging them with his rhythmic touch. "Remember when you wanted to prove to me that you would be the best submissive I'd ever been with?"

She nodded.

"This is me proving to you that I'm the best. By the end of the night, wax play's going to be on your Love It list." He glanced up to her for confirmation, and she saw the determination in his eyes. Hearing him, she almost believed him.

"I can see you don't quite think so," he said. "That's okay. I can be very persuasive." He took a leg in each hand and spread them. "I want you to stay like this. Do I need to bind you?"

"No, Master."

"I'm not going to blindfold you either, because it'll be much harder for you to remember the past when you're struggling to obey my command to keep your eyes closed."

Fuck. She hoped she could do this.

He moved to stand at her side, right near the table with the candles and the matches and the—

"Right now," he said sternly. "Close them."

She took a deep breath and closed them. *This is Jeff. This is Jeff. This is Jeff,* she repeated in her head until she'd calmed a bit.

"Good job," he said.

The room was absurdly still. She took another deep breath. Her hands fisted in the sheets at her sides, and she felt the weight of his cuff. The simple reminder that she was his calmed her further.

A match struck to her side, and the scent of sulfur filled the air.

She tensed but quickly relaxed when she reminded herself who it was holding the candle.

"Upper right arm," he said seconds before a trail of heat hit her arm.

She exhaled as the heat subsided.

"Upper left arm," he said, and a twin heat landed. "How does it feel?"

"Hot."

"Too hot? Do we need to stop?"

"No, Master. It's not near as bad as before."

He gave a grunt of satisfaction. "Knowledge. Technique. Proper candles." He took her hands and one at a time unclenched them, leaving them palm up on the table. "I'm not going to tell you where it's going to land anymore. You have safe words if you need them."

His reminder soothed her. She knew she had safe words, but no one had ever been so consistent in reminding her of them. For some reason, that simple act made her feel safer.

Three hot drops fell on her upper thigh. Two landed on her belly. And one dropped onto the valley between her breasts. Heat. She was surrounded by heat and it felt good.

"Where to go next?" he teased. "I have your entire body to play with. Here, you think?" He ran a finger along her inner thigh, and she gasped, imagining wax there.

"Here?" Warm air brushed her belly, but instead of wax, there was a sharp bite.

She muttered a curse. He chuckled.

"Or here?"

Her right nipple was encased in liquid fire. His mouth covered the other and sucked her hard and deep. It was as if a line of heat ran straight from her breasts, down her sides, and joined in an aching throb between her legs. Her body shook.

"Holy fuck," she gasped.

He blew a stream of air across her pussy, and she squirmed.

He wouldn't go there next, would he?

She didn't want him to.

Yes, she did.

No, she didn't.

Where was he?

The heat zigzagged across her belly, shocking the nerve endings that hadn't expected anything, and she cried out.

"Still okay?"

"Oh, God. Don't stop." The words rushed out without her even thinking them, and she surprised herself at how true they were. She wanted more heat. Needed it. Needed him. "Please."

"Please what?" The heat hit next in the inner crook of one elbow, followed quickly by the other.

"Please, please, please." She begged, desperate for something. She didn't care if it was him or more wax, just something.

He slipped a finger between her legs. "You're wet."

"Yes." Her hips jerked up in an attempt to get his finger deeper.

A sharp slap landed on her thigh. "Be still."

"Sorry, Master," she said, suddenly glad he'd had her close her eyes. She hated seeing him disappointed.

"I don't want your apology. I want your obedience." He placed his finger at her lips. "Clean it."

The temptation to open her eyes was strong; she wanted to get a peek at him badly. To see if the disappointment had left.

Instead, she sucked his finger inside her mouth and licked herself off. She'd rather it be his cock, but she'd take whatever part of himself he offered.

"Enough," he said, and he slipped his finger out.

There was a rustling to her side and another match was struck. At once, her heart pounded and her body tensed. She'd thought he was finished. She tried to remember how many candles were on the table and forced her eyes to remain shut.

"It pleases me to do this." His voice was soft but laced with iron. "You will take it for me."

Oh, fuck. What did that mean?

She yelped as hot rivers of wax ran over her midsection, pooled in her belly button, and dribbled down her sides. It barely cooled before another stream landed on the uncovered skin farther up her body. A third followed just as quickly. By the fourth, she was muttering uncontrollably. The fifth partially coated her breasts and was hot, so hot.

She waited for the sixth, needed the sixth, ached for the sixth. Instead, she shrieked when Jeff pushed two fingers deep inside her and started fucking her with them. Slow and methodical and brushing her clit with every inward thrust.

"Oh, God." She was going to come. Had he given her permission? She couldn't remember.

His fingers went deeper, stroking that spot inside her, the one he knew made her come, and she couldn't remember.

"Oh, God," she whispered. "Please let me come."

"I'm not God." His lips were so close to her ear, she could almost feel them, and his breath heated her further. "I'm the devil himself, sent to torture your angelic body in ways you can't imagine. And when I'm finished here, I'm going to fuck you so hard, so long, and so deep, you'll only think you're in heaven."

His touch. His words. "I can't . . ."

"Come for me, my wicked Angel. Come. Now."

He pushed a third finger inside her, biting her ear at the same time, and she shouted as her body shook with the force of her climax. Wave after wave of pleasure crashed through her. He kept moving his fingers, and she whimpered when a second orgasm overtook her, jerking and arching her back.

"Shhh," he whispered, and she realized she'd been babbling. "Shhh. It's okay. Open your eyes."

His lips were at her throat, placing kisses along her neck and whispering against her skin. She opened her eyes slowly, blinking in the low light. His face was the first thing she saw: dark hair, full lips, chiseled features, and questioning eyes.

He stroked her cheek. "How do you feel?"

"Wonderful. Sublime. Elated."

"That's a lot of adjectives."

"My mind's too fuzzy to pick just one."

He lowered his head and captured her lips in a kiss, cupping her face gently. It was only a soft kiss, but she felt her need and desire for him rise again. Amazing what he could do to her with a simple touch.

"You did great. Perfect," he said, pulling back, his voice full of pride and love shining in his eyes. He brushed a hair away from her face.

"Thank you, Master," she said in a sigh. "Thank you."

"You might want to hold your thanks." His smile was evil, and he picked up a flogger from the table and lifted it so she could see. "I still have to remove the wax."

Chapter Seven

Present day

Dena fell asleep in the passenger seat before Jeff pulled out of Daniel's driveway. Jeff remembered from playing with her in the past how sleepy she became afterward. When she'd told him she wanted to discuss expectations before leaving, he'd known she was fighting a losing battle. As tired as she'd looked, any meaningful conversation would have to wait until morning. He remembered, too, how loopy she became when tired.

He pulled onto the highway headed toward his cabin on the outskirts of town and glanced over at Dena. She'd leaned the seat back as much as the passenger side of his truck would allow. Her head was turned toward him in such a way that he could see her lips part slightly. The faint moonlight made her blond hair luminous.

Angel.

He had finally allowed himself to call her that the night he collared her. His sassy and sexy angel. When he thought back to their past, he still had a hard time believing a woman as wealthy and smart and beautiful as she was would want him—much less agree to wear his collar. Maybe he had never really been able to believe it. Maybe that was why it had been easy to let her go.

He frowned. He hadn't thought about it like that before.

But it made sense. Hadn't he always thought she was too good for him and that she'd realize it and leave? Did he take his collar back only because he didn't want her to break up with him first? He hadn't thought so at the time, but now, years removed, it made sense.

She smiled in her sleep, and he remembered seeing the same smile the first time they'd played together, as she'd looked up from between his knees. The night she'd proved her point about how good she was.

To this day she was the best he'd ever had.

He pulled into his driveway, knowing he'd have some explaining to do when she saw the moving boxes. He needed to brace himself for the hurt he'd find in her eyes. The hurt at both his leaving and possibly the hurt knowing he'd stayed for her. Or maybe that would be guilt.

He opened her door, unbuckled her seat belt, and scooped her into his arms.

"Perfectly capable of walking," she mumbled.

"Humor me."

"You have no sense of humor."

He smiled, remembering that fatigue always left her uninhibited. "Then maybe I just like holding you in my arms and carrying you."

"Mmm." She snuggled into his chest. "I like your arms. They're hot in that shirt."

He grinned. "Good to know."

Propping her up on his knee, he unlocked his door and stepped inside. Fortunately, he'd left some lights on in anticipation of arriving home late. What he had not anticipated was arriving with the bundle he currently had in his arms.

"Sheets on the bed are clean," he said, carrying her down the hall to his guest room. "I know you're a neat freak over things like that."

"Like you," she mumbled. "Remember . . . dirty . . . fuck."

His cock hardened at her words. He wasn't exactly sure which dirty fuck she was talking about. Hell, they'd had so many, and he was never one to be gentle.

"I remember them all—trust me."

He pulled the sheets down and tucked her in.

"Ass hurts," she said.

"I imagine it does. I'll check it out in the morning."

She smiled. "Check my ass out."

"Good night, Dena."

"'Night, Master." She snuggled into the bed, and his chest ached at the sight of her and the words she'd spoken.

Instead of going to bed, he went into the living room, where a small desk sat in the corner. He knew he wouldn't be able to sleep until he at least came up with a plan for finding out who was harassing Dena. He pulled out a notebook and a pen and jotted down his initial thoughts. There were several possibilities for who it could be, but he thought two most likely: someone she had prosecuted at work or someone trying to get to her father.

Tomorrow he would look into some of her closed cases and start with the assumption it was work related. That would be relatively easy in that the scope of the search was limited. Especially when you compared it to what he would have to do if it turned out to be related to her father. Jeff knew the man had to have made his share of enemies over the years.

Jeff considered himself a reasonable man. He got along with most people, though it helped that the majority of them simply left him alone. Dena had been the first person to really get under his skin. To know and understand him. How she came from the same genetic line as her father was a mystery he'd never solve.

He'd never forget his first, and only, conversation with Senator Jenkins.

He and Dena had been together only a few months when it had happened. He'd arrived at work one morning, and balancing the apple Dena insisted he eat on top of his files, he'd worked the lock with the other hand. He frowned when he got in, realizing he must have left the lights on all night.

But when he saw the man sitting at his desk, he jerked back and nearly dropped everything.

"Senator Jenkins?" he asked, recognizing Jenkins from his television appearances.

"Jeffery Parks, I presume?"

The guy spoke only those four words, but somehow managed to fit a world of disdain into them. Jeff disliked him immediately.

"That's what the name on the door says."

Jenkins ignored the barb and stood up. "You've led an interesting life, Parks."

Jeff shrugged, refusing to show any sign of surprise at Jenkins's words. Dena's father kept his gaze on Jeff, his look intense as he rose from his seat and started circling around him.

"In and out of trouble with the police from an early age. Alcoholic mother. Absent father. High school dropout. Though you did somehow manage to get your GED eventually, didn't you?"

"I'm guessing you didn't come all the way here to entertain me with stories of my past."

"I have one child, Parks."

"Dena." Of course, he'd known that was why Jenkins was there.

"She's on track to become a superior court judge. She will be an exceptional one."

Dena had told him of her father's obsession with her becoming a judge. She'd confessed to Jeff she had no interest in doing so because her passion was prosecuting criminal cases.

"She's an exceptional woman, Senator. I'm sure she'll excel at whatever she decides to do."

The two men continued to size each other up.

"Of course she will," Jenkins finally said. "As long as she's not . . . distracted."

"I suppose you consider me a distraction."

"She's had a conservative upbringing; I won't deny that. It's expected she'll feel the need to taste the other side. See what it's about."

"I see. I'm the distraction from the other side."

"Whatever you are, you aren't the same as us."

"You might want to run statements like that past your publicist before you make them. People tend to frown upon public officials drawing such class lines."

"I'm glad you find this conversation amusing."

"It's the only thing keeping me from telling you to fuck off. I'm sure I don't need to remind you that Dena's a grown woman, capable of doing whatever the hell she wants." Jeff had felt it was past time for the visit to be over. He walked to his desk and sat down. "Thanks for stopping by. You can show yourself out."

But the senator wasn't finished. "These are dangerous times, Parks. I hope you're careful. So much senseless violence these days. So many unprovoked shootings."

The enormity of the words hit Jeff solidly in the chest, and several seconds passed before he could breathe. "Did you just threaten me?"

"I did no such thing." Jenkins headed toward the door but turned right before he opened it to say one more thing. "I'm simply suggesting that it might be more beneficial to your health if you looked elsewhere for companionship."

"Asshole," Jeff had mumbled under his breath.

Now, thinking back on that day, words didn't exist to adequately convey the loathing he felt toward Senator Jenkins. And though he believed truth and honesty a pillar of any relationship, he'd never told Dena about the day he'd met her father.

She might not get along with the man, but that was a long way from her knowing just how manipulative he was. Was it wrong of him to keep that knowledge from her? Maybe, but he told himself he was just protecting her.

He brought his hand up to massage his temple, and when he did so, he caught the scent of Dena's perfume on his fingers. He held still for a second and breathed her in. It didn't seem possible she was in his house again, and he purposely didn't let his mind wander to how it would feel when she left.

With a sigh, he put the notebook away and headed to his bed with a heavy heart.

Dena walked into Jeff's kitchen the next morning, frowning. She had a sinking feeling she'd talked in her sleep the night before. No telling what she'd said and no telling if Jeff would tell her. Sometimes he would and sometimes he wouldn't.

He was sitting at the kitchen table drinking coffee. He made horrid strong stuff, she remembered. "'Morning."

She nodded in reply. "Two questions. What's up with all the boxes, and what did I say in my sleep?" It was downright embarrassing not remembering, but not knowing was worse.

"I'll tell you about the boxes after you have coffee. And 'dirty fuck' and 'sore ass.'"

She took the cup waiting for her on the counter and poured herself some. "This the same vile stuff as always?"

"Yes."

"Dirty fuck and sore ass. Not too bad. I've said worse."

"And you called me 'Master.'"

She stiffened in shock. "Fuck."

"Don't worry about it. I know how out of it you get when you're tired." He pushed back from the table, a determined expression on his face. "I did promise to check out your ass this morning, however."

Hurrying to the table, she sat down. "No worries. My ass is fine."

She couldn't explain why, but she knew she'd be mortified for him to look at her backside.

"I still need to look."

"No one else I'd play with would."

"Number one, I'm not anyone else. Number two, they damn well should. And number three, come here and let me see and I won't make you get over my knee."

When she wore his collar, he'd always made her come over his knee the morning after a hard spanking. "I told you I wouldn't be submissive in your house."

"I'm not asking you to be a submissive. I'm telling you, as the Dom who spanked you, that I need to check your ass."

"Kinda sounds like the same thing."

His sigh was heavy and sad. "Does the arguing ever get to you? Because it sure as hell wears me out."

"I told you this was a bad idea." He'd called it correctly once before: in the playroom they were fine, but once they stepped outside, they were toxic.

"And my other choice is what? Take my chances some maniac wrote you a note just because he was bored?" He shoved his hand through his hair. "This isn't forever—just until we get to the bottom of everything. Let's try not to hurt each other any more than we already have."

His eyes pleaded with her, and something inside of her softened. Surely she could do this. He was only acting out of his feelings for her. As much as they could claim otherwise, he wouldn't move anyone else into his house to keep them safe. He was too private and enjoyed his own space too much.

True, he would probably check anyone's skin the day after

giving them a spanking like he'd given her. But then again, that was just the kind of man he was.

She put her coffee mug down and pushed back from the table. Because she didn't have any other clothes, she still had his T-shirt on and nothing underneath.

It's no big deal, she told herself. *He's seen you naked plenty of times.*

Turning her back to him, she lifted the hem of the shirt and closed her eyes tightly. Last night at the party had been one thing; in his kitchen the next morning was different. But he was right; they should try to get along for the few weeks or however long it ended up being.

"Looks good," he said. "You can go ahead and sit down to eat."

"Good? That all you have? I have a great ass. Work out five days a week to keep it that way."

He took the olive branch for what it was and slapped her butt. "Yes, you have a mighty fine ass. Always did. Have a seat and I'll fix you a plate."

Jeff had always been the one to cook when they were together. He'd taught himself as a young child when he'd figured out that if he was going to eat, he'd have to be the one to prepare it. Dena, on the other hand, grew up with a personal chef and never learned how.

"Never understood how you could cook such a delicious breakfast and suck so much at making coffee," she said as he placed a plate of eggs, sausage, and toast in front of her. "Seriously, it's like drinking tar."

"You drink a lot of tar?"

"Only when I have breakfast at your place." She ate a bite of sausage. "Damn, I can't remember the last real breakfast I ate."

"Plenty more if you want it."

"This is good."

He refilled his coffee and sat across from her, silently keeping her company while she ate.

She waited until she'd finished most of her breakfast before asking, "Why all the boxes?"

He took a deep breath. "I'm going to Colorado for a while to help my dad prepare for retirement."

Her fork slipped from her hand and clanged against the plate. "What? Why? You hate Colorado."

He shrugged. "It's not forever—just to get him settled."

But still. It wouldn't be Wilmington without Jeff. Though they had broken up, there was still something inside her that needed to see him. Wanted to see him. Even when he played with other women, at least she was aware of what he was doing and whom he was with.

Her body shook. Jeff was moving. Across the country.

"It won't be for a long time," he repeated, but softer this time. "I'm going to help him wrap up the business."

"*You're* going to sell insurance?"

"That's what Daniel said. Why is it so hard to believe I'd sell insurance?" He was attempting to put a humorous spin on the situation, but he couldn't make his tone light enough to match his words.

"Probably because you'd scare the hell out of your customers with that scowl of yours." She couldn't believe she was joking about it. Jeff was moving, and she sat calmly at his table.

Because she knew if she didn't laugh, she'd cry.

"It felt like something I needed to do," he said.

"When?"

"Supposed to have been next weekend, but I called and told Dad I'd be delayed."

The breakfast she'd eaten sat like a rock in her belly. "Because of me."

"Yes."

She couldn't tell him she was sorry, because that would be a lie and she didn't want to lie to Jeff. "Were you going to tell me good-bye?" she whispered over the lump in her throat instead.

Something she couldn't make out lurked behind his expression. "Of course I was."

After breakfast, they took his truck first to Daniel's to pick up her car and then to her apartment to get her things. Jeff stayed with her while she packed, but he was quiet. The tension between them was back. Whatever tiny bit of frivolity they had managed to find had fled when he'd told her he was moving.

By midafternoon she'd made herself as comfortable as possible in Jeff's guest room. She'd brought over enough clothes for two weeks and all her active client files. Bentley, not pleased with the sudden upheaval, had taken up residence under Jeff's bed.

"Probably pissed about that name," Jeff had said in a rare moment of teasing. "Who names a cat Bentley?"

"This from the man with dogs named Ace and Bo. *Bo*? Would a little bit of originality kill you?"

He'd shrugged. "He looked like a Bo."

She spent the rest of the day reviewing work files in a corner of his living room. She'd noticed the small desk shortly after breakfast and had quickly claimed it. Without Jeff to remind her, she probably would have worked through dinner, but the enticing smells coming from the kitchen dragged her from her files.

After dinner she was back at it. Time flew by, and she didn't realize how late it was until Jeff quietly placed a glass of chocolate milk on the edge of the desk. Her heart clenched. So many people saw him as quiet and standoffish, but she knew the man under the gruff exterior.

Who would know him in Colorado?

"Thank you, Sir," she said. "I can't remember the last time I had some."

"You're welcome. I want . . . I want to make this as easy on you as possible."

"I appreciate that." She glanced down at her calendar and frowned. "Oh, I meant to tell you—I have a session with Daniel and Ron tomorrow afternoon."

Daniel was mentoring a new Dominant, and he'd asked her to help. As the most experienced submissive in the group, she was often asked to participate in training scenes.

"Why the frown?" he asked.

Dena sighed and ran a hand through her blond waves. "Ron keeps asking me to play outside of the mentoring sessions. I've turned him down I don't know how many times, but he keeps asking."

Jeff crossed his arms. Since he was being mentored by Daniel, Ron was able to play with submissives in the group, but it was surprising he kept asking one who'd repeatedly turned him down. "Do you want me to say something to him?"

"No. I can take care of it. Maybe he'll eventually get the picture."

"Or you could tell him you're not interested in being in a scene with him ever." He nodded as if he'd decided something. "I'll be going with you tomorrow."

She almost told him that wouldn't be necessary, but the look on his face and the determination in his eyes persuaded her not to. Accepting that this was how it was going to be for the foreseeable future, she simply nodded.

"I've been working on how to approach finding out who's been harassing you. I need a list of all the cases you've prosecuted, or at least the people involved. We'll start with that. How soon can you get it to me?" Jeff asked.

"I'll have it for you tomorrow," she said.

It was all sorts of odd with Jeff watching the training session the next day. But she couldn't put her finger on exactly why. There was no sex involved with the scene. Daniel was just teaching Ron a flogger technique. And she was naked, but Jeff had seen her naked plenty of times.

Maybe that was it, she decided as they drove back to his house. She was naked before him, but not naked *for* him.

"Daniel has his work cut out for him with that one," Jeff said, pulling the truck into the driveway of his house.

Dena shot her gaze his way, as these were the first words he'd spoken on the entire trip home. "Really? Why do you think that?" She had never noticed anything off about Ron before.

"There's just something in his demeanor."

"I didn't notice anything with his technique."

He pressed his lips together. "I noticed."

He'd stopped the truck and they got out. Probably he'd noticed because he was jealous. Or that's what she told herself. She watched as he opened the side door and let her in, enjoying the way his muscles flexed under his shirt. Not for the first time that day, she wished it'd been Jeff holding the flogger.

Because of the way the evening turned out at the play party, they'd never had their flogging scene. Of course, all it took was imagining Jeff holding a flogger to ensure she didn't think about anything else. Eating dinner, she'd watch his hands flex and imagine those hands on her. The movement of his biceps had her thinking of how he'd work a flogger.

Fuck, she wanted him.

So much for rules, expectations, and lines.

"Everything okay?" he asked the second time she almost dropped a dish she was drying after he washed it.

"Sorry; just thinking." And watching his lips. How full they were.

He took a step toward her, and he was watching her lips, too. "About what?"

Your lips on my body. Your hands bringing me to the edge. "Nothing."

"Liar." Another step closer. He put the dish down and dried his hands. "Tell me."

He was invading her space. And she loved it. She lifted her chin. "No."

"Yes." He was so close, she felt the warmth of his body. Any closer and he'd be touching her. They locked eyes. Time stilled.

She licked her lips. "You owe me a flogging."

"You want me to flog you?"

"Yes."

"Doesn't that go against your rules?"

"Screw 'em."

He crossed his arms. "I'm not going to fuck you."

Well, damn. But she'd take what she could get. "Fine."

He studied her for several long seconds before finally saying, "Playroom in ten minutes."

Chapter Eight

Three years ago

Jeff stared at the pregnancy stick in disbelief. Garbage was scattered all over the kitchen floor, thanks to a dog looking for table scraps, but the pale pink plastic stick may as well have been covered in flashing lights. "Dena," he finally managed to croak out. She was down the hall but should still be able to hear him.

"Just a minute."

It was as if he held a ticking time bomb in his hands. "I need you now."

Laughter came from where she was. "If I had a dime for every time I heard that one."

Less than a minute later he heard her footsteps in the hall. "Holy shit. Did Ace get into the garbage again?" she asked as she entered the kitchen and stepped carefully over the trash scattered across the kitchen floor. "Yuck."

He held up the stick, and she went pale.

"What is this?" he asked.

"I haven't confirmed anything yet. It could be a false positive."

Being knocked over the head with a brick would have felt better. "It was positive?"

She nodded.

"You're pregnant?"

"I haven't confirmed it yet."

"But you could be?"

It wasn't that he didn't want children. He just didn't want them now. He wasn't ready to be a father. A long time ago he'd decided exactly what type of father he would be one day: affectionate, protective, supportive. All the things his own father hadn't been. And he wanted to be able to provide for his family. His business was doing well, but with the economy the way it was, it'd be a bad time to take on that additional financial responsibility.

"Yes," she said. "I could be."

"But you're on the pill."

"Nothing's one hundred percent effective except abstinence."

He mumbled a curse under his breath.

"Yeah, well, that's why I didn't want to tell you until I confirmed it," she said, and kicked a banana peel for good measure.

He felt awful. He knew he should be more supportive. If he were a better man, he'd know just the right thing to say. Unfortunately, he felt like he'd been kicked in the stomach, and if he opened his mouth again, he was afraid he'd say something he'd regret even more.

"It's not like I'm jumping up and down with joy either, you

know," she said. "I have a whole list of things I want to accomplish before I become a mom."

A mom. Dena was going to be a mom. To his child.

She got a new trash bag and started picking up the scattered garbage. "We have to clean this kitchen up. The smell's making me sick."

As she knelt down on the floor, his eyes fell on her collar. His collar. The black leather band that labeled her as his. She was his lover and his best friend, but she was also his submissive. When he'd put the collar on her, he'd promised to care for her, to love and support her.

He was failing miserably.

"Don't." He stilled her hand before it could pick up a wet coffee filter. "You don't need to be in here if the smell's making you sick. Go sit down and let me do this."

"But I—"

"No buts. We'll talk later."

She nodded and left the room, leaving him with his thoughts and spilled garbage. He put the pregnancy test aside and went back to picking up the trash. Something about the mundane task soothed him. By the time the floor was clean, he felt calmer, although too many thoughts and emotions still filled his head. He poured a glass of chocolate milk and went to find Dena.

She was curled up, sleeping, on the couch. Moving slowly so he wouldn't wake her, he sat down and placed her head on his lap. Ever so softly, he stroked her hair, gently pulling his fingers through the silky blond strands. She stirred, and her eyes blinked open.

"I'm sorry," he said as she sat up. "I didn't mean to wake you."

"'S okay. If I sleep now, I won't be able to at bedtime."

He took the glass of milk from the table he'd put it on and gave it to her. She sighed a happy sigh and took a sip.

"Thank you."

"I didn't know if it'd make you sick."

"No. I've been craving milk."

"In that case, I'll get you more when you finish that."

She smiled at him, a bit hesitantly, and drank some more.

He waited until she'd finished half the glass before asking, "How late are you?"

She wiped away the remnants of a milk mustache but missed a tiny bit at the corner of her mouth. He thumbed it away.

"Week and a half," she said in answer to his question.

That long and she hadn't said anything? He knew her periods were usually as regular as clockwork. If she was ten days late, he thought there was very little chance it was a false positive. His stomach knotted, but he did his best to push those feeling aside and focus on her. She'd set her glass down, so he took her hand.

"I'm in a bit of shock right now," he said. "The very last thing I expected to find in the dumped-out garbage was a pregnancy test."

Her eyes searched his. "Much less a positive one."

"Yes. So I'm going to need some time to work out this news in my head. But, Dena." He cupped her chin. "We're in this together. I'm here for you. For you both."

She nodded and tucked a piece of hair behind her ear. "Thank you."

"It's just . . . Wow." He still didn't think he could form the words. "A baby."

"I know," she whispered.

The night grew silent around them. He didn't know how it would all work out, how they would make room in their very content and settled life for a child. He just knew they'd do it somehow.

Dena couldn't shake the feeling that something was wrong. No matter how often she told herself she was making it up, she never felt at peace with the pregnancy. She was nearly twenty weeks along, and the feeling had only grown worse lately.

Jeff, of course, had been wonderful, once he came around to the whole idea of fatherhood. Now he was fully engaged, scouring the Internet for baby names, making sure she got plenty of rest, and taking time off work to go with her to the doctor's office. She had thought he'd propose since she was pregnant, but so far he hadn't brought marriage up. He was probably waiting on her, looking and waiting for some signal she'd be receptive.

Her second-trimester ultrasound was in a few weeks. They were both looking forward to it. They'd decided not to find out if they were having a boy or a girl, though Jeff insisted it was a girl.

She rubbed her belly. As long as the baby was healthy, that was all she cared about. She frowned. Had long had it been since she felt movement? Should she lie down and see if she could feel something?

A quick glance at the kitchen clock told her Jeff would be home soon. He worked only half days on Saturday and said he'd stop weekend work altogether once the baby came. She decided to make a few sandwiches so they'd be ready when he got home. Food would probably wake the baby up and get it moving around. That would make her feel better. Plus, she had something she'd wanted to discuss with Jeff, and sitting down to lunch with him would give her a chance to do it. She could lie down later in the afternoon.

He walked into the house right as she finished the sandwiches. As always, she was his first stop. He met her with a sexy smile, hooked a finger through the metal loop in her collar, and captured her lips in a kiss.

"You made lunch," he said when he pulled back. "Any particular reason?"

Normally he did all the cooking, especially since certain smells had made her queasy in her first trimester. Plus, she didn't cook.

"It's just sandwiches."

He raised an eyebrow.

Damn man. It was like he could read her mind. "Yes, Sir. There's something I'd like to discuss." Hopefully, the 'Sir' would give him an idea of what.

They'd had sex since finding out she was pregnant, but he'd been so gentle, he treated her like she was fragile glass. On top of that, they hadn't been in the playroom at all since the positive test turned up.

She saw the desire flash in his eyes and knew he missed it just as much as she did.

"Well, now, Angel, why don't you set the table while I change and we can talk over lunch."

His use of her nickname made her heart race and her knees tremble. "Yes, Sir."

He kissed her hard and quick before walking to the bedroom, unbuttoning his shirt as he went. He didn't look at the closed door to the playroom, but surely he was thinking about it as he passed.

That's when the first sharp pain pierced her belly. She had turned to grab the plates from the countertop, and instead she had to grip it to steady herself. But it passed, and she moved to pick them up when the second hit. It hurt so badly, they slipped from her hands. The plates fell to the ground and shattered. She doubled over, not caring about the broken glass, just wanting the pain to end.

"Dena?" Jeff called from the bedroom. "Everything okay?"

"I'm fine. Just dropped a dish," she called back, hoping she sounded convincing. "Just fine," she added in a whisper.

For what seemed like forever, she stood, hunched over and breathing deeply through the pain. When it subsided, she timidly walked to the kitchen table and sat down.

Everything's okay, she told herself. *Just twisted the wrong way.* She'd just sit here for a minute; then she'd get the broom and clean the floor. And Jeff would be hungry; she needed to get the sandwiches.

Just the thought of food made her feel queasy, but this queasy was different from before. Before it hadn't made her heart race and her body feel clammy all over. A wave of nausea swept over her, and she jumped up and ran down the hall, hoping she would make it in time.

"Are you okay?" Jeff asked as she pushed by him in the hall.

She couldn't talk, couldn't open her mouth. *Almost there. Almost there,* she repeated in her head.

Finally making it to the bathroom, she jerked the door open, slammed it behind her, and reached the toilet just in time.

"Dena!" Jeff pounded on the door. "What's wrong? Let me in!"

He couldn't see her like this. She took some toilet paper and wiped her mouth. "No. Go away."

The pain hit her stomach again. She groaned and rocked back and forth, hoping that would help make it subside.

The pounding on the door continued. "I swear to God, Dena, open this door or I'll bust it down!"

She crawled to the door and opened it. Jeff rushed in, took one look at her, and fell to his knees.

"What do I do? Where does it hurt?" His hands ran over her body, looking for a way to fix everything, to make everything better.

Hot tears filled her eyes. *Oh, Jeff. I'm sorry.*

There was no fixing this.

The grief was overwhelming. Jeff felt it dragging him under, and he was unable to stop it. Every so often, he would float to the top and see Dena drowning in her own sea of sorrow, but he wasn't strong enough to reach her. Much less rescue her.

It was his fault, he knew, for not being excited about the baby in the first place. If he'd only embraced Dena's pregnancy from the start instead of being uncertain and worried. Maybe then he wouldn't be mourning his firstborn child. Their daughter. His perfect little girl who had never opened her eyes in this world before passing into the next.

The doctors hadn't been able to find exactly what had hap-

pened. They even said there was nothing in the way of them trying to conceive again in a few months. He wasn't sure either one
of them would be ready then, if ever.

Well-meaning friends came by the cabin to pay their respects,
tell them how sorry they felt, how it was for the best, and to
bring casseroles. He was caught between laughing over the number of casseroles in their freezer, crying over the outpouring of
sympathy, or yelling in anger, demanding to know how it could
ever be for the best.

Dena barely spoke, choosing to answer most questions in as
few words as possible. He didn't know how to reach her, and how
could he pull her from her abyss when he couldn't find a way out
of his own? Day after day, he felt her slip further and further
away.

When she suggested she move out for a while, just to get her
bearings, he agreed. She'd been living with him for years. Maybe
she needed to be away for a bit. He thought if they each could
grieve alone and without worrying about the other, maybe they
would heal faster. They could find their own peace and come together stronger.

But looking back, he could see his agreement for what it was:
the worst decision he'd ever made. Without her, the cabin
echoed with loneliness and despair met him at every corner.
Days after she left, he shut the door to the nursery, telling himself he'd wait until she came back so they could deal with the
room together.

She never came back. With time, they had each grown stronger, but they had also grown further apart.

"I don't get it," he told Daniel three weeks after she moved out. "Whenever we're together, it's like we're walking on egg-shells. Almost like we're scared of each other."

"I wish I knew what to say. I just don't. Has she mentioned moving back?"

They were at Daniel's house, having a few beers and pretending to watch the football game.

"Nothing," Jeff said. "Maybe I'll stop by and see her after work tomorrow."

"She still staying with Kelly?"

Mistress K was a Domme in their group. Since she worked for the Wilmington Police Department, their paths crossed often in both the vanilla and the kink worlds.

"Yes, but you know how Kelly can be."

"Bossy, demanding, and hard to get along with?"

"Exactly," Jeff said. "Just like someone I used to know."

Daniel put his beer down and leaned forward. "I can't say I know how you guys are feeling. I don't. But the loss you've experienced is a major one. It'll take time to come to terms with it."

"I wish I'd never agreed to let her move out."

"You can't keep her against her will."

"Maybe not, but I could have fought her on it instead of just agreeing." He thought back to the day she'd suggested moving out. "Do you think it's the house? Maybe it has too many memories?"

"I think it's a combination of things, but I know you have to accept the fact that you can't fix them for her."

Jeff knew Daniel was right. There were some things that were out of his control. He couldn't change what had happened; nor could he control Dena's feelings about it. She would have to work it out for herself, the same way he did. The only thing he could do was to try to be there for her while she did so.

He pulled up to Kelly's house later that evening and wondered if he should have called first. Dena's car was in the driveway, but Kelly's wasn't. With a heavy sigh, he parked his truck and made his way to the door.

Dena opened it at his knock, a look of surprise on her face. Her hand automatically went to her collar. "Jeff. I wasn't expecting you."

She moved aside to let him in.

"I wanted to stop by and see how you're doing," he said, once inside.

"You could have called for that."

"I wanted to *see* how you were doing. You talk to me on the phone but avoid actually being in the same room with me." By his calculations, it'd been almost two weeks since he'd seen her.

She led him into the living room, where they sat on opposite sides of the couch.

"I'm doing about as well as can be expected." She studied him. "How about you? How are you doing? You look tired."

"I'm not sleeping well," he said. *It's lonely without you,* he wanted to add, but didn't. For some reason, the words didn't make it from his head to his mouth.

She sighed. "Me either."

They sat, for what felt like eternity, without speaking. She picked at a thread on her jeans. He stared at the ceiling. It was like they were strangers.

"When are you coming home?" he asked.

She jumped when he spoke, almost as if she'd forgotten he

was in the room. "I don't know," she said. "I don't think I'm ready."

"Ready for what?" he asked. "It's our home. It's where you belong."

"It's not the house."

She went back to paying attention to the thread on her jeans. *It's you*, were her unspoken words. *It's you I'm not ready for.*

"I see," he said. And he did. It was his fault, after all. When they'd first confirmed she was pregnant, he'd thought about proposing. He'd been waiting for a sign she wanted him to. Now he knew why he never found one. He stood up. "I should be going. I just wanted to see how you were doing."

She didn't show him to the door.

They next saw each other a week later at a group social. He went because he thought it might be good for him to be around people. He'd missed the companionship of his peers, but he was surprised to see Dena there.

She still looked lost. She had always been thin, but she looked gaunt and her eyes were sad. She was wearing jeans and a long-sleeved tee. While she typically didn't wear her corset and heels to group socials, she usually didn't wear street clothes either. When she saw him arrive, he knew she was just as surprised to see him as he had been to see her.

No one came up to him. Most people simply stared at him and quickly looked away.

"How's it going?" Daniel asked, giving Jeff a slap on the back.

"Better now that I'm not being treated like I have the plague or something. Hell, it was a miscarriage; it's not contagious." He knew he sounded bitter, but he couldn't help it.

Across the room, no one was talking to Dena, either. As he watched, Kelly came and stood by her side. A feeling of gratitude swept over him.

He was at the buffet table, getting something more to drink, when Dena came up to him.

"I didn't know you were going to be here," she said.

He shrugged. "I didn't know it was my place to let you know my every move."

She shifted her weight. Her fingers drifted up to her throat and grazed his collar. "By that you really mean it's my place to let you know *my* every move."

"That is my collar you're wearing, isn't it?" Any other time, he would have insisted on knowing she'd be attending a group function ahead of time. Since the miscarriage, however, everything was a mess.

She looked past him to something over his shoulder. "Sorry, Sir. I thought it would be a good idea for me to come tonight. To see our friends in a neutral environment."

Yet she hadn't expected him to be there. He didn't want to examine that too closely, but he knew he would have to eventually. On the surface, her actions seemed to indicate she was moving on, but moving on without him. He closed his eyes in an effort to head off the pain of the realization that he'd moved on, too.

In that moment came the knowledge that this was what their future looked like. They would occasionally run into each other, and when they talked, there would be hidden meaning in their words. Their relationship had always held a certain measure of fire. It was what made her surrender to him in the playroom so intense—the fact that she was so unyielding outside those walls.

Even now, with her jeans hanging loose on her too-thin frame and her glorious hair pulled back into a ponytail, her spine held its undeniable strength. He had the unwelcome thought that she was turning that strength against him. Perhaps it was only by living separately from him that she had found the sense of self-preservation to move on from the loss of their daughter.

"We have to talk," he said, decided. "Come by the house tomorrow evening."

Dread filled Dena as she pulled into Jeff's driveway the next day at six thirty. Seeing him the night before had brought it all back: the pain, the grief, the guilt. And when those feelings overwhelmed her, she did the only thing she could—she took out her frustration on him. She loved him, but how could she live with that love when it broke her to pieces every time she saw him?

His expression was somber when he opened the door. "Dena."

She flinched. His use of her name hinted at how the conversation was going to go. He no longer saw her as his angel. Her collar felt tight around her neck. She didn't know how to address him, so she simply nodded.

Without speaking, he led her into the living room. She looked straight in front of her, afraid if she looked around the house, the memories of her loss would overtake her. How did he stand to live here?

He sat down on the couch, and she took the seat across from him. He looked hard and determined.

"It's been weeks," he said. "Are you planning on moving back here?"

Something about his tone rubbed her the wrong way. "I'm fine. How are you doing?"

"We're long past pleasantries, and if you were fine, we wouldn't be having this conversation."

She sighed. She knew he was right; there was no point in playing games anymore. "I don't know if I can ever move back. Being here, remembering." She shook her head, unwilling to tell him how much it hurt to see him. To see his grief and hurt. "I'm not the same person I was six months ago. Losing her changed me."

She wanted so badly to be her old self, to be the woman she used to be with him. It just didn't seem possible.

"You're not the same person, and you're not moving back," he said, almost to himself.

He slowly stood and walked toward her. She held her breath as he took a key from his pocket. His hands lifted her hair, and with a faint click, his collar fell from her neck.

"You're free," he said in a monotone voice.

"We're not going to discuss it?" she asked in a whisper. Her throat tightened in panic at the loss of his collar. Just like that he was going to take it back? Without talking?

"What's left to discuss? You said you aren't moving back in, and we've barely talked in the last month. Maybe neither one of us is the same person we were before."

She forced herself not to reach for her neck. Without his collar she felt naked.

Without his collar.

She balled her hands into fists. Jeff was breaking up with her. It felt too final, and she realized in that second, she didn't want him to leave.

"Why?" she croaked out, but didn't know what she was asking him to explain.

He sank into the couch, leaning forward with his head down, fingers clutching the black collar. "We're taking our grief out on each other, and it's not healthy. For either of us." He looked up and met her gaze with a pained expression. "Trust me."

"I've always trusted you. I wouldn't have worn your collar if I didn't trust you."

"This is for the best. We're better apart."

"For a time?" She forced it out past the lump in her throat. One day she'd be able to look at him and not feel pain and guilt; she just had to get to that point. She only needed time.

"No."

Hot tears filled her eyes and ran down her cheeks. This was happening. It was really happening. "One day . . ."

"Dena, don't. We're not good for each other."

"You're wrong."

His voice held the will of iron she knew so well. "I'm not. One day you'll see the truth."

Her chin raised just a notch. "No," she said, wanting to hurt him like he'd hurt her. "One day you'll beg me to come back."

Chapter Nine

Present day

Dena's hands trembled with excitement as she undressed in the guest room. He'd surprised her by agreeing to flog her. She told herself it didn't mean anything. More than likely, he needed some relief just as badly as she did. The events of the last few days had caught up with her, and if she was going to be worth anything at work tomorrow, she needed the release that came from turning her body over to someone who knew what to do with it.

Jeff was nowhere to been seen when she stepped into the hallway and made her way into the playroom. She purposely didn't look around, but kept her head down. The last time she'd been in this room, they'd played for Julie, and after, Jeff had kissed her with so much passion. She didn't want to deal with the emotions of being back in it. But she saw it in her mind's eye: the exposed-beam ceiling, the handmade oak cabinets, the light tan paint on the walls.

The hardwood floor had a knot in the wood grain right near the middle of the room. She remembered that and allowed herself a small smile when she found it. She went to her knees beside it, trying to make her position as perfect as possible.

Instinctively, she fell into her yoga breathing and focused on the movement of air in and out of her body. She felt rather than heard when Jeff walked to stand before her. Complete silence and then, finally, he spoke.

"Dena."

As always his voice soothed her as if he'd touched her. She sank deeper into herself. For now, for this moment, she would be his angel once more, even if he didn't say it. She let out a breathy, "Sir."

"Your posture today's even better than last time."

"I'm glad it pleases you, Sir."

"I didn't say it pleased me. I said it was an improvement."

"Sorry for assuming, Sir."

He didn't say anything, but simply snapped his fingers. *Yes.* At his signal, she dropped to her elbows and slid forward. Part of her had wondered if he'd have her do this and she was secretly thrilled he had. Her lips lightly brushed the top of his right foot.

"I am yours," she whispered into his skin.

Keeping her head low, she moved to his other foot. She'd always loved kissing Jeff's feet. Kneeling before him, offering herself for his use but able to touch him, to kiss him and show with her lips how much she wanted him. Her lips had just left his left foot when he spoke again.

"Kneel."

Reluctantly, she moved back into her waiting position and waited for further instruction.

"You asked me to flog you—is that correct?" he asked.

"Yes, Sir."

"I'm fairly tense after the last few days. I need to make sure you can take what I'm going to give. It won't be anything like the so-called flogging Ron gave you. I'll get you into subspace, but you're going to feel it in the morning."

If he meant for his words to cause her to change her mind, he would be disappointed. They did the exact opposite. She needed this. Needed him.

She lowered her head to the floor. "Please, Sir."

He didn't hesitate. "Stand."

She slowly rose to her feet. She knew above her head were restraints he'd hung from the ceiling. If he had an intense session in mind, that's where he'd bind her.

"Arms above your head."

Her heart pounded just a little faster, knowing she'd guessed correctly. He took one wrist and then the other and buckled them in the cuffs above her head.

"There's no fear in your eyes tonight," he said.

"No, Sir. Never when I'm alone with you, Sir."

There was victory in his eyes; she was certain of it.

"Tell me this." He walked closer to her, blocking her view of anything but him. Not that she was interested in looking at anything else. He wanted her; she was almost certain. He lowered his head and whispered in her ear, "Are you wet for me, Dena? Are you excited knowing I'm getting ready to use you?"

Fuck, yes. "Yes, Sir."

He nipped her ear and then backed away and walked to his cabinets. He took two floggers, hesitated, and took two more, then turned to face her. "Close your eyes."

He was so unfair. He knew how much she enjoyed watching.

"Now," he said. "Or else I'll call another submissive to come over, and you can watch me get her off."

Bastard.

She closed her eyes.

He could move so quietly, she might not hear him when he approached her again. She forced her body to relax, but she still jumped slightly when the first blows fell.

He was using a light flogger and the blows were soft. For Jeff that only meant he was warming her up so she could take more and for longer. Bound as she was in the middle of the room, he had access to both sides of her body and he made use of it. Across her thighs, lighter across her belly, a touch harder on her breasts.

There was no pain with his light touch, and she relaxed her muscles, gave herself over to him.

"There you go," he said, obviously noting her surrender. "That's it."

She fell into a rhythmic breathing pattern and barely noticed when the flogger started landing harder. He picked up speed, or maybe he was using more than one; she couldn't tell. And to be honest, she really didn't care. All that mattered was the thud of the tails hitting her skin and the warmth that slowly spread throughout her body. She hummed in bliss.

"You're fucking beautiful."

His voice sounded fuzzy, and some part of her recognized that he had switched floggers. The thuds were landing harder. She gasped as one came precariously close to her clit and then moaned when it didn't hit again.

"Please," she begged.

"Not even close to being finished."

As if to prove his point, there was a switch of floggers and he went back to the lighter one. So light it almost tickled as it brushed between her legs. She shifted her feet.

"Need to come, Sir. Please."

"No."

He let her come down from her endorphin high, but just slightly, and then he worked her back up and she was flying again. Fuck, she missed this. She spent too much time working with newbie Doms who didn't know what they were doing.

He leveled off with his strokes and kept her where she was, once more working all sides of her body until she toed the pleasure/pain line and balanced between almost too much and never quite enough.

"Want to come?"

The leather struck between her legs and she rose on her toes. "Yes, Sir." She made a garbled sound when it flicked her clit. "Please, Sir. Touch me. I need your hands."

She wasn't sure where those words came from, and they must have surprised him as well, because there was a pause in his strokes. *Idiot.* She felt the high leave and she started the descent back to reality.

"I'm sorry, Sir." *Why did I open my mouth?* "I didn't mean to. . . . I'm sorry. . . ." She was babbling. She couldn't help it. What had possessed her to say that?

"Look at me." His command left no room for disobedience.

She didn't want to see him; she was too afraid of what she would find in his eyes. But she looked anyway, and there was nothing to be found but masculine lust. He cupped her ass and pressed his hips against her, his erection rubbing her just the right way, even through his jeans.

"You want to feel my hands?" he asked, starting a rocking motion that would probably have her climaxing within seconds, all the while looking straight into her eyes.

"Yes, Sir." *Fuck.* The roughness of his jeans against her was almost more than she could take.

"Come for me." He kneaded the flesh of her backside roughly and held her in place as he rolled his hips into her and pressed hard against her clit.

She sucked in a breath as she came. "Oh, fuck. Yes."

He stayed where he was as her climax passed. His arms moved up her back and held her close to his chest. When the last tremor left her body, he gently removed her wrists from the cuffs and swept her into his arms.

For a second, she thought he was taking her to his bed, but instead he carried her to the guest room. Once there, he placed her on the bed and held her close to his side. And though it felt decadent to be in his arms again, something was missing.

His strong hands held her close and his thumb brushed back and forth against her skin, but unlike last time, there was no sweet kiss, no soft words murmured. She could have kicked herself for saying what she had about needing his touch. All that had done was further prove how awkward and distant they'd become around each other.

She shifted slightly, and in doing so, brushed against his still-present erection.

That was what was missing. And it made her angry.

"Forget something?" she asked.

He looked unconcerned at her outburst. "I don't know what you're talking about."

"How many times have we played together?"

"Are you looking for an exact number?"

"A lot," she said. "And guess how many times you've still had a hard-on after the scene was over?"

"Dena." He said her name in that low, warning way of his.

"One." She rolled out of his arms and propped herself up on her elbow. "Today. What exactly are you trying to prove?"

"If you want to discuss the scene, it'll have to wait until you've calmed down. Right now I'm going to take a shower."

He moved to get off the bed, but she put a hand on his chest. "Are you going to jerk off in there?"

His eyes narrowed. "Move your hand."

"Look at you. Your cock's so hard, it's got to be painful in those jeans. Bet you're ready to take them off and stroke yourself into some relief." She scooted closer to him. "Will you think of me when you do? Pretend they're my hands?"

He tried to roll away, but she moved quicker than he did and pushed him back on the bed and straddled him.

"Did you tell yourself that if you didn't come in the playroom, you'd somehow be proving something about us?" She reached out and touched his chest. "You still going to think that while you're in the shower, fucking a memory?" Her fingers trailed downward. He was breathing heavily. "Is it easier to fuck my memory than the real me?"

His hand grabbed her wrist just before she slipped her fingers into his pants. "Stop. I told you I wasn't fucking you."

She leaned down and dragged her lips across his belly, noticing he'd broken into a light sweat. "Fine. My mouth. Your cock."

"I said 'no.'"

With a quick jerk, her hand was free. She unbuttoned his jeans and stroked his erection. "You're trying to prove some asinine point to yourself. But I know you. You want me. That's why you're breathing so hard and why you're gritting your teeth. Want me to stop? Safe word."

She teased aside his boxers, wanting to feel skin, knowing she was taunting him. It'd serve her right for him to say his safe word.

"You think you know me?" she asked, wrapping a hand around his cock. "I know you just as well. One word and I'll stop. Say it."

He closed his eyes and took a deep breath. She braced herself for him to say *red*. Instead, he grabbed her hair.

"Suck it," he growled.

Waves of sweet relief and victory surged through her as she moved down his body, taking his pants down as she went. His erection sprang toward her and she took it in her hand.

"Remember the time you had me suck you off during the presidential debates?" She didn't wait for him to answer, but continued talking, all the while stroking him. "I'd done something to piss you off, and you thought you were punishing me. You held off for nearly an hour."

"Best thing you can do with that mouth is fill it with my cock."

"We're not in the playroom, and you took your collar back years ago. You have to play by my rules for the moment." She was pushing him, pushing him hard. How much more would he take? "You thought it was a punishment, but I loved every second—your taste, the feel of your hand holding me down, kneeling for you." She kissed his tip. "I fucking loved it."

He thrust his hips forward.

"Maybe I'll stay here and stroke you softly for an hour or two." She blew on him. "Consider it payback?"

"Fucking suck my dick. Now."

She hid her smile. He was almost there. Lifting her head to look at him, she blinked innocently. "Make me."

That was all it took. With a growl, he flipped them over and half pulled, half dragged her up the bed, so her head rested on a pillow. Keeping her head steady with one hand buried in her hair, he knelt by her face and thrust his cock in her mouth.

He was rough. Just like she wanted, what she'd been missing. "This what you want?" he asked. "My cock fucking your throat?"

She couldn't answer verbally, so she wrapped her arms around him and sucked harder, relaxing so he could go deeper. He wasn't going to last long. He'd already been on the edge after their time in the playroom.

"Damn it, Dena." He fisted her hair harder.

Tears prickled her eyes. Whether from his use of her or because he still wouldn't call her "Angel," she wasn't sure. He didn't say anything else, but kept up a steady, almost punishing rhythm, and she wasn't surprised when her own arousal grew. It had always been that way between her and Jeff.

He jerked in her mouth. When he held still, she prepared herself and swallowed as he came.

Too soon. It was over too soon.

And she wanted more.

He slipped from her mouth and sat down, pulling her up beside him. Now would come the part she hated. He'd withdraw from her once more. She resisted the urge to grab her knees and rock, choosing instead to look at the bed. It hurt too much to look at him. But he knew her too well.

"Look at me."

She'd do it for him. Only to him would she give that part of herself—the vulnerable, the unsure, and the needy part of her.

She met his eyes.

"God, what you do to me," he said seconds before crushing his lips to hers.

She gave herself over to the kiss, relishing the feel of him. In those seconds she knew he gave her the hidden parts of himself as well. His thumb stroked her cheek, and she nearly hummed in pleasure.

But then he pulled away and it was agony.

"Three hundred eighty-two," he whispered in her ear.

"What?"

"The number of times we've played together."

She sat speechless as he kissed her cheek, hopped off the bed, and walked off to shower.

*   *   *

Two weeks later, Jeff looked around Daniel's guesthouse and sighed. He should have skipped the monthly meeting for the group's Dominants. Neither his heart nor his mind was in the right frame of mind. He'd given a few obligatory grunts at appropriate times, but other than that, he'd been worthless.

When only Daniel and Nathaniel remained, he addressed them. "I need some help, guys."

Something in his tone of voice must have startled the two men, because they both had concerned expressions on their faces when they looked at him.

"What's up?" Daniel asked.

Jeff decided he should start at the beginning. "A lot of things. I had a call from Colorado today."

"Your dad?" Daniel asked.

"His nurse, actually."

"Nurse?" Nathaniel's forehead wrinkled. "What's that about?"

The call had caught him off guard. Even now, hours later, it was painful to think about, much less bring up in conversation.

"Dad's not retiring. He's dying."

Nathaniel placed a hand on his shoulder. Daniel looked like he'd been punched in the gut.

"Prostate cancer," Jeff continued. "Terminal."

"I'm so sorry," Daniel whispered.

"What can we do?" Nathaniel asked.

Jeff took a deep breath. "I'm going to have to go to Colorado, which is a problem because I haven't been able to find the person threatening Dena."

"Nothing?" Daniel rubbed his temple and didn't wait for an

answer. "Obviously she can't stay by herself. I would tell you she could stay here in the guesthouse, but Cole's due back next week."

"She can stay with us," Nathaniel said. "She's welcome in New York, and the estate is safe."

"I appreciate the offer," Jeff said. "But you have kids. I wouldn't want to put them in danger."

"You won't be putting anyone in danger," Nathaniel assured him. "The grounds are gated, and there's a security system in place. I don't anticipate any trouble, but I will tell you that if it comes, I'm calling the police."

Jeff nodded. "I understand, and thank you. I'll talk to Dena tonight."

"You haven't had any luck figuring out who's been threatening her?" Daniel asked.

"No. I had her pull together a list of people she's prosecuted, but that was a dead end." Jeff got angry every time he thought about someone harming her. Who could imagine hurting Dena? She had dedicated her life to serving others. "Unfortunately, now I have to look into who might be using her as a way to threaten her father, and that's not as straightforward."

"It goes without saying, but I'll say it anyway." Daniel glanced at his phone and sent a quick text. "If you or Dena need anything, let me and Julie know."

He was a fortunate man to have such good friends, Jeff thought later, driving to his house. Other than Dena staying in New York with the Wests, there wasn't much else either of the two men could do, though. He tapped his fingers against the steering wheel. It was such a bad time to leave the city.

He needed to call his partner, Tom, and fill him in on the investigating he'd done on Dena's case. As much as he would like to handle it personally, he had no idea how much time he'd have to devote to the case once he arrived in Colorado. He needed someone he could trust working on it while he stayed with his dad.

And while he stayed with his dad, Dena would be with Nathaniel and Abby. The case she'd been working on had pleaded out, which meant there was no reason she couldn't work remotely. He thought about asking her to come with him to Colorado but decided she probably couldn't be that far away from work. He wasn't looking forward to having that conversation with her. She would not be happy about moving in with the couple.

She'd kept mostly to herself for the last two weeks, working in the evenings at his desk. Not once had she complained about his overbearing manner. After the flogging scene a few weeks ago, he'd thought she might want to play more, but so far she'd given no indication that she was interested.

He pulled into his driveway and scratched Bo's ear when the large dog trotted up to him. He needed to find someone to feed them while he was gone.

Tom was on the front porch, sitting on one of the weather-worn Adirondack chairs Dena had insisted on buying years ago.

"Thanks for staying," Jeff told Tom. "I feel much better knowing she isn't alone."

"It's no problem. Noting to report. She came home from work and has been inside ever since. No sign of anyone here."

"Fucker knows better than to come on my property." But that

was okay. It was only a matter of time before his luck ran out and Jeff caught him.

"I'm going to head home now if you don't need me anymore," Tom said.

"I have it covered. Thanks again."

He waited until the taillights of Tom's car disappeared into the night before unlocking the house and stepping inside. He looked for Dena at the small desk in the corner, but she wasn't there. He glanced at his watch. Seven. Usually at that time of day, she'd be nose deep in the next day's work.

Maybe she was in the bathroom. That would give him a few more minutes before he had to tell her she'd be packing for New York while he headed to Colorado. He walked toward his bedroom, planning to change, when he noticed the door was half-closed and the light was on.

Was Dena in his room? Why? Snooping through his socks?

He pushed the door open with a grin, but stood frozen at the sight that greeted him.

Dena was naked and kneeling on his floor.

Images of days long since past ran through his head. The numerous times she had knelt for him, the evenings he'd come home from work to find her waiting exactly like she was now. Seeing her in the same position nearly knocked the breath out of him.

"Dena," he whispered, and she flinched.

"I had a rough day in court, Sir."

So that's what it was. He shouldn't be surprised. She'd requested play sessions after bad days before. It was only that seeing her in his bedroom, waiting. He'd thought . . .

It didn't matter what he'd thought. She needed him to take control, to use her, and to allow her the escape and release necessary to ease her physically and mentally. He could do that. He would give that to her.

One last time before he left.

"I'll take you to the playroom," he said. "But I still won't fuck you."

"I understand, Sir."

He didn't know why he insisted on that, what point he was trying to prove. Maybe he was only trying to show that he was over her and didn't want her. But any fool could see that wasn't true.

"Stand up and walk in front of me to the playroom." He wasn't going to do anything in his bedroom. Not the room they used to share. It had been hard enough the last time to get over the memory of her being there.

Dena rose to her feet, unaware of his inner turmoil, and brushed her hair back from where it'd fallen. If he closed his eyes, he could remember the smell. His fingers knew how soft it'd be.

Hell, who was he fooling? He wasn't over anything.

Dena's hips swayed as she walked, and he knew it'd take every ounce of his self-control not to take her. He was uncomfortably hard as it was.

"I want you bent over the padded table," he said, running through his head what he planned for the evening. "I forgot how much I enjoyed spanking your ass until I did it the other night."

She sucked in a breath, obviously remembering the spanking he'd given her the night of the botched demo. But she walked over to the table like he asked and bent over it, her ass facing him.

He washed his hands at the sink he'd had installed in the room and then took an anal plug, lube, and a wooden paddle and moved to her side.

She didn't jump when he touched her, but groaned softly when he placed the collected items beside her head so she saw them. Anal play wasn't one of her favorite things to do.

"Is someone regretting asking to play?" He gave one butt cheek a swat.

"No, Sir. Someone's regretting not being more specific when she asked."

"Too damn bad." He squeezed a fair amount of lube onto his finger and teased her anus. Pushed the tip in slightly. "You said you had a rough day in court. I'm going to help you forget."

She started to speak, but he slapped her ass. "And if you're smart, you won't speak unless you're asked a question. Of course, if you'd like a repeat of the last spanking I gave you . . ."

She was silent.

"Good choice. I'd much rather use pleasure to help ease the stress of your day."

With that, he took his time pushing his finger inside her while teasing her slit with the fingers of the other hand. She stayed still and silent, taking what he gave her.

"I'm going to push the plug in now," he warned her. "Then I'm going to spank the bad day out of you."

She tensed her backside, but he was quick to tease her clit, causing her body to relax. While one hand continued the tease, he used the other to gently push the plug in.

"Damn, you're tight. How long has it been?"

"Please, Sir."

He didn't understand what she was asking. "Please what?"

Her reply was so low, he had to drop his head to hear. "Please don't ask me that, Sir."

"Tell me, Dena." He tenderly swept her hair to the side and placed a kiss on her temple. "There have never been secrets between us in this room. Let's not start keeping them now."

She took a shaky breath. "You were the last, Sir."

If he thought finding her naked in his bedroom had knocked the wind out of him, that was nothing compared to her confession in the playroom. He couldn't get his muscles to move. "What?" he asked, noting her knuckles had turned white from the way she was clutching the edge of the table so tightly.

"You stopped." There was a catch in her voice.

He brushed a hand down her body. She wanted him to continue, but he wasn't ready to resume the scene yet. "Do you play with anyone outside of a training scene?"

Her deep sigh told him she had resigned herself to answering his questions. "Very infrequently."

"When was the last?"

"About nine months, Sir."

He thought back, trying to remember when he last saw her with anyone at a party and realized with a start he couldn't.

Nine months.

Nine months of nothing but Doms in training who wouldn't know how to play her body, drawing the exquisite pleasure out of her. His plan for the evening changed immediately. "Turn around, Dena."

She didn't want to. She moved slowly and hesitantly. But she wanted to obey him more, so she complied. Her questioning eyes met his.

"I'm not stopping," he assured her. "I just decided I'm not going to spank you." He nodded to the table. "Hop up with your ass to the edge."

The relief was evident in her expression as she followed his directions, but there were still questions in her expressive blue eyes. He took her legs and spread them, not bothering to tell her to keep them where he put them. She knew his expectations.

He kissed the inside of one thigh. "How long has it been since someone who knew what they were doing tasted this delicious pussy?"

A tremor shot through her legs. "A long time, Sir."

"I want a number."

"Ten months."

Ten months. Unreal. He beat back the jealousy he felt while wishing he'd known she was spending all her free time in training scenes. She deserved better.

And if you knew, what would you have done? Asked her if you could stop by her house for a quickie?

No. He wouldn't have done that, but maybe he could have done something to make sure she was getting some sort of satisfaction.

"Does what you're doing with the training sessions fulfill your needs?" He placed a kiss on her other thigh.

"Some of them, Sir."

"And have you spoken to Daniel about needing more?" Since Daniel was the Dom working with her in the training sessions, he would be the one she should talk to first.

"I hinted that we could play a few months ago, but I think he'd already met Julie. He didn't take me up on it."

The jealousy roared to life again, but he knew he'd have to bring that up with Daniel. His friend's mind might have been preoccupied, but he still needed to make sure a submissive in his care was attended to properly. If Daniel didn't want to play with anyone other than Julie, that was fine, but at least ask another Dom to help.

Like you? he asked himself, not bothering to answer.

Taking his own advice, he pushed all thoughts of Daniel to the back of his mind and focused on the beautiful submissive currently in his care. "You're not allowed to move," he told her. "But you can come when you're able, and there's no need to be silent."

"Thank you, Sir."

He brushed his mouth back and forth across the juncture where her thigh met her body. "You're welcome."

He placed tiny kisses along the apex of her legs, ignoring for a moment the spots he knew longed for his touch. Making her wait for it would only increase her pleasure. From kisses, he progressed to nibbles and then to a soft bite on the flesh above her clit.

"I can't wait to taste you," he murmured against her skin.

"Please, Sir."

He leisurely licked her entrance from one end to the other, dipping his tongue into her briefly. On his next pass, he ended with a lick to her clit and then settled his mouth over her and flicked that sensitive area with his tongue.

"Oh, fuck, yes," she panted.

Her muscles tensed as she tried to hold back her orgasm. He

took the end of the plug and moved it in and out in time with the actions of his tongue. She wouldn't be able to hold back much longer, and he wanted to drive her to the brink.

From their years together, he knew exactly where and how to touch her, and he used all that knowledge to drive her closer and closer to the release her body craved. He fucked her with his tongue and ran his teeth along her sensitive flesh.

Within minutes, her body tensed further, and she softly came around his tongue. Wanting to push her into a second release, he pulled the plug out while at the same time pushing two fingers inside to press against her G-spot.

"Fuck!" she screamed as the second climax hit.

Satisfied he'd made her forget whatever happened at work, he climbed up on the table and pulled her into his embrace so they were spooning. She sighed and snuggled against him.

"I'm not finished yet." He spoke coarsely into her ear while dropping a hand between her legs and pumping two fingers inside her. "Come for me again, Dena. Give me your pleasure one more time."

"I can't, Sir." But already he felt her body tremor as her arousal grew.

"Are you lying to me?"

"I didn't think I could, Sir," she panted. "But, *fuck,* I think I can."

"Oh, I know you can." He pushed his fingers deeper. "Fucking you with my fingers feels so good. You're pushing your ass against me, trying to make me go harder."

She bucked against him, brushing his erection, and for a minute he thought he might come in his pants, but he did his best to ignore his need and turned his energy toward her. He brushed his thumb around her clit, and her inner muscles tightened around his fingers as her third climax crashed over her.

He stroked her back while her breathing and racing heart calmed. Dropped his head into her hair and inhaled, breathing in the smell of her. His chest hurt because he knew he had to tell her now. He couldn't wait until morning.

"Will you let me take care of you, Sir?" she asked, snaking her hand behind her.

"Not right now," he said, surprised at the catch in his voice. "It's not a good time."

"Why not?" She turned in his arms and stopped cold when she saw his expression. "What's wrong?"

"Dad's dying," he stated simply. "Prostate cancer. Advanced. He's not retiring."

"Oh, Jeff." She palmed his cheek. "I'm so sorry."

He nodded.

"You have to go," she said.

"I know. That's what I wanted to talk to you about. I haven't had any luck finding out who's threatening you. I've been through your old cases and I've been able to rule out anyone you've prosecuted."

"I'll be fine. You need to be with your dad."

"You know damn well I'm not leaving you alone right now."

Her forehead wrinkled. "So what are you going to do?"

He took a deep breath. "Nathaniel has agreed for you to stay with him and Abby in New York while I'm gone." He waited for her to explode and argue that she wasn't going to do it, but though her face showed shock, she didn't say anything at first.

Finally, she spoke slowly. "I think that would be the best option for everyone."

"You're not going to argue with me?"

"Give me some credit, why don't you. I'm not the important one in this equation. Your dad's dying and you need to be with him. If my staying with Nathaniel and Abby will help you get through this time, I'd be petty to argue."

He was in awe of the woman in his arms. Just when he thought he understood her, when he thought he knew exactly what she'd do, she'd surprise the hell out of him. He tightened his arms around her. "Thank you."

Chapter Ten

Present day

Hours later, Dena rolled onto her side in the guest bed. Her mind wouldn't slow down enough for sleep to catch her. Between thinking about Jeff moving to Colorado and her own move to New York, paired with the orgasms she'd had earlier, she decided she'd probably be awake for another few hours.

Jeff hadn't said when he was heading across country, but she had the feeling it would be soon. After all, from the way it sounded, his father didn't have much time left. She wasn't ready to leave Jeff's house, but she hadn't put up a fuss about moving in with Nathaniel and Abby, partially because she didn't want to go back to her empty apartment.

With Jeff leaving, there was one thing she had to do before moving out of his house. She had to face the empty nursery at the end of the hall. The door was always closed, unlike every other door in the house, and she wondered why. Had Jeff shut that door in an attempt to shut off his feelings associated with it?

Maybe, she thought, if she could deal with seeing the nursery again, she'd be able, once and for all, to put that part of her past behind her. She'd never felt as if she had closure after her grief over the miscarriage. Hell, she'd never really even spoken about it with Jeff.

She sat up and swung her legs to the side of the bed. Yes, seeing the nursery would be one of the final steps in her healing process. She left her room and walked softly down the hall. Jeff's door was closed. Once again he'd ended a scene without taking his own release, but she felt certain he'd done something about it once he was by himself.

She decided not to dwell on how much that hurt. Why wouldn't he allow her to pleasure him? Surely he knew how much she loved getting him off.

Later, she decided. Maybe she'd talk to him about it in the morning. Right now she had to deal with *that* room.

She stood before it, unable to twist the knob.

"It's a room," she whispered as if not to disturb the secrets inside.

"Just a room," she repeated.

With a deep breath and a determined twist, she opened the door. It was several moments before she could move or even form a coherent thought.

"Oh, Jeff," she whispered in the stillness. "You didn't."

But he had. He had kept the room untouched for more than three years.

She blinked back the tears that gathered in her eyes, but it was useless. They ran unbidden down her cheeks.

The curtains were drawn, but a faint light from outside lit the room. She walked to the far corner and, without thinking, brushed her fingers across her belly.

The crib before her stood exactly as it had three years ago. Back when everything had seemed so right. So complete.

They had not planned for her to get pregnant. Jeff had been so upset at first. When he'd come around, though, everything had been perfect. Or so she'd thought. Her pregnancy had actually marked the beginning of the end.

But for a brief moment in time, she'd believed she had all she'd ever wanted. Then that moment had passed, and now she was alone.

There was no bedding in the crib, just a bare mattress. Jeff had been convinced the baby would be a girl, however, and had even gone so far as to get his grandmother's rocking chair with a delicate pink floral print and put it in the nursery. It was still there, just as they'd left it.

Dena smiled through her tears, remembering the way she'd stood in this very room with her hands on her hips, telling him that was a fine way to ensure they had a boy.

"It's a girl," he'd said. "A daddy knows these things."

She remembered now how he'd originally set up the nursery to surprise her and as a way to show her he'd accepted the idea of the baby and grown excited about it. She'd come home from a long day at the office and he'd barely been able to contain himself, leading her down the hallway with his hands over her eyes.

He showed her the crib he'd bought and put together. For hours that night they sat on the nursery floor and spoke in excited whispers about their hopes and dreams for their child.

Five weeks later and for reasons unknown, barely twenty weeks into her pregnancy, she'd miscarried. Their tiny daughter was born too fragile to even take her first breath.

Excitement had turned to grief and their grief had become bitter.

"Never found the strength to put her things away."

Dena jumped at Jeff's voice, but she didn't turn around.

"She'd be just over three now," he continued. "Too big for a crib. We'd have to get her a bed. . . ."

He remembered her. Thought of her. Missed her. A father's love, unchanged by death.

"Sometimes at night," she whispered, "I put my hand on my belly. It's almost like I can feel her kick."

"I only felt her that once." His voice was laced with pain.

"I tell myself she was . . ." Dena paused, wiping at the tears running down her cheeks, but it didn't do any good; others fell in their place. "She was too perfect for this world. She left before anything bad or evil could touch her."

Nothing from Jeff. She looked up to the window but couldn't see his reflection.

She closed her eyes. "Then I think, what if it was me? What if she had to leave because I would have messed her up?"

"For God's sake. Dena, no." He was behind her in a second, his hands rubbing her shoulders, and she resisted the urge to sag against him. "It wasn't you."

"She was all that was good and whole and pure." A sob ripped from her throat. The doctors had been unable to tell her what had gone wrong. They said it could have been any number of things. "And I wasn't good enough to hold on to her."

His hands tightened on her shoulders. "You are. You are good enough."

She turned to face him. She had to see his face when he answered her question. She didn't know why she could ask him now when they'd gone so long without talking about it. Maybe it was because he was moving away for who knew how long or because they'd been intimate. Maybe she'd finally gotten to the point where it didn't cause her physical pain to talk about it. "Then why aren't I good enough for you?"

He turned white. "That's what you think? That you're not good enough for me? Christ, Dena. What have I done to you?"

"I know you're leaving for Colorado because of your father. But it feels like you're leaving me. Again. What is it I keep doing that makes you not want me anymore?"

"That's not it. That was never it." He cupped her cheek. "Letting you go ripped a hole in my heart so big it aches every time I breathe."

Standing so close to him, she almost believed him. But it was easy to say the words. Words were cheap. "I don't believe you. You won't even let me get you off, much less *really* take me. What am I supposed to think?"

"I want you." He ran his thumb over her lips while he gazed into her eyes. "I'll want you till I die."

She'd balled her fists so tight, her nails dug into her palms, but she forced her chin up. Words. Again with the words. She wanted more. "Prove it."

"Dena."

"I'm not asking for anything beyond tonight. Just tonight. I need you. I need to feel . . . something."

He wouldn't do it. She knew he wouldn't. He'd turn her down, and in the morning she'd be ashamed to face him, but she couldn't stop herself from asking.

"Make love to me. I know I said you'd have to beg me, but now I'm begging you. Please."

"Don't, Dena." He kissed the tears from her cheeks. "Don't beg me. I want you. I need you. And I'm finished pretending otherwise."

He nearly shook with the knowledge that she blamed herself for the miscarriage. Was that why she'd left him so many years ago? Out of guilt? Did she think he blamed her? The doctors had told them there was nothing she could have done differently. Damn it all. He should have made her talk to him instead of just letting her move out of his house.

He should probably talk to her now, but he couldn't stop touching her. His lips needed to be on her and his hands needed to feel her.

Later, he promised himself. *We'll talk later.*

He swept her into his arms, picking her up and eliciting a whimper of surprise from her. Effortlessly, he carried her down the hall to his bedroom. "You damn well belong in my bed."

She stared at him wide-eyed as he deposited her on the bed and stood back to undress.

"I'm an ass, Dena. I'm an overbearing, know-it-all, selfish ass.

And I've hurt you. I've made you feel unwanted, undesirable, and unloved." His shirt fluttered to the floor, and he went to work on his pants. "Let me make it up to you. I can't come close and it's not nearly enough, but it's all I have."

She sat up and started to take her shirt off.

"No," he said. "Let me. I don't want you to do anything but let me bring you pleasure."

"Damn it," she said, and she took her shirt off anyway. "What will it take to make you understand that serving you brings me pleasure?"

She amazed him. She always had. And he didn't deserve her. But if she wanted him, he wasn't going to argue tonight.

"That's the way you want it?" he asked.

"Please. Sir."

He grew harder, and he forced his voice to remain low and soft as he spoke the words he knew he needed to give her. "Come to me, my Angel."

Her eyes darkened and her breath hitched. One lone tear streaked down her cheek, but she rose to her knees and made her way to him.

"Don't cry," he said, taking her in his arms. "Please, don't cry."

"Say it again."

He brushed his thumb under her eye, capturing a new tear. "Angel."

She sighed, and her breath was shaky. "Thank you."

"You will always be my Angel."

She looped her arms around his neck, and he dropped his lips to hers. He wanted to show her how much he still needed her after all their years apart, and suddenly he couldn't touch enough of her. He kissed her like a hungry man, drinking in the smell and feel of her, relishing in the warmth of her skin.

He gently pushed back on her shoulders so she rested on the bed, and he held himself over her. She stroked his cheek softly. The hole she'd made in his heart by leaving didn't feel quite as empty anymore.

He nuzzled her neck, knowing it was one of her most sensitive spots. He was just getting ready to nibble her ear, another favorite spot, when the phone on his nightstand rang. Dena stiffened under him.

"Ignore it," he said.

"Phone calls this time of night are never good."

He shifted to the other side of her neck and peppered it with kisses. "Then I won't answer. Ignore it."

"What if—"

"Relax, Angel. I've got everything under control. Nothing's going to interrupt us." He ran a hand down her body, tracing her curves.

He continued teasing her with his lips and touch. He'd once known every inch of her. He'd known how and when to touch her. When to stroke. Where to bite. The places she loved his fingers. And the parts that went wild for his tongue.

Gradually, he felt the tension leave her body. Just as gradually, her arousal grew and her breathy sighs became moans of pleasure. He dropped his head and suckled a nipple, remembering her taste.

She clutched his hair in her hands. "Harder. Fuck, Jeff. So hard."

He obliged, giving her exactly what she asked for. When she writhed against him, he slipped a hand between them and teased her wet entrance. "I'm going to take you now, Angel. I'm going to sink inside you so deep, I may never leave."

She didn't say anything, but he saw the need in her eyes, the longing and the desire. Even more, he saw want and acceptance. He nudged her knees farther apart and settled himself between them.

Her eyes remained on his as he gently pushed inside her. It took most of his self-control not to thrust in completely, all at once, but to take his time and to ensure they each felt every movement of his penetration.

"Oh my God, *yes*," she said as he went deeper and deeper.

"Never again," he whispered as he moved within her. "You'll never be without me again."

He kept his thrusts slow and purposeful, watching as her pleasure grew while keeping his own need in check. Even when he finally started moving faster, he couldn't keep his eyes off her. She raked her nails down his back, and he groaned in his own pleasure.

It had been too long since he'd had her, and neither one of them was going to be able to delay their release. As he drove them both toward their climax, he knew no other woman would ever satisfy him. Just her.

His Angel.

He thrust harder and faster, dropping a hand between them to tease her in a way he knew would have her coming within seconds. She closed her eyes, and with the next pass of his hips, she gasped and stiffened as her climax rippled through her.

Jeff wasn't far behind, his own release following on the heels of hers. He was panting when it was over, and he wasn't sure he'd ever come so hard.

Afterward, she was soft and pliable in his arms. She nuzzled his chest with her head, and he wrapped his arms around her, more content than he'd been in years. He kissed her forehead and was interrupted by the phone.

"Damn it," he mumbled, and whipped the handset off his nightstand. "What?" he nearly shouted.

"Mr. Jeff Parks, please."

"You've got him. Make it fast."

"Mr. Parks, this is Amy, the nurse caring for your father. I know you're planning to come here, but I want you to know you should probably come as quickly as possible. He doesn't have much longer."

Chapter Eleven

Present day

The afternoon of the following day, everyone met at Daniel's house for lunch. Nathaniel and Abby had planned to stay a few more days, but when they learned about Jeff's father, they decided to head back to New York earlier. Jeff was surprised to see Sasha there, but Daniel caught his quizzical look and took him aside to explain after everyone had finished eating and they stood around chatting.

"Julie was shopping with Sasha this afternoon when I called her. I assumed she wanted to say good-bye to Dena, but Julie told me she thought Sasha was kicking around the idea of rejoining the group."

"The way she ran out of the last meeting she attended, we need to think that one through."

"Agreed," Daniel said. "But I thought it'd be a good idea for her to be here for something not group related."

It had been a casual lunch, just make-your-own sandwiches. They ate sitting in the kitchen, and Jeff thought Daniel's idea to slowly integrate Sasha back into the group was a good one. But at the moment he wasn't able to think about Sasha. He looked to his right to where Nathaniel was talking to Abby and met the Dominant's eyes.

"When will you be leaving for New York?" he asked.

"I thought we'd head out later this evening," Nathaniel said. "What time's your flight?"

"Later this evening."

"You know, by moving Dena to New York, you're really going to mess with her stalker. I think we'll either see an increase in activity or nothing at all while he plans what to do next."

"If he makes any sort of move, I want you to call me. It doesn't matter what time of day it is."

Nathaniel nodded. "Will do. Any luck finding out who it is?"

"No, but I have a pretty good idea of who it isn't."

"That's a start."

"I had hoped to know a lot more by this time."

"Going to dig into people who have it out for the senator?" Daniel asked.

"Yes," Jeff confirmed. "And it's a damn long list."

"Come on, now. He's not all that bad," Dena said with a roll of her eyes, and Jeff again felt a momentary sense of guilt for not telling her about the details of his meeting with her father all those years ago.

"He's not all that good, either," he said.

She opened her mouth to protest, but just then someone new

came into the room. "I parked at the guesthouse since your driveway's already overflowing with cars."

Everyone's head spun to the doorway at the sound of the smooth British accent. Daniel's close friend Cole Johnson stood with a backpack slung over one shoulder. He was smiling, but the smile quickly faded as he glanced around the room.

"Have I interrupted something? I apologize," he said.

Daniel stood and walked over to Cole. "I didn't expect you until next week." He punched his arm. "Don't you ever call?"

"I rang twice on the way here, but you didn't pick up. I rang the doorbell, but no one answered. It was unlocked, so here I am." He shrugged. "You always tell me to make myself at home."

Cole was an award-winning journalist and had been on assignment in India for the past several months.

"You're always welcome," Daniel assured him. "Let me take your bag. I think you know everyone."

Cole passed him the bag and walked over to Julie. "Julie." He took her hands and kissed her cheek. "So good to see you again. You've made Daniel very happy."

Julie stood up straighter and squared her shoulders. "Thank you, Sir. The feeling's mutual."

"*Cole* is fine when we're not with the group." He winked at her. "I'm only an arse in the playroom."

Daniel snorted. "That's debatable."

Cole ignored him and moved to Sasha. He didn't touch her, but simply stood before her with a kind smile. "Hi there, Sasha. Good to see you again. How are you?"

Jeff was glad Cole remembered Sasha's trauma and brought

up the incident indirectly. But then again, it had been Cole who'd held her after she'd nearly fallen.

At Cole's greeting, Sasha stood. "I'm afraid I don't remember much of our first meeting, but I'm doing well." She held out her hand. "Sasha Blake. I understand I owe you thanks for your help a few months ago."

Cole shook her hand. "Cole Johnson. And no thanks required. I'm glad I could assist."

"The guesthouse is ready," Daniel said. "I had it prepared for you after the last play party."

"Excellent," Cole said. "So tell me what I walked in on today."

Daniel explained what had happened to Dena and where she was going.

"If you don't want to go to New York," he said when Daniel finished, "you're more than welcome to stay at the guesthouse with me. Or I could find something else and you could stay by yourself."

A jealousy like he'd never experienced rushed through Jeff, catching him off guard. "Frankly, I think it's better that she go out of town. That way we throw him off her trail, at least for a while."

"I'd like to do something to help," Cole said. "You have dogs, right? I can take care of them."

"I have a cat, too," Dena said.

"I could bring them here to the guesthouse. I miss having a pet." Something almost wistful-looking flashed in Cole's eyes for a second, or at least it appeared that way to Jeff, and he quickly agreed for Cole to keep his dogs and Dena's cat.

Nathaniel looked at his watch. "We need to be hitting the road soon."

Dena nodded and made her way to Jeff. "Can I speak to you alone for a few minutes?"

Her expression showed resignation, and though he wondered what was on her mind, he had a strong feeling he didn't want to know.

"Last night was wonderful," Dena started, and something in his heart broke because he knew there was a "but" to follow. "But I don't want what happened between us last night to distract from time with your father. Let's put our relationship to the side, and we'll deal with it when you get back."

By the time she finished speaking, he wasn't heartbroken anymore. He was angry. "Don't you think we've put our relationship to the side long enough?"

"We can pick up where we left off when you get back."

"Fuck that. I'm tired of putting us last."

"Jeff, don't—"

"Don't what? Act like we're important? I'll tell you what. Forget Nathaniel and Abby. Come with me. Come to Colorado with me. Let's face the coming days as a couple." He wanted her to acknowledge that the night before meant *something*. That their relationship was still a priority to her.

"I can't. There's too much work and a court case and—"

He held his hand up. She didn't even appear to have thought about going with him. That told him everything he needed to know. "I know. You're busy. The thing is, Dena, you complained about me not wanting you, but let's not forget who moved out. I think you like playing the part of the wounded party. The truth is, you're the one who didn't want *me* anymore."

He'd hurt her with his words. There was pain in her eyes. "I can't believe you think that."

He shrugged.

"Don't end it like this," she begged.

"I'm not the one ending it."

"Jeff," she called, but he was already walking away.

"Good-bye, Dena," he said without looking back.

Chapter Twelve

Present day

A week and a half into her stay with Nathaniel and Abby, Dena was ready to move back into her apartment. Nothing against the Wests as hosts—they were welcoming and accommodating—but she missed her own space. Besides, there had been no harassment or threats of any kind since she moved in. Her reasonable mind told her it was probably because whoever it was didn't know how to find her, but she counted it as a positive anyway.

Childish giggles drifted down the hallway. Nathaniel must have just gotten home. She was fortunate her current caseload allowed her to work remotely, but part of her wished she could miss the daily homecoming chatter.

The giggles escalated into peals of laughter, and Nathaniel's low voice added to the sounds of the family's happy reunion. It wasn't just that she missed her own space, Dena knew, but also that little Elizabeth and Henry were a constant reminder of what she'd lost. And the worst was when she'd spend the evenings with Nathaniel and Abby. Especially those nights when Abby would settle on the floor by Nathaniel and he'd look at his wife with such intensity and passion that it caused Dena's heart to ache.

Her phone rang. Without looking at who it was, she snatched it off the nearby table. "Hello."

"Think you can hide, bitch? I'll always find you."

Dena froze. Her entire body turned ice-cold, and she couldn't remember if it was better to talk to him or to stay quiet. Whoever it was used a voice distorter and the gravelly sound was frightening. But at the same time, there was something to it . . . the cadence or the words . . .

The person on the other end laughed, and the sound sent shivers down her spine. Not caring if she should keep him on the line or not, she ended the call and sat for long seconds until her body stopped shaking.

When she felt steady enough to stand, she made her way down the stairs to where she knew the West family would be gathered in the kitchen, catching up on the day.

Abby's back was to her, but Nathaniel saw her. She must have looked terrified, because he set Henry on his feet and rushed to her. "Dena? What's wrong?" He took her gently by the elbow and guided her to a chair.

"He called again," she said once she had sat down.

"Elizabeth," Abby said. "You and Henry go play in the living room for a bit, okay? I'll be there in a few minutes."

Nathaniel waited until the kids left before turning to her. "He called? Just now?"

Dena nodded and told him the details. "The strange thing is, I think I recognize the voice." She squinted, trying to remember. "He used a distorter, but I recognized something about him."

Nathaniel leaned back in his chair and crossed his arms. "That means it's probably not connected to your father. Unless it's someone you both know. That's not much of a clue, but it's the first one we've had."

She needed to call Jeff. Her stomach sank just thinking his name. She hadn't spoken to him since he left, and she knew he'd be upset to learn the calls hadn't stopped. And she felt guilty for not calling to see how he was doing and if his father had gotten worse.

"Someone should call Jeff." Abby put a glass of water in front of her on the table. "And the police."

Dena agreed. There were children involved this time. She wouldn't put them in danger.

"Anything else you remember about the call?" Nathaniel asked.

"No, but the phone number was listed as private." She'd looked when she'd disconnected.

Nathaniel had his phone out, making notes. "I'm going to call the police, get them involved. And then I'll call Jeff." He looked up at her. "Do you want to talk to him?"

Dena shook her head, doing her best to not to acknowledge the disappointment in Nathaniel's eyes. When he left the kitchen, she dropped her head to the table.

Abby patted her shoulder. "They'll find him."

"I know. I just wonder what my frame of mind will be like by the time they do."

"Let me pour you a glass of wine. That'll help it a little."

"Thanks." Dena rolled her shoulders. "What I really need is about two hours with a Dom who knows what he's doing." As soon as the sentence left her mouth, she remembered. "Fuck."

Abby set the wineglass down in front of her. "What?"

"I have a damn training session with Daniel and Ron tomorrow. I swear when Ron's finished with his training, I'm not doing any more mentor sessions for a while."

"Do you play with anyone other than Ron?"

"Not lately. Jeff and I did, before he left. . . ."

Abby nodded.

"I shouldn't have let him leave like he did. I thought I was being helpful, but I hurt him." It had been an amazing night. Even now, almost two weeks later, she still recalled every detail: his moan of pleasure when her nails raked down his back, the fullness of him inside her, the sharpness of his teeth as he nibbled her skin.

Then she compared that to the look of despair—no, it had been more than that. She remembered the look of betrayal on his face when she'd told him to go to Colorado without her.

Abby placed her hand on top of Dena's. "You'll work through it."

"I wouldn't count on it. Jeff and I don't have a stellar record in the work-through-it department."

"You're both older now, with a lot more life behind you. And you know what it's like to live without him."

"What if he doesn't come back?" It was her newest fear. That he would stay in Colorado. That her words had killed whatever small spark they'd managed to reignite.

"I've seen the way he looks at you. He'll be back."

Nathaniel walked back into the kitchen. "I talked with the police and then a company about setting up private security for the house. I had to leave a voice mail for Jeff, but I did have a call from Daniel."

"Daniel?" Dena asked. "About me?"

"He can't do the mentor session tomorrow and was wondering if you'd mind if Cole ran it sometime next week. He thought it might work better if Cole and Ron came here. You can use my playroom."

"That sounds good. I wasn't jumping up and down to head back to Wilmington anyway." Not anymore, not since the phone call.

He slipped an arm around Abby's waist. "You're welcome to stay here for as long as you want." His cell phone rang and he pulled it out of his pocket, nodding to Dena when he read the display. "Hello, Jeff."

Dena held her breath and hoped Nathaniel would stay in the kitchen. She'd told Nathaniel she didn't want to speak to Jeff, but just knowing he was on the phone made him seem so close, and she didn't want to give that up.

"I was calling to let you know Dena received another phone call. Yes, just now, less than thirty minutes ago." There was a pause as Nathaniel listened, head nodding. "I notified the local police and called a private security company." He glanced her way. "She's shaken up, but holding it together. This time, though, she thought she recognized the voice."

Dena shivered just thinking about the mechanical laughter on the other end of her phone. The sound would echo in her sleep, and she was so glad she wasn't alone in her apartment.

"That's what I was thinking," Nathaniel said to Jeff. "Probably work related." More silence followed. "We know you want to be here, and we all understand why you're not. How's your father?"

It was probably eating him alive that he couldn't be here, and she wondered, just for a minute, if they shouldn't have told him. He had enough stress dealing with his father and his business. But just as quickly she realized she could never keep the truth from him.

"I'll let you know if anything changes," Nathaniel said, and then, looking at Dena, he added, "I will. I'll protect her as one of my own."

"What are you doing here, Dena?"

Cole had approached so quietly, she hadn't heard him. She turned from the window in the Wests' kitchen. The mentor session had ended twenty minutes earlier, and Cole had sent Ron back to Wilmington as soon as it was over. "Cole, hey. I didn't hear you come in."

He tilted his head toward the kitchen table and waited for her to sit down before taking his own seat.

On the surface, Cole was easygoing, but those in the community knew he was also a Dominant. And not just any Dominant, Dena thought, watching him sit down. He was called the Badass Brit by many submissives. Just never to his face. Dena didn't know from personal experience; this was a case where his reputation preceded him.

"I came to get some water," she answered, not understanding why he asked.

"I don't mean here in the kitchen. I meant, why are you here in New York and not in Colorado?"

She sucked in a breath at hearing the words, and memories of Jeff flooded her mind. No one had—

"I know everyone else tiptoes around the subject," Cole continued, undeterred by her obvious anguish or perhaps spurred on by it. "Or at least those who know of your history with Jeff. The both of you did a relatively good job at keeping your emotions hidden from everyone."

They had, she would agree. Too good of a job.

"But frankly," he said, "I've never been very good at tiptoeing around things, and I've never seen the point in pretending something is other than what it is. So, the question is: why are you here and not there?"

He was certainly bold; she'd give him that much. No one else had the nerve to ask her about Jeff. Still . . .

She raised an eyebrow at him. "And why do you think I want to discuss it with you?"

"I have no doubt that you *don't* want to discuss it with anyone, but . . ." His expression grew slightly softer. Just slightly. If she hadn't been watching him so closely, she'd have missed it. "The truth is, I do know something about running away from your past."

Kate. His ex. Dena knew they'd been together forever, and now they weren't.

"Sounds to me like you're the last person I should talk to," she said. "Why are you here and not there?"

His lips tightened. "It's complicated."

She snorted. "Hell, Cole, we're all complicated. You think Jeff and I are simple?"

"I know there's some history between you two."

Against her will, she started to feel angry. "You know the problem with most Dominants? You guys think you know the answer to everything. You think you can fix anything. Well, guess what. You can't fix this."

"I never thought—"

"Yes, you did. You thought you could come up to me and give me a little talking-to and I'd go running to Colorado and fall gladly into Jeff's arms like nothing happened."

"I just wanted to give you something to think about."

"There you go again. You think I haven't thought about it? I don't think about *anything* other than Jeff."

He opened his mouth to say something, but then closed it. After several seconds he said, "Very well. I'll tell you about me. Kate and I were together eight years, and she was more than my submissive; she was my slave."

He stopped for a moment, obviously knowing Dena needed time to process the information. She must have had a shocked look on her face, because the corner of his mouth lifted.

"Are you okay? Shall I continue?"

"Please," she squeaked out, still trying to wrap her head around the fact that Cole and Kate had lived such a lifestyle. She'd met Kate once and never picked up on the fact the couple was Master and slave. Normally, she had a sixth sense about such things.

"There's a certain type of intensity involved in a twenty-four/ seven relationship. I'm not sure anyone who hasn't lived it can fully understand. I was her Master in every way. She worked outside of the house and she went out with friends, but we both knew she belonged to me." He looked at his hands, flexed his fists, and looked back up to her. "Do you know why Kate and I broke up?"

She shook her head.

"She wanted kids and I didn't."

"Oh. Wow."

"We didn't argue much, but when we did, it always came back to that. We tried to discuss it reasonably, but eventually she'd tell me I was being a selfish son of a bitch by not giving her a child, and I'd tell her to go to her room and write an essay on the problems with overpopulation." He sighed. "One day I told her if she wanted a kid so badly, she could just find someone willing to give her one. She looked me straight in the eyes and said she would. She moved out that afternoon. I kept waiting for her to come back. She never did."

His eyes held a pain his normal personality hid. It'd been close to six months since they had broken up, and he was still hiding the hurt. She wondered how long it would take for the pain to ease and knew there was no easy answer. Jeff had broken things off with her more than three years ago and her heart still hurt when she thought about him.

"Do you wish you could take it back?" she asked. "The things you said that day?"

He smiled. Just barely. "That's a question I ask myself every day. Would I do it differently if I had the chance? Should I have done it differently?" He shook his head. "I don't know."

She had asked herself the same question after Jeff took his collar back. If she had it to do over, would she have moved out? Looking back with the knowledge she'd gained in the years since, she didn't think she would have. She liked to think that she would have stayed with Jeff, found a way to talk with him about her grief and guilt. If she had done that, they would probably still be together today.

She tilted her head. "You wouldn't have changed your mind about having a baby, though, right?"

"No." Cole's sigh was a sad combination of grief and resolution. "No. I wouldn't have changed my mind. I'm not having children. I just think maybe I could have handled it better."

"I miscarried four years ago." She made the confession before she could think about what she was going to say and change her mind. "Jeff and I got pregnant unexpectedly and the baby died at nineteen weeks."

His eyes widened, and he looked like she'd knocked the wind out of him. "Damn, Dena. I'm sorry. Here I am talking about not wanting a child and you lost one."

"No. It's okay. I only brought it up because it was after that that Jeff and I got in trouble and ended up splitting up. When I think about it now, I wish I had handled it better. Differently."

He nodded. "Sad to live a life filled with regrets."

"Yes, but don't you see? There were two people in the relationship. It didn't just fall apart because of something you did. And if you can think of things you would have done differently, I'm sure Kate can, too."

"I'm sure of it, but that doesn't change the fact that children aren't an area you can compromise on." He snorted as if remembering something. "And though I'm somewhat of a—what's the word? Oh, yes: 'badass.' Even though I'm a badass in the playroom, I'd like to think I'm a reasonable man otherwise."

They caught each other's gaze, and for a few seconds the room hummed with anticipation. Dena gave him a once-over. He was undoubtedly a breathtakingly handsome man. His dark brown hair was just long enough to curl slightly at his collar. His eyes were a deep bluish green that could change from warm to cold and unyielding in seconds. But it was the sculpted cheekbones and angular jaw that set apart his face and made him look so uniquely handsome.

His lips curled into a seductive smile, and she realized he'd been appraising her, too.

"Why have we never played together, Dena?" His voice was a promise of pleasure and sin that wrapped her in a warmth she'd never thought she'd feel again.

"Seriously?" She was surprised at how husky her laugh sounded.

He took her hand. She didn't stop him. "The playroom is empty and I have all afternoon. Would you like to join me there?" His thumb stroked her palm. "I can give you pleasure, Dena. Allow you to forget for a while."

His words made her shiver. She bet he could, and she let herself imagine it. He would be tough and demanding, probably more so than Jeff. Cole promised an afternoon of sexual delights with no strings. She was so tempted.

"I don't know," she confessed.

He stroked her cheek with his knuckles and she leaned in to his touch. "When was the last time you played? And not in a training scene."

"Almost two weeks ago. With Jeff. You?" She wouldn't allow him to hide; if he demanded truth from her, he could offer the same.

"There were several willing submissives in India."

Of course there were. She was willing to bet he rarely had an empty bed if he wanted company. Unlike her bed, which was perpetually empty.

He was a knowledgeable and experienced Dominant, one who promised a few hours of stolen pleasure. His touch would be nothing like the mentees she worked with under Daniel's supervision. Maybe an hour or two with Cole was exactly what she needed.

Telling herself she wasn't going to think too much about it, she stood up and dropped to her knees beside his chair. She closed her eyes when he stroked her hair. The touch brought to mind faint echoes of Jeff. Cole's hand was rougher, but with her eyes closed, it might be easy enough to pretend.

"What are your limits?"

"Master Covington has a copy of my checklist in his office."

The hand in her hair tightened. "I didn't ask for your checklist, sub. I asked what your limits are. And I expect to be addressed as 'Sir.'"

She nearly groaned. Yes. This was what she needed. His response was similar to what Jeff's would have been. "Sorry, Sir. Blood play, breath play, knives, body fluids, and fisting are hard limits."

"Noted. I'll discipline you for those two trespasses once we make it into the playroom. What's your safe word?"

"Win—"

She froze.

When she played with Jeff, they used "wings." Whenever she

played with someone else, she used "red." That she almost gave Cole "wings" as her safe word stunned her. She looked up at him in shock.

"Dena?" he asked with a puzzled look on his face.

He wasn't Jeff. He never would be. No one would be.

Not even with her eyes closed.

She shook her head and stood. "I'm sorry, Sir. I can't."

Cole didn't say anything.

"It wouldn't be fair to either one of us," she said. "We both know if we went into that playroom, it wouldn't be just the two of us. There'd be four people present." As much as she had imagined him to be Jeff, she knew there was a good chance he pictured Kate in her place. "We deserve better."

He sat and thought for a long moment. "You do at least," he finally said, then looked at her with a serious expression. "Do me a favor and ask yourself one last time why you're here and then think about whether that reason is worth what you're giving up."

"Sir?"

He stood. "You're living with a ghost. Either bury it once and for all, or banish it by fighting for the real thing."

A week after her talk with Cole, Julie and Sasha came to visit her at the Wests' estate. Abby welcomed them inside. Nathaniel took one look at the group of women gathering in his kitchen and told Abby he was taking the kids out for ice cream.

As much fun as it was to sit, drink wine, and gossip with her friends, Dena found that Cole's words from the week before refused to leave her alone. They had run through her head nearly nonstop. They taunted her at work. And at night they echoed in her empty room, keeping her from sleep.

She'd thought she'd done the right thing by letting Jeff go. She'd given him up so that he could take the business over from his father. She told herself it would have been selfish to ask him to stay. If she thought about it enough, she could almost convince herself it was noble of her to sacrifice him like that.

During the day when she was busy, she could convince herself she'd made the right choice. But at night, when there was only herself to listen, she knew better. The truth was, Cole was right; she had let Jeff go because living with his ghost was easier than facing her fears and fighting for the man.

It was useless to try to keep her thoughts hidden from her friends. They were always able to see through her.

Julie raised an eyebrow at her. "You're awfully quiet today. It's not like you."

"Just a lot to think about." She had told her friends about the call she'd received and how the voice sounded familiar.

"Have you figured out who you thought it sounded like?" Sasha asked.

"No." She hadn't, which was irritating. "I keep thinking if I try harder, I'll know. But no luck so far. And I feel so guilty. I know Jeff's working on it, and he shouldn't be. He needs to be with his dad."

"It'll come," Abby said; then, as if sensing Dena didn't want to talk about it, she looked to Julie. "How's Daniel's grand-mother?"

"Doing much better, thanks. He'll be able to do the next session with Ron." She laughed. "Just as well. I think Cole scared him."

"Probably good for him." Dena knew she should talk about it, and this was her chance. "Speaking of Cole, I had an interesting conversation with him the other day."

"Oh?" Julie poured herself more wine. "He's certainly an interesting guy."

"I can't imagine talking with him," Sasha said. "He seems so . . . different. But in a hot way."

Julie shook her head. "He's a nice guy. Out of the playroom, that is. I can't imagine submitting to him."

"I almost did," Dena quietly admitted.

Her three friends stared at her in shock and spoke at the same time.

"You did?"

"What about Jeff?"

"No way."

Dena nodded. "After the mentoring session we did together, after Ron left, Cole found me in the kitchen and we just started talking."

"Must have been one hell of a talk," Julie said. "I can't imagine anything making me want to play with him."

"Please." Sasha punched her arm, and Dena was glad to see some of her old playful spirit. "You can't imagine playing with anyone other than Daniel and you know it."

"True. But even if I could, it wouldn't be Cole."

"I don't see why not. He's hot. And that accent?" Sasha sighed, then looked over at Dena. "It was the accent, wasn't it?"

Dena had almost forgotten she was the one talking, she was

so flustered at Sasha's remark. As far as she knew, this was the first time Sasha expressed an interest in any guy following the scene with Peter that had put her in the hospital months ago. And she really couldn't believe it was over a Dominant with Cole's reputation.

She tried to cover her surprise. "No. It wasn't his accent. I think it was because so many of his actions and responses reminded me of Jeff."

Julie looked down at the table. Sasha absentmindedly twirled her wineglass. Abby met her gaze but remained quiet.

"You know, he said to me that all my friends tiptoed around it. And he was right," Dena said. "Look at you guys. And I let you do it. I'm a big girl. I can talk about Jeff without breaking into pieces."

"We don't want to make you feel uncomfortable," Julie said.

"Yes, that's true. But it's also true that I should know better." Sasha looked especially pained. "I remember my first group meeting after . . . Peter. Everyone would look at me and whisper, but it was all, 'How's work going?' when they worked up the courage to talk to me. And I let them avoid the subject. I was hiding."

"It's okay," Dena said. "I've been unwilling to talk about it for so long, I should probably put a sign around my neck that says 'It's okay. I can say the word "Jeff."'"

"Tell us what you and Cole talked about," Abby said.

"We went through our sob stories. Mine with Jeff. His with Kate. After a while the room just hummed. You know that feeling?" The women nodded, so she went on. "We never made it to the playroom, though. I realized Jeff was too much in my mind to be with anyone else."

"If it had been a different situation, would you have done it?" Julie asked.

"You mean if both of us still weren't hung up on our exes?" At Julie's nod, she continued. "I think so. He'd certainly be an interesting Dom to play with. But I couldn't—not with Jeff so fresh in my heart."

Everyone held still, waiting for Dena to continue.

"He said something, though, that stuck with me. He claimed I was living with a ghost and I needed to either bury it or banish it by fighting for the real thing."

"What are you going to do?" Abby asked.

Dena took a deep breath. She'd gone over her plans in her head, but she'd yet to vocalize them. This would be the first time she spoke them out loud. "I'm thinking about taking some time off work. A month or two. I have the time coming to me."

"Are you going to . . . ?" Julie looked at her with excitement growing in her eyes.

Dena found it so easy to say the words with Julie sounding so excited about what she was going to potentially say. "Yes. I'm thinking about going to Colorado. To fight for the real thing."

Abby burst into a big smile. "I knew it! I knew you guys were going to work it out."

"Whoa, there," Dena said. "I said I was thinking about going to Colorado—not that I was. And even if I do go, Jeff might show me the door as soon as I arrive."

"Have you ever even seen the way he looks at you?" Julie

asked. "There's not a woman in this world who wouldn't kill for a man to look at her just once the way Jeff looks at you."

"There's so much history between us. I'm not sure we can overcome it."

"Love conquers all," Sasha said, lifting her glass. "Or so I've heard."

"Sometimes life gets in the way." Dena wasn't aware of how much of her history with Jeff Abby and the others knew about, and she didn't feel like talking about her lost pregnancy at the moment. "We've tried to fight it before."

"You have to keep trying," Julie said. "That's what makes it so sweet when you finally make it. It's like that with everything. You value what you've had to work for."

Julie would know. She'd had to fight her own inner demons before she was able to find her happily ever after with Daniel. Her fight had been worth it. It was obvious to anyone how happy they were as a couple.

"We had a really awesome night just before he left," Dena said. "But I messed up the next day."

"Everyone messes up," Abby said. "Remind me to tell you about my first few months with Nathaniel sometime."

Dena shook her head. "You didn't see him. I think I went too far. I think he's over me for good."

"Not possible," Julie said. "I've seen you two together, and I've seen the way he looks at you. Trust me. You guys could live on separate continents and he wouldn't get over you."

"I agree," Abby said in an almost whisper.

Dena looked over to Sasha and raised an eyebrow. "You believe that, too?"

"I want to," she replied. "I've never had a relationship like yours. Or Julie's. Or Abby's."

Julie took her friend's hand. "You just haven't met the right guy yet. Your time's coming."

Sasha whispered a "thank you."

"And you," Julie said with a determined look on her face. "You need to get yourself to Colorado. We'll help you pack."

Jeff hated everything about Colorado. At night, when he couldn't sleep, he'd play a game with himself where he'd try to come up with a list of things he liked about the state. He always fell asleep before he could think of one.

When he'd arrived three weeks ago, he'd been shocked at just how bad his father looked. Even though he knew hospice had been called and his dad had only weeks to live, seeing him with the IVs giving his skeletal body morphine had taken his breath.

"You should have told me sooner," he told his dad.

His reply was a raspy, "Would you have gotten here any faster?"

Jeff didn't have an answer for that. Not one he could voice. The truth was, he didn't think it would have mattered. He'd probably have stayed with Dena. His father had never been a real father to him. The sad fact was, his dying didn't change that. But Jeff felt guilty whenever he admitted that to himself.

Hell, he was tired of feeling guilty.

One more thing he hated about Colorado—the guilt he felt whenever he was around his father. Apparently, Wilmington, Delaware, didn't hold sole rights to his guilty conscience.

Nearly two thousand miles hadn't kept Dena from his thoughts. She was on his mind constantly. He considered it a small victory when he went half an hour without thinking about her. Or worrying. It killed him that she'd received another phone call and he was so far away. He felt like a failure. Even though Tom was working on the case, Jeff worked late into the night after his father was asleep, looking over files and running searches. There was something somewhere he overlooked, and he was determined to find it. He wouldn't be able to live if something happened to her.

During the day he pictured her at work. He'd seen her in court once. Snuck in without telling her he was going to show up. Seeing her work the courtroom, so confident and sure of herself, had been an instant turn-on, made all the more intense by the silver cuff she'd been wearing that marked her as his. He'd been surprised to discover he wasn't jealous of the unabashed way men had stared at her with longing and desire in their eyes. She didn't once pay them any mind, and he knew whose bed she'd be in when night came.

But the nights in Colorado were far worse than the days. Alone in his childhood bedroom and all the memories that came with it—finding his mother drunk and passed out on the kitchen floor, his father's absence—had him tossing and turning all night, wishing Dena was beside him. Even with all those years of sleeping apart, it'd taken only that one night together for his body to remember how it was to share a bed with her.

Jeff sighed as he washed the breakfast dishes on his fourth Tuesday morning in his father's house. They were the same blue and white flowered china he remembered from childhood. When his father died, he was going to throw them away.

His father had had an appointment with his oncologist the day before. The doctor had told them it was only a matter of time. His father had refused to listen.

"Damn quack doctor," he'd snapped. "Said that a month ago, and I'm still here."

Jeff had been silent, but later that day when he'd entered the living room quietly, thinking his father was asleep, he'd found him instead sitting on the side of the bed, crying. Jeff stood frozen, hesitating. He'd lived with his father's anger his entire life. He didn't know what to make of his fear. But his feet eventually moved him forward, and he put a hand on his dad's bony shoulder. It was the first time he'd touched him in years, and the contact made his father crumple. He reached his arms up and embraced Jeff, and they'd both wept until they'd exhausted themselves.

The doorbell rang while he was in the middle of washing a plate, snapping him out of his thoughts. He put the dish towel down and jogged to the front door. His father was taking a nap, and he didn't want the doorbell to ring again.

He couldn't imagine who would be coming by the house. His father had very few friends in the community. Even the local church had eventually stopped coming by, thanks to his ability to offend even the most patient visitors.

He opened the door and stopped short.

"Surprise!"

He stared at Dena for what seemed like hours. Surely she was a hallucination he'd conjured up to ease the misery of being in Colorado. She wore all white from head to toe, and her beautiful blond hair peeked out from under her hat. She looked like an . . .

Like an angel.

He stopped himself before he said it.

"What are you doing here, Dena?" he asked instead.

Chapter Thirteen

Present day

Jeff knew her well enough to see through her almost perfect fake smile. Not only that, but her lips quivered for a brief second while she stood in the doorway. She was trying to act like she had everything together, but he could see that inside she was scared as hell.

Of him?

"I, uh, probably should have called." Her gaze looked behind him, over his shoulder, to the ground, anywhere but at his eyes. "But I wasn't sure you'd answer your phone if you knew it was me." She rushed on before he could say anything. "Okay, that's a lie. I know you would have answered, but I was afraid you'd tell me to go back home."

Hell, no, he didn't want her to go back home.

"Come inside," he said, holding the door open for her. He wanted to ask her a hundred questions, but they could wait. She was probably tired, and his father would be up soon. It was supposed to turn cold later in the day. Already the temperature was dropping. He looked over her shoulder. "Got any bags?"

"I'm staying at a hotel. I'm not so uncouth that I'd show up unannounced and expect you to put me up."

He nodded and let her pass him into the house. He'd just closed the door when he heard his father call out from the living room.

"Who the hell's ringing the doorbell at this hour?"

Dena stopped walking and raised an eyebrow.

"My father," Jeff said.

The look on Dena's face spoke of her sympathy, but before she could speak, his father called out again.

"Who are you talking to?" his dad asked. "Tell them we're not interested."

Dena started walking toward the living room.

"Dena," Jeff tried to warn her. "Watch out. He's . . ."

But she was already gone. He followed her.

"Hello, Mr. Parks," she said. "My name's Dena. I'm a friend of Jeff's. From Delaware."

"You must be what kept him there so long."

"Well, Jeff and I do go way back. We're close." She draped her coat over the arm of the couch, then placed her hat on top and gave her head a shake. Her blond hair bounced around her shoulders.

His father looked her up and down, probably trying to determine just how close they were. "You and Jeff? Nah."

Jeff watched, amazed, as she walked over to his father's hospital bed and sat down on the edge.

"Between you and me, it shocked the shit out of a lot of people," she said.

Then his father did something Jeff hadn't heard since he'd arrived weeks ago. He laughed.

"I think I might like you," he said in that raspy voice. But when a big smile broke across Dena's face, he added, "I said I *might*. You two go and let me get some rest."

They walked silently into the kitchen, and Jeff picked up a dish to wash. "Figured if you charmed my dad I'd let you stay?"

She looked pained, and he immediately regretted his sharp statement, but she only smiled and said, "Yes. Exactly that."

"I'm sorry. You came all this way. I shouldn't be such an ass."

"At least not this soon."

He smiled at her attempt to lighten the mood. "Why *are* you here?" And then another thought crossed his mind. "And by yourself? I can't believe Nathaniel let—"

She held her hand up. "Cole flew with me and drove me here. He's staying with friends." She had told him it was the least he could do following the pep talk he'd given her. "I'm going to tell you the truth because you deserve it and you'll know if I'm lying anyway." She bit her bottom lip. He'd never seen her do that before. "I couldn't stand to be away from you anymore."

They were words he'd dreamed of hearing, but part of him feared it was much too late. They never seemed to be able to work things out permanently.

"I know we can't start over," she continued. "There's too much history between us. And I don't think we can ever be just friends. For the same reasons."

He nodded. "Some people were never meant to be friends."

"I don't want to be just your friend, either, but there are things we need to deal with."

Is that why you're here? he wanted to ask, but he waited for her to speak.

Tears gathered in her eyes. He'd always hated her tears. Hated even more that he was often the cause of them.

"We've always been so honest with each other," she said. "About everything except *her*."

His heart broke anew just thinking about his daughter. "Dena," he said in a broken whisper.

She held up a hand. "It's true, and you know it."

He did.

"I came because I want us to try to work things out. You told me you wanted to face things together. Do you still?"

"It can't be like it was," he said. "Neither one of us can go through that again."

"I know," she said softly.

"God, I can't believe you're here."

"I have to tell you, I almost played with Cole."

His heart pounded. He couldn't bear to think about another man's hands on her. Surprising since such thoughts had never bothered him before. Hell, there had been gossip that she and Daniel were a possible item. All before Julie, of course. "I have no claim on you," he said, calmer than he felt. "You're allowed to play with anyone you want."

"That's not why I'm telling you. I realized I wanted to play with him only because he reminded me of you."

"I don't know if I should be flattered or worried."

She chuckled at his honesty. "I know we can't capture what

we were, but maybe, if we try, we can create something even better."

Could they do that? Become something different, something more together than they were before?

His smile was slow, but he hoped she heard the truth of his words. "I think I'd like that."

When Dena smiled, her real smile, not the fake plastic one she wore to political fund-raisers, she transformed from merely beautiful to ethereal. She made it hard to breathe.

"Oh, thank God," she said.

He leaned a hip against the countertop and crossed his arms. "I'm sure you have lines, rules, and expectations already planned out?" he asked, half joking.

"I have a few suggestions."

He smiled. "Of course you do."

"Let's have no lines, rules, or expectations."

He didn't even try to cover his shock. "Do I know you?"

She playfully held out a hand. "Hi, I'm Dena J. I'm rich as sin, the daughter of a senator, and a lawyer who has no interest in becoming a superior court judge. I'm outgoing, have a sarcastic sense of humor, and tend to get into trouble easily."

He threw his head back and laughed.

She beamed. "Your turn."

"Hi, Dena J.," he said, shaking her hand. "I'm Jeff Parks. I dropped out of high school, never went to college, and likewise have no interest in becoming a superior court judge. I'm introverted, hard to get to know, and have no originality in naming my dogs."

"Pleased to meet you, Mr. Parks."

Jeff kissed her hand, grinned, and for the first time in years, felt something a lot like hope.

Dena hadn't been sure how long she would stay. She'd told Cole not to go too far away, but he'd just laughed and said to text if she needed him, but he doubted she would. It pained her that Cole had more insight into Jeff than she did, because it'd taken only one look at Jeff's expression when he opened the door to know he was glad to see her.

After talking with Jeff in the kitchen, seeing him smile, and hearing him laugh, she couldn't leave. She wanted to stay. Especially when the hospice nurse called and said she was running late.

"Hell," Jeff said, hanging up the phone. "I don't know what to do with him."

She pressed her lips together. She knew he didn't get along with his father. It must be hard on him now to return to this house to care for his terminally ill dad.

"I can help," she said.

"You get queasy putting on a Band-Aid."

She opened her mouth to argue but promptly closed it. He was right.

"He's sleeping right now anyway," Jeff said. "It might be that he'll stay that way until the nurse shows up."

"What are the doctors saying?"

"That it's a matter of time."

"Didn't they say that a few weeks ago?"

He nodded. "He's hanging on."

She touched his shoulder tentatively. "And you're having to deal with this all on your own."

"You do what you have to do." He said it with a shrug, like it was no big deal, but she saw the fatigue in his eyes and the tension in the way he held himself. He wasn't sleeping well.

The idea hit her so suddenly, she didn't even think about it before letting the words flow from her lips. "Let me move in here and help."

She'd rarely seen Jeff speechless, but that did it.

"What?" he finally asked.

"Let me help. I'll clean. I'll . . . Well, I don't cook, but I can help with anything else. At least if I'm here, you can get some sleep knowing someone else can watch your father for a while."

"You know this will be the opposite of putting our relationship to the side."

"I'm sorry." She put her hand on his arm. "I wish I could take those words back." And not just those. There were many words, said by both of them, she wished they could move beyond.

His expression softened and he placed his hand over hers. "I'm sorry." He exhaled deeply. "Yes, please stay."

Relief flooded her. "Do we need to make your dad lunch? How long will he sleep?"

"Now I know aliens have invaded your body. You're going to make lunch?"

She was so glad easygoing Jeff was back. "When I said, 'Should we make lunch,' I meant 'Should you make lunch.'"

"Thank goodness. You really had me worried there for a minute."

Neither one of them moved, and they both seemed to remember at the same time that he still had his hand over hers. He squeezed it and brought his lips to hers. "Thank you."

Her heart pounded at the brush of his mouth on hers. "You're welcome."

He pulled back with a moan, saying he needed to start the soup for lunch. He said it was one of the few foods his father could keep down. Dena watched as he worked in the kitchen. She'd always enjoyed being in the kitchen while he cooked. They used to chat while he prepared meals. Some of their most intimate discussions happened in his kitchen.

But at that moment, she couldn't settle on any one question to ask to get the conversation started. Once upon a time, words had flowed freely between them. Now it was just awkward.

"Nathaniel said you thought you recognized the caller's voice the last time he called," Jeff finally said, breaking the silence. "Which makes me think I overlooked someone when I was going through your past cases."

She knew that possibility was eating him alive. "Seriously, I think it's nothing or else he would have done something else by now. Escalated it somehow. Besides that one note, he's still just calling. That's probably all he means to do."

"Careful with the assumptions there, Counselor." He ladled some steaming beef broth into a bowl to cool. "You and I both know nothing good comes from assuming things. And this time it's dangerous."

"Yes, but in this case—"

"Dena, stop."

His sharp tone surprised her so much, she actually stopped talking. She pursed her lips together and waited for him to continue.

"We're not going to change each other's mind," he said. "Let's not argue about it."

He was right. She needed to learn to pick her battles when he was involved. The world wouldn't collapse if she didn't get the last word in. "Agreed."

"I have my notes on my laptop. We'll go over them together in a bit. Right now I'm going to take this to Dad. There's some left-over beef stew I cooked for my dinner last night if you're hungry."

While he fed his father, she warmed up two bowls of stew. Nosing around the cabinets, she found some crusty bread and cut a few slices. When Jeff came back into the kitchen, she had everything prepared and laid out.

He didn't hide his delight at finding lunch waiting for him. To see him happy, especially over something as minor as lunch, made her heart hurt for him. Not to mention how it brought back memories of the ways she used to take care of him. When he had allowed it, that was.

"Thanks," he said, putting his dad's used bowl in the sink and sitting at the table. "You didn't have to warm mine up."

"I know."

They ate in silence for several minutes, which gave Dena the chance to study him closer. Fatigue lined his features in a way she had never seen before. The way he rolled his shoulders, al-most stretching, was something she had rarely witnessed either.

"How's your dad's business?" she finally asked. "Have you sold it yet?"

He took a bite of stew, then replied. "It's on the market." He looked up at her. "How are things at home? How's Daniel? I ha-ven't had a spare moment to talk with him."

"Great." She blew a stream of air across her spoon. "Julie's moving in with him."

He gave her one of his rare smiles. "I saw that coming. She's perfect for him."

"He's perfect for her." She laughed. "Of course, she was giving him hell about something when I left."

"Good. He needs a woman with spunk." His voice lowered. "How's Sasha?"

Dena nodded. "Believe it or not, I think she's coming around. I recommended a therapist, and she's been going a few times a week. I'm not sure, though, that I think it's a good idea for her to get back involved just yet."

"Why is that?"

"Master Greene's just now allowing Peter back into group meetings."

"Really? Took him long enough."

"Exactly. I think it'd be best for one of them to integrate themselves back without the other."

Jeff nodded. "It'll take a patient and determined Dom to work with Sasha when she's ready."

"I think she's already thinking about one in particular," Dena said, remembering what Sasha had said about Cole.

"Anyone I know?"

"Maybe, but I would never break her confidence. Besides, it'd never work. The one she has her eye on would eat her for breakfast."

Jeff raised an eyebrow.

"Not like that." She swatted at his arm and then froze at the look he gave her. Her hand had just brushed his arm, but it was enough. Just the simplest touch was all it took to bring to mind all the history and intimacy between them.

Not only that, but whenever she'd playfully swatted at him in the past, he'd dragged her over his knee for swats of his own. Just briefly, she saw his eyes darken with desire, and she knew he was remembering, too.

"Want to play, do you?" he'd ask, and she would only be able to moan a reply as his hand traveled to land between her legs.

How had they gone from that to where they now were? Eating leftover beef stew in a strange house, acting like strangers.

She pushed back from the table. It was too hard to sit at the table with him during the awkward silence following her statement. "I can clean this up," she said, picking up her bowl.

He held out a hand to stop her. "Not this time."

She sat back down in her chair. "Not this time, what?"

"You're not going to leave just because you got uncomfortable. If we're starting fresh, we're starting fresh."

She thought just for a minute about telling him she wasn't leaving because she was uncomfortable. After all, they didn't know how much longer his father would sleep or what he might need when he woke up. But Jeff was right. They didn't need to fall into old habits. And if she told him she wasn't uncomfortable, he'd know it was a lie.

She looked up and met his gaze. "Do I do that a lot?"

"No, but you've done it enough."

"Sometimes it just seems easier to work things out alone. Inside my head."

"But when you do that, you shut me out." He reached over and took her hand. "I want to help you work things out."

The sincerity in his eyes took her breath away. "When did you get so smart?"

He grinned. "Hell if I know. It definitely didn't happen in this house."

Looking around, she wondered how much had changed since he'd lived here as a boy.

"Is it hard being back?" she asked.

"I've had easier assignments." He looked around the kitchen. "I'm going to sell this place as soon as I can. Be rid of it once and for all."

Silence fell over the room, and she thought he'd forgotten about her trying to get up until he spoke again.

"Tell me what made you want to leave the table," he said.

She took the napkin from her lap and twisted it. "When I play swatted you, it made me remember what used to happen when I did that."

"When I'd pull you across my lap?"

"Yes, and I knew you wouldn't, but I remembered it and I figured you were remembering, too. And then it felt awkward, sitting at the table, both of us remembering what would have happened years ago and what would not be happening now."

"Would you like for me to pull you across my lap?"

"Yes." There was no way she would be able to lie about that, even if she were so inclined. "But with your father asleep in the living room and a hospice nurse on her way, it wouldn't be the best thing to do at the moment."

He took in all her words without a change in his expression, and when she finished, he simply asked, "Do you still want to leave the table?"

The truth surprised her. "No."

"See what a little bit of talking things through can do?" he said in a not-quite-teasing voice.

"Hmmm." She let her gaze travel over his chest downward to where his waist was hidden by the table. "Your turn. Tell me what you're thinking."

His voice grew low and rough. "I'm thinking I wish my father wasn't taking a nap in the living room and a hospice nurse wasn't on her way because I'd very much like to take you over my knee."

"I missed you," she blurted out.

He moved closer, his eyes locked on her lips. "I missed you, too."

She sucked in a breath and leaned forward. The napkin fell from her hands. It was probably a bad idea to kiss him. They had agreed to start over, start fresh. Kissing now might be too much too soon.

She told herself that, but her body wanted him. And from his body language, he wanted her just as badly. The space between them grew smaller and the hint of their indecision hung between them.

Just go for it.

No sooner had she decided to throw caution to the wind and kiss him than his father called from the living room. It sounded like he was in pain.

"Damn," Jeff mumbled under his breath as he pulled away from her. "I'll be there in a second, Dad."

"Now I'll clean up the kitchen," Dena said, gathering the bowls.

Later that night, the awkwardness returned. After calling Cole and having him bring her bags to the house, she realized she hadn't given much thought to the sleeping arrangements. Jeff had been an only child, and there were only two bedrooms in his small childhood home.

Jeff picked up on her unease as she stood in the hallway with her suitcase. "I can take the couch. You can have the bedroom."

"I can't kick you out of your bedroom."

"You're not. I volunteer."

His old bedroom was furnished with a queen-sized bed. *Technically,* there wasn't any reason for either of them to sleep on the couch. Or to sleep alone, for that matter. She had told herself they were going to take things slowly and make a fresh start, and if they shared a bed, she had a feeling the slow plan wouldn't happen.

Even so, she surprised herself by saying, "Don't sleep on the couch. Share the bed with me."

His jaw tightened at her words, like he was restraining himself. "Only if you want."

"I wouldn't have asked otherwise."

He nodded. "I'll keep my hands to myself," he said, before heading down the short hall to check on his father one more time.

Dena took her suitcase into the small bedroom and took out her pajamas and toiletry bag. She'd packed her regular pajamas, a white cotton long-sleeved two-piece set. She wondered if she would have packed something different if she'd known she'd be spending the night in Jeff's bed. With Jeff in it.

He hadn't returned to the bedroom when she was finished getting ready, so she climbed into the bed and scooted as close to the edge as possible. She was still hesitant and unsure enough about where they were headed that she didn't want to tempt him. He'd said he'd keep his hands to himself, and she wasn't going to make it difficult for him.

He came into the bedroom ten minutes later and silently crawled into bed. She noticed he scooted as close as possible to his edge, too.

"How's he doing?" she asked.

"He's sleeping. He's slept much more today than normal. I think it must really be the end this time." He seemed to hesitate before asking his next question. "How long are you here for?"

She rolled over to look at him and replied with a gentle whisper, "As long as you need me."

The silence in the room was deafening. Her heart pounded so hard, she felt it in her ears.

"Fuck, Dena," he whispered coarsely. "I'll always need you."

Her answer was just as rough. "Then take me."

He didn't pause to ask questions or to make sure she meant it. Her statement was all the encouragement he seemed to need, and he rolled her over to her back, coming with her, so he rested hard and heavy on top of her.

Fuck, it feels so good to be under him. She shifted her hips, trying to ease him closer, but he resisted and nipped her ear instead.

She yelped, and he covered her mouth with his hand. "You have to be quiet. The night nurse is in the living room." He rocked his hips. "Unless you want her to hear all those pretty little sounds you make when I fuck you."

"I'll be quiet," she said against his skin, running her hands down his back and grabbing his ass, pulling his shorts away. "Now. Please. In me."

He pushed her pajama pants down and shoved his free hand between her legs. "Already so wet. Do you have any idea what it does to me, feeling how your body reacts to mine?"

While he whispered, he worked his fingers along her entrance, brushing and teasing until she shook with need. She squeezed her eyes shut, wanting to hold off until he was inside her. He removed his hand from her mouth and, taking hers, placed it on his cock.

She wrapped her fingers around his base, stifling a moan when he continued whispering. "I've been in this bed alone for the last few weeks, imagining what I'd do to you if you were here. All the positions I'd fuck you in, how many ways I'd make you take my cock, and the number of times I'd let you come before I gave in and rode you as hard as I could for my own pleasure."

She wiggled under him. "Please."

"Show me. Take my cock and put it where you want it."

Right at that moment, she'd have taken it anywhere. But she loved the feel of him on top of her, so she spread her legs and placed him at her entrance. "Here. Hard, fast, and deep. Give in and ride me for your own pleasure, because I'll fucking explode with you inside me."

He pulled back and entered her with a hard thrust, covering her mouth with his and swallowing her groan at the feel of him. She clawed at his back, urging him deeper, harder. She was already so close. She worked her hips, meeting him thrust for thrust and getting lost in the feel of him filling her over and over.

Her release bubbled low in her belly and spread outward, touching every part of her body until she was coming around him. Her response only made him move faster and harder, until he jerked inside her and dropped to the bed, panting.

Neither one of them said anything. He simply pulled her into his arms, and within minutes, they were both asleep.

The next morning after breakfast, Dena joined Jeff in his father's office to go over the notes he had on her stalker. He knew he was overlooking something key, and he wouldn't feel at ease until he figured out what.

"I need you to go over this list," he said, handing her the paper with the people he thought he could rule out. "I don't think the guy is on here, but look over this and see if there's a name I'm missing. Or if it triggers something."

She scanned the list, her forehead wrinkled and her lips pressed together. "The thing is, it could be anybody: someone's uncle's cousin's son-in-law."

"Right, but you recognized the voice."

"I *think* I recognized the voice."

He sighed and ran a hand through his hair. "I think the best thing to do is bring in the police. They have resources I don't."

"Fine. I'll do it. When we get back home."

His head shot up from the computer screen. "What?"

"If it'll bring back the easygoing Jeff of last night or the Jeff who actually smiled while he made breakfast? I'll do it." Her own smile faltered for a brief moment. "It's almost like you're more at home in Colorado."

"No. That's not it. I wasn't like this before you showed up. It helps, having you here," he confessed. "Keeps the past at bay."

"You never talked much about your childhood," she whispered.

"It's not a topic I enjoy." He remembered coming home from school and finding his mother drunk and passed out. His father was never home, preferring to work instead of coming home to a kid and an alcoholic wife.

"I'm a good listener," she said. "I'm sure being here has brought back memories. Maybe it would help to talk about it."

"Yes," he said. "It's probably about the same as how the house felt to you . . . after."

Her breath caught as if she hadn't expected his discussion of *her* to be so blunt. "I wasn't . . . I didn't . . ."

"We've got to talk about it sometime."

"I know." She looked down and brushed her hands against the papers in her lap. "I just wasn't expecting it to be quite so soon."

"It's been years."

"I know," she whispered.

"My childhood was mostly horrible. I hope you can't say the same for our life together."

Her head shot up. "You know that's not the case."

He needed the truth. After all they'd been through, all they'd meant to each other, surely she owed him that much. "Then why did you leave me?" he asked.

"For a hundred reasons at the time, and now it's hard to remember just one."

"Why did you leave me, Dena?" he asked again.

She closed her eyes tight. He knew it wasn't a time she wanted to relive, but if they were to have any hope of anything in the future, they had to be honest. "I thought," she started and then stopped. "I thought you hated me."

"How could I have hated you for what happened?" he asked, pained to think she honestly felt that. "It was a miscarriage. Nothing you did caused it, and nothing you could have done would have prevented it."

"You can't say that. You don't know."

"Then tell me. Tell me why you've carried the guilt for this all these years."

"That day, the day it happened, I didn't feel her move. I realized it about the time you made it home from your office." She paused, bit her lip, and looked away.

Jeff didn't say anything. He simply waited, knowing his silence would persuade her more than words.

"I was thinking about how long it'd been since we'd played. Since we'd been in the playroom," she said. "I wanted you to take me there. I thought we could discuss it over lunch. So instead of seeing if I could feel her move, I made sandwiches. Don't you see?" She looked him square in the face. "I decided sex was more important. If I'd just checked it out, maybe she wouldn't—"

"Stop." He knew where she was going, and he couldn't let her think it anymore.

She took a deep shuddering breath and glanced out the window.

"You've thought all these years it was somehow your fault because you didn't check for movement? You think you could have prevented it?" He didn't wait for her to answer. "Dena, look at me. You didn't do anything wrong. By the time you realized what was happening, she was already gone."

"You don't know that, and even if it's true, if I'd been paying closer attention—"

"It wouldn't have changed anything. It was nothing you did. Nothing." His voice was soft but firm. "I was living with you, remember? You did everything right. It just wasn't meant to be."

"It's so much easier to blame myself."

"That's because you want there to be a reason for everything, and in the absence of finding one, you make one up. The fact is, sometimes there's not a reason. Sometimes things just are what they are."

She blinked tears away. A faint glimmer of hope danced in her eyes, showing him how much she wanted to believe his words.

"Every time I saw you after it happened," she said, "I'd remember how I'd pushed my concerns away and I'd hate myself more."

"I thought you blamed me."

"You?" She wrinkled her forehead. "Why would I have blamed you?"

"Because of the way I acted when I found out you were pregnant." He frowned, remembering his reaction at finding the pregnancy test in the scattered garbage.

"You were surprised, and it wasn't something we'd planned. I didn't expect you to turn cartwheels."

"And then, when you suggested that maybe you should move out, I thought it was because you couldn't stand to be around me."

"Only because it reminded me of my guilt," she replied softly.

Silence fell over the room as each of them thought through the other's words.

"That day in the bathroom," he said, shaking his head. "I'd never felt so damn useless. You were sitting there in pain, going through hell, and I couldn't do a thing."

"You were there. That's what I needed. Even though I told you

I didn't want you in the bathroom, deep down it comforted me to know you were with me."

"I'm a man," he said with a small smile. "I thought I should be able to do more. I like to fix things."

She snorted. "Don't I know? And you get all pissy when you can't."

"I take offense at the word 'pissy.'"

"That doesn't make it untrue."

Their gazes caught, and the lighthearted moment turned serious.

"What happened to us, Dena?" He reached across the desk and stroked her cheek. "How did we go from what we were to where we are now?"

Her skin was soft under his fingers. He wanted to pull her close and never let go. To somehow shelter her from the ghosts of their past. No matter what happened between them, whether they were able to start again or not, no one else would ever make him feel the way she did.

"I ask myself that all the time," she said.

"Have you ever found an answer?"

"No."

"Then the question becomes how do we move ahead?"

She took the hand he had on her face and laced her fingers through his. "I don't know the answer to that one either, but I think we're making a good start."

Falling into a routine was as easy as breathing. In the mornings Dena would keep Jeff's father occupied while he cooked. After breakfast his father would nap and either Jeff would work on getting the insurance business taken care of or he would look over the notes he had on Dena's stalker.

She joined him in the kitchen while he cooked lunch and dinner, taking a break from her laptop and the remote casework she was doing. He remembered how much she used to enjoy being in the kitchen while he prepared a meal. Before they'd met, he had been used to cooking alone, and it took time to grow accustomed to having her there after she moved in. Eventually, he not only got used to it, but he got to count on it. Their talks during that part of the day became something he looked forward to. And something he'd missed horribly after she left.

The Friday night following her arrival, though, he decided to change their routine. He made alternate arrangements with the nurse on duty and waited in the kitchen. When she came in to chat while he cooked, she raised an eyebrow at the sight of him standing and doing nothing.

"I have a change of plans for us this evening."

"Oh?" A playful light glimmered in her eyes. "This doesn't involve me cooking, does it?"

"No. Will you go to dinner with me?"

"Like a date?"

"Yes, like a date."

She smiled that smile that never ceased to stop his heart. "I'd love to have a dinner date with you."

He'd made reservations at a nearby steakhouse that had recently opened. The afternoon nurse had gone on and on about it when he'd asked for a place to take a date. The truth was, he didn't care where they ate; he simply wanted some alone time with Dena, away from the house. Sure they talked, but part of his attention had to be on his father. He wanted time to focus on her.

"If I'd known we were going out, I'd have worn something else," she said, frowning at her jeans and sweater.

He bit back his laugh. She would always be the daughter of a senator, would always feel the need to look picture-perfect. Which meant he would be the one who had to talk sense into her.

"Look at me," he said, lifting her chin. He smiled when their eyes met. "You are beautiful. Don't worry about your clothes. The restaurant's casual."

Even so, she didn't seem relaxed until they stepped inside the restaurant and she took note of the casual way the other diners were dressed. The building was an old restored warehouse, and echoes of its former life were evident in the brick walls and over-head wooden beams.

They were soon seated at a secluded booth in the back corner. Dena picked up her menu and peered at him over the top of it. "Did you request this booth?"

"No. Why?"

"No reason," she said, and dropped her eyes to read the menu. "I just remember you did request a certain table in the back corner of a darkened restaurant once. Or twice."

His cock grew hard as memories of one of the nights in question flooded his mind, and he swore softly.

"Sorry," she said, still reading the menu. "I probably shouldn't have brought it up." The tone of her voice indicated she wasn't sorry in the least. "But just to make sure, I am allowed to speak to people other than you, right?"

One of their favorite things to do when she wore his collar was to subtly play in public. He often instructed her not to speak to anyone other than him. She usually messed up. For someone with a vivacious personality like hers, it was difficult to curtail the chatter.

Though he suspected she often messed up on purpose.

"Yes," he said through clenched teeth. "Of course."

"Mmmm." She went back to looking over the menu.

He tried to focus on his own menu, but since she'd brought up the past, the only thing he could focus on were memories.

Telling her to go to the bathroom and remove her panties.

Having her masturbate at the table and to come with no one noticing.

Playing with her under the table and having her suck his fingers clean when he finished.

"Remember the restaurant with the long tablecloth?" she asked after they ordered drinks. She sat back in her seat and appeared to be enjoying watching him sweat. "You had your hand under the table, your fingers inside me, when that client of yours came up to the table and wanted to shake your hand."

That memory hadn't been one of the more erotic ones. Instead, it had been awkward and embarrassing. The client had been excited to see him and had wanted to introduce him to his dinner companion. Jeff had been coaxing Dena through an orgasm when he walked up.

Not wanting to shake the guy's hand with Dena's arousal on his fingers, he'd pled messy hands as a result of dinner and excused himself to the bathroom to wash them.

"Not that one either," he said. "That one's just downright embarrassing."

She laughed. "It was that way for me, too. You left and went to wash your hands. I was alone at the table, highly aroused, and had to make small talk like everything was normal."

"I'd apologize," he said, "but if I remember, I more than made it up to you once we got home."

Her eyes darkened as she remembered. "You did. Definitely."

He was uncomfortably hard. "Let's talk about something else." *Before I fuck you on the table,* he almost added.

"Just as well," she said. "I need to decide what I want to eat."

They silently studied their menus until the waitress came by for their order. After she left, Dena looked at him with a familiar naughty look in her eyes, and he knew he was in trouble unless he took control back.

She started to speak, but he stopped her by placing his finger over her lips. "Shhh. This table has some pretty long tablecloths, too. Typically, we talk before dinner, but tonight you'll use your mouth for a different purpose. Namely, you can't eat until you've sucked me off."

Dena had always loved their public play, and by the gleam in her eyes, nothing had changed.

"That's my favorite appetizer, Sir."

"Then what are you waiting for?"

Without another word, she disappeared under the table. Within seconds, her hands were on him, undoing his pants. He fisted the tablecloth as her warm mouth engulfed him.

Fuck. What where they doing? They were acting like teenagers. He should pull her back up to the table and act like an adult.

Then she took him so deep in her mouth, he reached the back of her throat, and he decided maybe she could keep it up a little bit more.

"Excuse me, sir." The waitress was suddenly standing by the table, and he could have kicked himself for not seeing her approach. "I didn't ask what kind of salad dressing your friend wanted."

He wasn't sure, but he thought Dena was laughing around his cock.

"Uh, salad dressing?" he asked.

"Yes, sir. We have Italian, French, honey mustard, ranch, blue cheese—"

"Blue cheese. Yes, that's it." He remembered she'd ordered blue cheese once.

He thought.

But under the table, Dena shook her head "no" around his cock.

"No, wait. Not blue cheese." He tried to think. Fuck, it was hard to concentrate on anything other than Dena's mouth. "What were they again?"

"Italian, French, honey mustard . . ."

Dena's head started nodding at "honey mustard."

"Honey mustard," he said in a tight voice.

The waitress wrote something down. "Got it. So," she said, leaning against the wall to the right of the table. "I haven't seen you before. Are you new in town?"

Fuck. Was she going to stand there and *talk?*

Under the table, Dena didn't stop; in fact, she took him deeper.

He sucked in a sharp breath. "I'm caring for my father. He's sick."

"Where are you from, I mean if you're just visiting here to help your dad?"

Damn it all. Yes, she was going to stand there and talk. And, yes, he was certain Dena was laughing under the table.

"Delaware," he said, fisting Dena's hair in order to still her.

It worked, and she kept her head still. But he was buried deep in her mouth, and she decided to suck harder and run her tongue up and down his shaft. With every sweep of her tongue, Jeff felt his release building. He would have to do his best to hold it back.

Fortunately, the waitress seemed to lose interest upon hearing he lived so far away. She pushed off the wall and left with an "I'll go put this order in."

As soon as she left, he thrust hard into Dena's mouth and released down her throat, swearing under his breath. Seconds later, she slid up into her seat, wearing a grin and licking her lips.

"I thought that woman would never leave," she said while he leaned back and gathered his breath. They locked gazes and laughed.

"Me, too," Jeff admitted. "Thank God I'm not from around here or she'd probably still be here."

"That was fun. We should do it again."

He was getting ready to voice out loud that they were walking down a dangerous path when the waitress delivered their salads.

"Ah," he said, looking down at the bowl of lettuce. "Saved by food."

"Saved?" Dena cut into a tomato. "How so?"

Because I'm about ten seconds away from fucking you on top of the table. He cocked an eyebrow at her. "Best not ask that question."

She gave him a sly smile that told him she knew why she shouldn't be asking that question. She sighed. "Okay. If you insist."

"I do." He was operating on too little sleep and too much emotion to properly control himself if she continued playing him.

She seemed to understand his difficulty and thankfully changed the subject. For the next little bit, she caught him up on all the Wilmington gossip.

"How's that mentee you've been helping Daniel with?" he asked halfway through their main courses.

"Ron? He's doing okay, a little on the slow side. Daniel's having to go over the same things repeatedly, and I can tell he's not completely pleased with his progress. He had to have Cole run a session."

"How'd that go?"

She took a bite of salad. "Pretty good. And by that I mean Cole didn't make him cry."

"What do you think?"

She took her time thinking through her reply. "I believe with enough work, he'll become adequate, but he'll never be a great Dom. There's something inherent in the great ones. You guys are born with it. Not that there's anything wrong with being adequate. He'll be fine for someone looking for light or infrequent play."

"Have you discussed your thoughts with Daniel?"

"Yes, several times. He agrees. Right now he's just trying to give Ron enough knowledge so that he doesn't hurt himself or anyone else."

Daniel would do everything he could to ensure everyone's safety. Plus, he had the patience and nature to firmly but kindly instruct and reinstruct. That was one of the reasons Jeff never took on a mentee. While he had some patience, if he had to reinstruct too many times, he had to admit he lost it.

He snorted. "Daniel should let Ron be the bottom in a scene or two; that'd help him."

"He's already arranged a session with Mistress K."

His jaw dropped. "Shit. Kelly will rip him to shreds only so she can put him together and do it again."

"Exactly." Dena laughed. "You should have seen the look on Ron's face when Daniel suggested it. He told Ron he didn't have to agree to it, but that it'd go a long way in completing his mentorship. I think they were going to try to set something up this weekend. Kinda sorry I'll miss it."

"Daniel wouldn't have let you watch anyway."

"I know. But still."

He narrowed his eyes and studied her carefully. "Not a big fan of Ron's?"

"Not really, no." She caught his gaze and smiled. "Hard to be satisfied with adequate once you've had great."

His heart raced, but he forced his voice to remain calm. "Flattery?"

"You know better. The night you collared me and made wax play something I craved, you proved you were the best."

If anyone would ever ask him why he'd never collared anyone after Dena, he need only look to that night for the answer. When she'd looked up at him from his table, there'd been fear in her eyes. Though he didn't know exactly how the last wax scene she'd taken part in before that had gone, something had spooked her. Yet even in her fear, the trust that radiated from her body spoke far louder.

It was that trust. The unguarded, raw trust she had in him that lit her eyes. He could play with every woman on the planet and he'd never find a more beautiful sight than the trust in Dena's eyes.

Unless it was the love in Dena's eyes.

He reached across the table to take her hand, but before he could, his phone rang. He dug it out from his pocket with a frown. He'd asked not to be called unless it was an emergency.

"Damn," he said. "It's the nurse."

"Hello?" he said, answering the call.

"Mr. Parks, sorry to interrupt your dinner. It's your father. We're losing him."

There was a ritual to death that was oddly comforting to Jeff. A schedule of events to follow and plenty of people to ensure everything got done. He supposed it happened that way to make it easier for those in mourning. Not that he truly grieved the loss of his father; but now that the man was really gone, Jeff realized the depth to which he grieved the relationship they could have had.

Through it all, Dena was right in the thick of things. She handled the business associates and the few friends of his father graciously. Jeff supposed being a senator's daughter had groomed her for such a role. Even still, every once in a while, he'd look and find her thanking someone for coming by or shaking the hand of a former client of his father's and she would stun him with her poise and gentility.

She looked so out of place: a queen in the midst of the lowly home of his childhood. He wondered what she would say if he shared his observation with her. Likely as not, she'd laugh and say he was crazy. Then she'd narrow her eyes and playfully tell him she had no desire to be queen.

After the funeral, they drove back to the house. Finally, for what felt like the first time in days, they were alone together.

Dena shrugged out of her coat. "Ugh. I forgot how exhausting funerals were."

It felt oddly quiet in the house. The hospital bed had been removed from the living room, and the noisy hum of equipment no longer filled the silence. Gone, too, was the flow of visitors.

Dena hung up their coats, closed the closet door, and raised an eyebrow at him. "Are you okay?"

"Yes, just thinking about how silent the house is." He sighed and looked around the room. "Guess I'll start boxing up things pretty soon."

"You're going to sell it that fast?"

"I don't see why not. There's no reason to put it off. Most of the furniture and stuff I'll give to Goodwill." He walked toward the kitchen. "Do you want something to drink?"

"Sure." She ran a finger over the top edge of the well-worn couch. "Is there anything you're going to keep?"

"There's nothing here for me. Nothing I want." He took two glasses down. "The sooner I get this place settled, the sooner I can get back home."

"I can help pack things up," she said, following him into the kitchen.

"You've already done so much. You don't have to help me pack." He crossed the room to where she stood and cupped her cheek. "I haven't said it enough, but thank you for all your help. You've done so much the last few days. I truly appreciate it."

Her eyes grew soft. "You don't have to thank me. You'd do the same for me."

"Regardless, thank you."

He almost dropped his head to kiss her, but stopped himself at the last minute. It didn't feel right to kiss her in his father's kitchen, not many hours past his burial.

"You're welcome," she whispered.

He stroked her cheek and stepped away to get the iced tea from the refrigerator. "A bit sad most of the people who came today were old business associates and not friends, don't you think?"

"Maybe a lot of people had to work and couldn't get off."

He snorted. "I don't think so. The business was his wife, child, mistress, and best friend all wrapped in one."

"Then yes, that's sad."

"I can't remember how it was when Mom died. I was too young, I guess."

They carried their drinks into the living room and sat down on the couch. The couch was so small, their knees touched, and he knew if he sat back, he'd brush her shoulder as well.

"How old were you when she died?" Dena asked.

"Six," he said. "And I hated her for leaving us. Hated that she loved her booze more than she loved me."

She took a sip of coffee. "How did your dad react to her death?"

"I think in some ways it was a relief to him. He had one less person to look after." He set the glass on the table, suddenly not in the mood for it anymore. "That's all I ever was to him, something to look after."

Dena was silent. She'd never talked about her childhood much either, but he had a feeling the senator hadn't won any Parent of the Year awards.

"I found her," he said, admitting something he'd never shared with anyone. "It was horrible. I was six, but that was the day my childhood ended."

"Oh, Jeff," she said, and there were tears in her eyes. "I'm so sorry."

"I came home from school and wanted a snack. I knew she kept the cookies hidden on the top shelf of the pantry. I figured she wouldn't notice if I took one or two." He stopped. Remembering back, being in the house, it was almost like reliving it. His sigh was shaky. "I went looking for cookies and found Mom sleeping on the floor. I didn't understand why she wouldn't wake up."

Dena put a hand on his knee. "Oh, Jeff."

"Something like that happens these days, you put the kid in therapy," he said, not surprised to hear the bitterness in his voice. "You think I got sent to therapy? I got sent to my bedroom and was told to stay there. I think it took my dad two days to remember I was in the house."

"I . . . I had no idea."

"Can you see now why I was in such a hurry to leave this godforsaken place and never come back?"

Silent tears ran down her face as she nodded.

"Soon as I turned sixteen, I was out. I wasn't sure where I was headed, but I thought anywhere was better than here. Hitchhiked my way to New York, where I joined up with a group of petty thieves. We lived hard. Probably would have died on the streets if it hadn't been for Grandma."

She sniffled. "Your grandmother followed you to New York?"

"Not my biological grandmother. Grandma was an older lady who lived in a small apartment I broke into. She caught me."

"What happened?"

"She cooked me dinner," he said with a smile.

"She what?"

"She told me she'd cook me dinner and all I had to do was listen to her." He shrugged. "I figured a hot home-cooked meal in exchange for listening to an old lady gabber? Easy as pie."

She'd told him he looked like her son, all dark and dangerous and ready to pick a fight with anyone who looked at him wrong. Over dinner she said he could be a thug and fight for the wrong reasons, like her son, and die too young, like her son had. Or he could be a man and fight for the right ones.

"You picked the right ones?" Dena asked.

Jeff grinned. "Actually, I looked at her and said, 'Hell, Grandma, I'll fight whoever you damn well want me to if you'll cook me dinner again.'"

Dena laughed.

"So she became 'Grandma.' I lived with her until she died of a massive heart attack. She's the one who encouraged me to get my GED and join the NYPD. And she was the only person who came to my graduation from the police academy. After she died, I moved to Delaware. Worked on the force there for a few years and then quit to open the business. I was able to afford it because she left everything to me. Best damn woman I ever knew." He smiled at her. "Over sixty, that is."

"She saved you."

"She did."

"Why Delaware?"

"Why not? I figured with all the big businesses in Wilmington, there'd be need for my services."

She looked at him quizzically for a long time. "Why did I not know this about you before?"

"I don't like talking about it."

"We lived together for how many years?"

"Are we going to fight about this? Is that what you want?"

Her arms were crossed and her iced tea sat beside his, neglected. She looked pissed.

"No," she said. "I don't want to fight. I'm just angry you have this whole past I knew nothing about until today."

"You've never been exactly forthcoming about life with Daddy Dearest."

"What's there to tell? I was raised by nannies and dragged out on important occasions to smile and look pretty." She shot him an evil glare. "But my dad never sent me to my room and forgot about me for two days."

"No, your dad just threatens to shoot people if he doesn't get his way."

Her arms fell to her sides and her jaw dropped. "What?"

"Fuck, I didn't mean to tell you like that."

Horror replaced the shock in her expression. "Didn't mean to tell me like that? Do you know what you just accused my father of?"

His rotten day had just got a hundred times worse. He dug his fingers through his hair. "Dena, let's sit down and discuss this reasonably."

"Reasonably?" She shot up from the couch. "I think reason left the room the minute you suggested my father would do something like that."

He could kick himself for blurting it out like that. The only reason he could think of was that the day's emotions had overwhelmed him. He might tell himself he didn't grieve his father, but that didn't mean his death didn't affect him.

Dena had moved across the room as if needing to put as much space as possible between them. He weighed his options and then decided to go with instinct.

"Sit down," he said in a tone of voice guaranteed to either get her attention or earn him a kick in the balls.

Multiple emotions rippled across her face. "I'm not your—"

"I am *fully* aware of that, but I said to sit down." He pointed to the couch. "I buried my father today. He might have been a worthless bastard, but he was still my father. The least you can do is let me explain."

She sat down. "You have two minutes."

Without moving his eyes from her face, he told her about the day Senator Jenkins had paid him a visit. He left nothing out. Not the insinuation he wasn't good enough for her, her father's plan for her on the superior court, nor the veiled threat if he didn't leave her alone.

By the end of the story, her bottom lip was trembling. "I don't believe you."

"Christ, Dena, what reason would I have to lie?"

She didn't answer.

"You don't want to believe me," he said. "But deep inside, you know it's true."

He tried to put himself in her place. She might not have had

the best relationship with her father, but there was a big difference between thinking someone's a jerk and allowing for the
possibility of that person being capable of cold-blooded violence.
Especially when the person in question was your father.

Jeff wasn't going to argue his point. He'd told her the truth,
and it was up to her whether she believed it or not.

She sank into the nearby chair and buried her face in her
hands. "Oh, God."

"I was trying to protect you by not telling you." All those
years he hadn't told her. Had he done more harm than good? He
didn't know if he'd do anything differently if he had the chance
to do it again.

"You and my dad are so similar. You always think you know
what's best for me. One of these days you're going to have to let
me stand on my own." She stood up, wiping her cheeks and
brushing the hair back from her face. "I need to go think."

She was calmer when they talked later that evening. After
spending the afternoon thinking things through, she realized she
could have no future with Jeff until she confronted her father.
Jeff said he understood, but the easy camaraderie they had
enjoyed days before was gone.

Dena decided to head back home before Jeff did. Jeff called
Nathaniel, and he volunteered to send his jet for her to fly home
on. And of course, he said, their house was always open and she
could stay with them until Jeff got home.

It was late when she arrived at the Wests' estate, and she
mumbled a quick "hello" to Nathaniel and Abby before heading

to the guest room and crashing. The toll of Colorado's emotional highs and lows finally caught up with her, and she was asleep within seconds of falling into bed.

She awoke disoriented, and it took her several minutes to remember where she was. According to the alarm clock on the nightstand, it was after nine; it'd been years since she'd slept that late. Her fingers fumbled putting on a robe, and she headed down the stairs.

After making a cup of coffee in the kitchen, she found Abby in the library. Her hair was pulled up on top of her head, and she was intently focused on the laptop screen in front of her. At Dena's arrival, she broke into a smile.

"There you are. I was starting to think I should make sure you were breathing."

"Hard week," Dena said. "Mind if I join you?"

"No, not at all." Abby picked up her own coffee mug and joined her on a leather couch.

"I love this room. It's so warm and welcoming." Her father's house had a library, but she'd never felt comfortable in it. Even as an adult, she was afraid to touch anything.

"It's my favorite, too. Nathaniel actually gave it to me shortly after we met. He wanted me to have a space that was completely my own."

"He gave you a room?"

"It was probably more symbolic than anything." Abby sighed and looked at the piano. "There are a lot of memories here."

Jeff's words about his memories of his childhood home came back to her. But what different reactions to memories. Abby looked blissfully happy. Jeff had been miserable.

"Memories," Dena said. "I battled memories the entire time I was in Colorado. My own. Jeff's. Why do we carry the past around like a weight?"

"Because we're afraid of losing it. Or we think if we don't carry it around we'll forget who we are."

"I learned so much about who Jeff is from being with him in Colorado. He had a horrible childhood."

"You didn't know that before?" Abby asked.

"Not so many details. He'd always avoided talking about it when we were together before," Dena said. "But being in that house and coming back to this." She swept her arm around. "I can feel the difference and see part of why he was always caught up in the fact that I come from money."

"It's a legitimate issue. It took me a while to get used to Nathaniel's wealth."

"We were together for years."

"You also have to remember Jeff's a man, and it's harder for them to deal with their partner being better off."

Dena hadn't thought of that. "Because he's supposed to be the breadwinner, according to society?"

"Yes, and he feels he needs to provide you with the lifestyle to which you're accustomed."

"But I have plenty of money. I don't need his."

"Exactly the problem. Men want to feel needed."

Dena sighed and leaned back into the couch. "Sometimes men are hardheaded. Seriously? Who cares who has the money?"

"I agree. It shouldn't be an issue. And you think men are stubborn *sometimes?*" Abby laughed "How about most of the time?"

"True." Dena took another sip of coffee. "He also had a run-in with my father a few years ago he didn't tell me about."

"Oh?"

"You have to understand my dad. Scratch that. There's no understanding him."

"I take it Jeff and your father don't get along?"

Dena snorted. "That's putting it mildly. My dad has always had a plan for my life: where I should go to school, what job I should have, whom to marry. That sort of thing. If he could find a way to arrange my marriage, he would."

"Sounds like a tyrant."

"He is. I went to law school at Harvard because that's where he went, though the truth is I wanted to go there. But after I graduated, I did my own thing, and that's always made him mad." She sighed. "Apparently, when Jeff and I were together before, my dad threatened him if he didn't leave me alone."

Abby gave a low whistle. "That's pretty bad."

"I know. I can't believe my dad did that, and I can't believe Jeff didn't tell me."

"I take it you've discussed your feelings with Jeff. Are you going to discuss them with your dad?"

She had thought about that on the trip back from Colorado. Would it do any good? Her dad wouldn't really hurt Jeff, would he? What was the best way to approach him?

"I need to," she finally answered.

"I agree, especially if Jeff's going to be a more permanent part of your life." There was a question in Abby's eyes.

"I certainly hope so."

Her phone buzzed with an incoming text, and she smiled when she saw it was from Jeff.

Coming home in two days. Miss you.

She ran her finger over the words on the display as if touching them brought her somehow closer to him. She sent a simple reply.

Miss you more. Waiting.

Since she had a few more days off before she had to go back to work, she made sure she was waiting in her father's home office at the end of the next day. Nathaniel arranged for the private security company to take her.

Her father hugged her. "Dena. Darling. How lovely of you to stop by."

She pulled away from his arms. His hugs always felt fake to her. Almost as if he'd read a book on parenting and was just following the rules.

Get tree for Christmas. Check.

Hug child. Check.

Threaten daughter's lover. Check.

He frowned when she pulled away. "What brings you by?"

She looked around the massive office with the huge wooden desk and the faint smell of cigar smoke. She hated this room. Hated that every detail of it was focused on making the person behind the desk look big and the person on the other side feel small. When she was little, she wasn't allowed to enter it, and she'd imagined it a magical place where laws were made and the country's problems solved. Then she'd grown up and realized its only purpose was to stroke her father's ego.

"I've been out of town," she said in reply to his question. "Jeff's father had cancer, and I went to help. He died a few days ago."

"I'm sorry to hear that, of course." He spoke with no emotion noticeable in his voice, though he winced when she spoke Jeff's name. "But glad you're back home where you belong."

She didn't even know what to say to that.

Her father didn't seem to notice. Or else he did and just didn't care. "I have to say, I am disappointed you've taken back up with Jeffery Parks. If I've taught you nothing else, you should know appearance is everything. Especially if you're looking to be elected into the judicial branch. That man will be seen as a handicap. Honestly, Dena, he didn't finish high school."

"He got his GED," she said through clenched teeth.

He waved as if shooing away something unpleasant. "GED. Please. I raised you better."

He said something else, but blood pounded in her head so loudly, she didn't hear it. Her plan had been to have a reasonable conversation with her father, but it didn't appear that was going to happen. She smacked her palm on top of the wooden desk so hard a pencil holder fell over.

"Let me settle something," she said, interrupting whatever her father had been going on about. "Jeff Parks is the best man I know. He's smart. He's honorable. He's hardworking. And he's honest. Frankly, that's a hell of a lot more than you are."

"You will not come into—"

She shocked herself by snapping her fingers, a move Jeff had made numerous times. Her father must have been shocked as well, as he suddenly fell silent.

"I am not finished," she said. "You will *not* interrupt me."

He looked at her with ire but remained silent. She straightened her spine. If her dad wanted to play dirty, she would respond in kind.

"Certain—let's call them *classified*—conversations have been brought to my attention over the past few days. The fallout of which could be very damaging to a political career. Especially for someone short-listed for the vice presidency. Are you with me so far? Nod 'yes' if you understand."

"For crying out loud—"

She slapped the desk. "I said nod!"

He nodded.

"Good. Now, I might be just a lowly attorney, but I have connections you wouldn't believe. I've helped a lot of people, and I'm not afraid to call in favors. Not only that"—she smiled sweetly at him—"but I'm prepared to lie. I'm prepared to make up shit so rotten you'll be headlining the gossip rags for years. You'll be the punch line of every late-night-show joke. I'll lie my ass off and it'll work. Know why?"

He shook his head, his face ominously expressionless.

She planted her hands on top of the desk and looked him straight in the eye. "Because the American public loves a scandal, and they like nothing more than to see pompous rich assholes fall off their pedestals."

With those words, for the first time ever, she saw fear in her father's eyes.

"Here's the deal," she continued. "I love Jeff, and if he'll have me, I plan to spend the rest of my life with him. He'll be the father of your grandchildren, if we're lucky enough to have kids. So I'm going to walk out that door, leaving you with the knowledge that if one hair on Jeff's head is hurt, I'll call a press conference faster than you can say 'impeached.' Are we clear? If so, nod your head." He opened his mouth, but she shook her head. "Best not."

He nodded.

"Excellent." She straightened up and brushed her palms as if wiping something off. "I'm glad we had this chat." As she walked to the door, she looked over her shoulder. "Oh, and one more thing. You can screw the judicial branch. I have no intention of ever being a judge."

Chapter Fourteen

Present day

If there was one thing Jeff hated, it was being late. He demanded punctuality of his employees, clients, and the submissives he played with. He himself made sure he arrived to appointments at least five minutes early.

Unfortunately, driving across the country had a way of throwing obstacles in your way. Especially, it seemed, when you were trying to get home in time for something. He'd hoped to make it back to see Dena before tonight's play party. To be frank, he wasn't in the mood to go to it, but Nathaniel and Abby were spending the weekend in Delaware and no one was comfortable with Dena being by herself. Plus, Dena had said she wanted to be there to offer support to Julie, who was doing her first public demo. There was no way he'd be in the same city with Dena and not see her, so it looked like he was going to a party.

He only wished someone had told the traffic.

"Come the fuck on," he said, once more coming to a stop in the middle of the interstate.

He glanced at the clock on his dash. From the way it looked, he'd have just enough time to stop by his house and take a quick shower. Even then, he would be a little late to the party. Which meant no time to talk to Dena beforehand.

With a frustrated sigh he used his voice command to call her.

"Hello," she answered with a smile so evident in her voice, he could almost picture it.

"Hey," he said. "How are you?"

"I'm doing great," she said. "I can't wait to tell you all about it."

"I can't wait to hear."

"I feel better than I have in ages. And let's just say, I'd have made one kick-ass Domme."

He laughed. "Now I have to know what you've been up to, especially since I know there's not a sexually dominant bone in your body."

"Ewwww. There was nothing sexual about it, and I'll tell you when you make it home. I promise your patience will be rewarded," she said in a low and seductive voice that shot straight to his groin. He cursed the traffic again. "Something wrong?" she asked.

"No. I'm stuck in traffic and growing impatient." He signaled to change lanes. Why did it always seem like the other lane moved faster than yours until you got in it?

"Are you not going to make the party?"

"I'll be there. I'll just be late. I'd hoped to see you before we went, but I guess I'll just meet you there."

"Okay, as long as you're there." She paused for a second. "I have a new corset. I think you'll like this one."

He was now certain the closest thing to hell on earth was being stuck in traffic with a massive erection. He shifted in his seat the best he could. "Fuck, Dena. I like all your corsets."

"This one's special," she nearly purred.

"I'm getting there as fast as I can."

"You better."

"Mistress K's place this time, right?"

"Yes."

"See you soon."

Even so, the party had been going on for at least an hour and a half when he pulled into Kelly's driveway. He parked his truck on the street and walked up to her door.

Evan Martin opened the door at his knock. "Master Parks, the she-devil who owns this joint said you'd be here tonight. Good to see you again."

"Thanks." Jeff shook his outstretched hand. "Who'd you piss off to get assigned door duty?"

Evan leaned against the doorframe and crossed his arms. "The she-devil."

"What'd you do this time?"

"It was either the she-devil comment or the insinuation that she spanked like a girl. Master Greene heard me, said I was being a bad example and I should take over the door."

Jeff shook his head. Kelly and Evan were always butting heads. They seemed to get off on insulting each other, and everyone tolerated it because it didn't appear to be harmful. He was going to have talk to Daniel. Before he'd left for Colorado, Kelly and

Evan's arguments had intensified. It was beginning to look as though someone might need to intervene.

Jeff slapped the other man on the shoulder. "Well, good luck with guarding the door. I'm going to find Dena. Do you know where she is?" She'd asked him to text her when he was ten minutes away, but said to check with whoever was working the door to find out where she'd be.

"Oh, that's right." He snapped his fingers. "She said to tell you she'd be waiting in the she-devil's office."

"Which is where?"

"Down that hall, third door on the right." He waggled his eyebrows. "She was wearing a raincoat, wouldn't let anyone see what was underneath. If she's still looking to play when you finish, I'll find someone else to guard the door. Will you tell her?"

"I'll relay the message," he said in a gruff voice, though it was probably the last thing he'd ever do.

He left Evan at the door and walked toward the office with one thought on his mind. A few people spoke to him as he passed, but he couldn't remember if he replied or not.

He knocked on the closed door three times in rapid succession. "It's me."

"Come in."

The room was dimly lit, and it took a few seconds for his eyes to adjust after the bright light in the hallway. But when they did . . .

He grasped on to the chair in front of him. "Dena?" he croaked.

"You like?"

The corset was flesh colored and covered in lace, so you

couldn't tell what was fabric and what was Dena. The cups uplifted her breasts in offering, and the faintest hint of a nipple showed. At least, he thought it was a nipple. A matching garter belt, thong, and stockings completed the outfit.

Her hair had been curled into spirals that fell gently to her shoulders, and on her feet were four-inch heels that screamed "fuck me."

He stood for a long moment and just devoured the sight of her. When he regained his composure, he answered, "Hell, yes, baby. I like. I fucking love it."

It took four long strides to close the distance between them, and when he made it to her, he took her in his arms and crushed his lips against hers. He held nothing back, pouring out the emotions of the last weeks in his kiss. She moaned and pulled him closer, parting her lips and allowing him to take the kiss deeper.

It'd been too long since they'd kissed, but their bodies remembered and their flesh rejoiced at the reunion. He ran a hand down her side and cupped a breast, brushed his thumb over the nipple and smiled at her groan.

"I'm not taking you here," he said through heavy breaths. "I'm going to make us both wait. Make it better. In the meantime." His right hand traveled down to her thigh and slipped under her knee. He lifted her leg so her barely covered pussy was exposed to him, and he rocked his erection against her clit. "No coming without my permission."

"You're so unfair." She pouted.

"Good girls get rewarded," he said with another rock of his hips.

"I'll be good. I'll be so, so good."

He kissed her again, softer this time, but he still held her leg, still pressed against her. "You always are," he whispered.

She whimpered and pushed herself closer to him. He placed a soft kiss on her cheek and forced himself to take a step back. If he didn't, he feared he'd shove everything off Kelly's desk and take Dena on its gleaming wooden surface.

"Not yet," he said, lowering her leg and running his hand up her body. "Not here."

"Let's leave," she suggested, and he strongly considered it.

"I need to talk with Nathaniel, and you said you wanted to support Julie."

"The demo's over, but I know where Nathaniel and Abby are." She held out her hand. "Come with me?"

Like she had to ask. He wasn't about to leave her side. As she reached for the door handle, he remembered his conversation with Evan.

"Master Martin wanted me to tell you he'd find someone else to watch the door if you were interested in doing a scene with him."

"I'll pass." She looked over her shoulder. "Did he still have his teeth when you left him?"

"I'm not that much of a Neanderthal, am I?"

She didn't answer but opened the door instead. "Let's go find Nathaniel."

"Am I?" he asked again.

"I'm trying really, really hard to be good," she whispered. "Don't make me lie. Oh, look. There he is."

He followed behind her, assuming she was taking him toward Nathaniel but not really paying much attention. He was too focused on her ass and the sexy-as-fuck lingerie she wore. Images and ideas of what he'd do when he finally got her alone filled his mind. He tried not to think about the fact that he'd probably have a raging erection for the duration of the party.

She came to a stop in the living room, and Jeff looked up to find Nathaniel and Abby sitting with Julie and Daniel on the couch. Julie was dressed in a fluffy robe and sat curled up in Daniel's lap, her head tucked under his chin as she spoke with Abby.

"There he is," Daniel said, seeing Jeff approach. "Glad you're back, but I'm sorry to hear about your dad."

Jeff nodded. "Thanks. It's good to be back home. How'd the demo go? No stomach issues this time?" he asked Julie.

Something danced in her eyes, but she replied with a simple, "No, Sir. Everything's good."

"Glad to hear it."

"She's being modest," Daniel said. "The demo went great; she was wonderful."

Julie lifted her head for a soft kiss.

Nathaniel looked around the room and put his arm around Abby. "Now that you're here, we can tell our news."

Jeff held his breath. *They are pregnant.* He told himself if that was their news, it was okay. That all he had to do was smile. Beside him, Dena stiffened. *Damn*, he wished they hadn't picked tonight to share their news.

"We made an offer on a house here in Delaware and found out this afternoon it was accepted," Nathaniel said.

The air left Jeff's body in one big whoosh.

"That is the best news," Dena said, clearly relieved she wouldn't have to offer pregnancy congratulations. "I can't believe you didn't tell me. What about your New York places?"

"I didn't want to jinx it," Abby said.

"We'll be living here part-time. We're not selling anything," Nathaniel explained.

Everyone started talking at once. Dena let go of his hand and sat down beside Julie and Abby. Soon the women were talking with their heads together. Daniel shifted Julie so she could better talk with them while still keeping his arms around her.

Nathaniel was discussing the new house with Daniel, but Jeff couldn't pay attention to the conversation. His focus kept slipping to Dena.

It was several minutes before he realized the two men weren't talking anymore.

"Why do I have the feeling I'm going to have to find a new submissive for my mentees to work with?" Daniel asked.

A streak of possessiveness like nothing he'd experienced shot through Jeff's body. It shocked him; he'd never had a problem with Dena helping with the mentor program before. And yet he heard himself answer, "Because you probably will."

Daniel gave a resolved sigh. "Guess I better start looking through files."

"Last I heard you were switching it up." Jeff chuckled, thinking about Ron and Mistress K. "Literally."

"Yeah, but that was just a onetime thing. Now there's the potential I'll have to look into replacing her permanently."

Jeff crossed his arms and cocked his head. "If you're waiting for me to say I'm sorry, you'll be waiting a long damn time."

"No way in hell am I wanting you to apologize. If that's the way it turns out, it'll just create a slight headache for me."

A movement in the corner of his eye caught Jeff's attention. "Speaking of mentees."

Ron, Daniel's mentee, approached the group and nodded at the men. "Excuse me, Master Covington, Master Parks, Master West. I wanted to speak to Dena."

Something in the way he looked at Dena made Jeff want to pick him up by the nape of his neck and kick him out the door. It wasn't necessarily a leer, but it wasn't a look of honor and respect either. Not that Jeff could fault the young man. Dena looked fucking hot in the cream-colored outfit. Besides, he didn't want to prove Dena's Neanderthal comment right.

The two other men looked to Jeff, and Jeff nodded, appreciating the subtle request for his permission.

But apparently the request was too subtle for Ron to pick up on. "Ladies," he said, interrupting whatever the women were talking about, and Jeff growled deep in his throat.

"Ron, hey," Dena said, a slight look of irritation in her expression.

Ron didn't seem to pick up on that either, though he did grimace a bit at the use of his first name. *Too damn bad,* Jeff thought. The term "Master" would never be bestowed upon someone still in the mentor program.

"I was wondering if you'd like to join me in the upper bedroom, Dena?" Ron asked.

Doesn't he see she's with someone? Jeff took a step forward, but Daniel held out a hand. *Let her handle it,* he seemed to say.

"Sorry, but I'm not playing tonight," Dena said with a fake smile.

"Your outfit suggests otherwise."

I'll rip his—

Daniel's fingers dug into Jeff's upper thigh as if he knew what Jeff was about to do. It gave him momentary pause. "Control your mentee, Master Covington, before someone else does it for you," Jeff ground out.

Daniel's grip didn't loosen. "Ron, you extended an invitation and you were refused. It may be cliché, but in this group no means no."

"Yes, but—" Ron started.

"If you argue with me or disrespect a submissive again, you will be removed from the mentee program. Now apologize to Dena."

He paused a bit too long for Jeff's liking. "Now."

"Sorry, Dena," Ron said. There may have been concession in his voice, but there wasn't a trace of remorse.

"It's okay," Dena replied.

"It sure as hell is not okay." Jeff still didn't like the look on Ron's face or the halfhearted manner of his apology. If that made him a Neanderthal, so be it. "Dena, let's leave."

She gave Julie and Abby hugs, promised to call soon to set up a lunch date, and rose to her feet. "I arrived early, Master Parks. I'll have to see if I can get my car out."

Jeff kept his eyes on Ron as the younger man stalked off. "Leave it here. We'll take my truck."

They bade everyone a hasty farewell and then stopped back by Kelly's office to get Dena's coat.

"You really didn't have a chance to talk to Nathaniel," she said as they made their way outside. "I think they're going to have dinner with Daniel and Julie. I could change and we could join them."

"I'll call him later," he said, opening the door for her to get into the truck. "And no way. We're spending the evening alone."

She didn't say anything, but she looked pleased they weren't joining the other couples for dinner. Jeff pulled onto the street. "Mind if we go to your place? Mine's still a mess."

"Sure. Did you bring your bag?"

"Overnight bag or toy bag?"

"Either one. Both."

"Yes."

"You didn't really answer my question."

He grinned in the dark. "I know."

She mumbled something under her breath but didn't say anything else. As he drove away from Kelly's house, he felt the tension of the night ease. No matter what happened at the party, he was with Dena and they were headed to the privacy of her home.

Because it'd been a while since she'd been at her apartment, Jeff insisted on looking over everything. Nothing appeared out of order, and there was no new note waiting.

When they made it inside, Dena hung up her coat.

"You need to put on a robe or something," he said, looking over her outfit. "I want to talk for a bit, and it'll be damn near impossible with you wearing that."

She kicked her heels off. "If you insist."

"I'll pour us some wine," he said, walking toward the kitchen while she disappeared into the bedroom. He didn't know his way around Dena's apartment since she'd rented it after they broke up, but he knew she had excellent taste in wine. Though he preferred a good craft beer, he had grown to appreciate some of her recommended vintages.

"Help yourself," she called from the bedroom.

He opened the refrigerator, deciding he'd open a white wine, and found a four-pack of his favorite local brew sitting on the shelf.

"You're a dream come true," he said, taking out a bottle for him and a Riesling for her. "Has anyone ever told you that before?"

"Once or twice."

He turned to find her standing in the doorway. She'd slipped a robe on that somehow matched what he knew lay underneath. Her feet were bare, and she'd rearranged her hair so it was swept to one side, the curls spilling over her shoulder.

"You want to talk?" she asked.

No, not really. Not with her looking like she did. But he knew they needed to. "I have to hear about you being a Domme."

Her laugh was soft and seductive as she took the offered glass of wine and led him into the living room. She sat on the couch and patted the seat beside her. "Yesterday I went and had a little chat with my dad."

He took the offered spot. He sat just close enough to feel her presence without actually touching her. "How is Senator Jenkins doing?"

He listened as she recalled her visit and her threats. When she got to the part about lying, he gave a low whistle. "You would actually do that?"

"Without thinking twice. Would it actually work?" She shrugged. "Who knows? He thought it would, and that's all that really matters."

He took her hand. "I shouldn't have kept his threats secret. At the time, I thought I was protecting you. I see now it implied you weren't strong enough to handle it."

She set her wineglass down and shifted to face him. With her free hand she brushed the hair from his forehead. "In a way, I'm glad it happened like it did. I don't know if I'd have had the confidence to confront him all those years ago."

"You had it."

"You always have thought I was capable of doing more than I thought I could."

He leaned closer; she still smelled like flowers. "I just see you more clearly than you see yourself."

"And who do you see now?"

"A beautiful, strong, courageous woman. Who would have made a kick-ass Domme."

"Oh yeah? And what are you going to do?"

He let go of her hand so he could stroke her cheek. "I'm going to start by kissing her."

With a patience he didn't know he possessed, he took her in his arms and kissed her. Though he was tempted to rush things along, he'd been wanting this moment for days and wasn't going to hurry through it.

She sank into his embrace as though she'd never left, lifting her head and meeting his kiss with one of her own. His lips traced the curve of her jaw, and he allowed his hand to slip under her robe and caress her shoulder.

Moving as slowly as possible, he drew the robe down to expose her collarbone to his lips. He nibbled along, following the path that led to the hollow of her throat, and he smiled in satisfaction. "Your heart is racing."

"You're killing me."

"Good." He gave her shoulder a small bite, and she rewarded him with a groan.

"Isn't this when you go get your bags?"

"No," he said, starting at the other shoulder and following the same path.

"No?"

"No," he repeated. "If I go get my bags, I'll be tempted to rush. This way"—he slipped the robe off her shoulders completely—"I'll be sure to take my time."

She arched her back and hissed in pleasure when he teased the upper skin of her breasts with his lips. "I'm not sure I follow your logic."

"That's okay." He ran his tongue along the lace edge of her corset. "All it means is I'm going slow tonight. I'm going to bring you to the edge while you're still in this gorgeous outfit, and then I'm going to have you take it off for me. And when you're finally naked, I'm going to kiss every inch of your skin. Watch you squirm and listen to you beg. And when I think you've had enough, I'm going to slide between those pretty little legs and ease my cock inside until you're completely filled." He'd made it back up her body, so he nibbled her earlobe and continued whispering. "I'll hold still for a bit, let you get used to my dick, because when I pull out and start to fuck you, I'm not holding back. I'm going to pound into you so hard and deep you'll remember my claiming you for days."

She bucked against him. "God, Jeff. Fuck me now. Please."

"But I can't. You're nowhere near the edge yet."

"Oh, trust me." She shifted her body and tried to pull him on top of her. "I'm on the edge. I'm hiking the edge. I've set up a picnic on the edge."

His fingers skirted the wet fabric of her thong, gently rubbing her clit through the cloth. "Impossible. I've barely touched you."

"You're that good." She grinded her hips to get more friction. "Please, oh please."

"Sounds like I need to slow down even more," he whispered against her lips.

He'd just given her a soft kiss when a noise from outside caught his attention. His head shot up. "What was that?"

"Didn't hear anything. Come back."

"Sounded like something by your door."

She tried to pull him close again. "Probably the neighbors."

He heard it again. "I'd better check it out."

"If you leave me on this couch alone, I'm stripping out of this lingerie without you watching."

"If you're naked when I get back, I'm making you watch me jerk off alone," he warned, rising to his feet.

She huffed. "You're impossible."

"No. I just like having my way."

"Same thing."

"Say another word and I spank your ass after I check things out."

Desire and playfulness filled her eyes, and she kept her gaze on him when she replied, "Word."

He pointed at her and grinned. "That's ten. Hands and knees on the bed, your ass in the air, waiting for my hand. Then I'm moving you to your back so you can hold your legs open while I give that naughty pussy ten more."

Her only response was a low moan of eager anticipation.

"Let me take care of this first." He opened the door, expecting to see darkness, but instead finding Ron.

"What the hell?"

Chapter Fifteen

Present day

From her place on the couch, Dena tried to peer around Jeff's body. "Is someone out there?"

"Call the police. And you," he said, reaching for whoever it was outside, "don't even try to run unless you want me to break every bone in your body." With a jerk, he pulled the person inside and something fell to the ground. "Not that I'm not sorely tempted to do so anyway."

Dena gasped as she saw Ron. What was he doing outside her apartment? She looked down at his feet. With a can of red spray paint?

"There's a red W on your front door," Jeff said, his voice filled with barely controlled anger. He shook Ron. "You little fucker. I bet you're the one who's been harassing her." He glanced at her. "Dena. Police."

His voice snapped her into action. Ron? Why?

She reached for the phone and hesitated. "Is that really necessary? The police? Can't the group handle him?"

Jeff still had Ron by the scruff of the neck. "At least call Daniel," he said, and then addressed Ron. "The only reason I'm not beating you into a pulp right now is because it'd cause problems for Dena. If you're smart, you'll explain what your problem is before I decide I don't care and beat the shit out of you anyway. What the fuck were you thinking, threatening a woman?"

Ron looked like he was about to throw up. Whatever he'd been expecting, being caught by Jeff wasn't one of them. "I—I—I," he stuttered.

Jeff shook him. "Speed it up."

"You weren't supposed to be here," Ron said.

"What?" Dena asked.

"I thought you were going to Jeff's house."

"What does that have to do with anything?" Jeff asked.

"She wouldn't play with me," he rushed out.

"I wouldn't what?" she asked Ron, scrolling through her contacts. Her finger trembled as she pulled Daniel up.

"Outside of a session with Ma-Master Covington." Ron looked from her to Jeff. "She would never do a scene with me. She always turned me down."

"And you thought harassing her would change her mind?"

"I just wanted to scare her."

"Fucking asshole," Jeff said with a growl.

"Hello?" Daniel answered his phone. From the silence in the background, she guessed he and Julie were at dinner with the Wests.

Her voice shook while she explained what had happened, and

he let out a string of expletives before saying he and Julie would be right over.

"They're on their way," she told Jeff, who was still towering over Ron with his arms crossed and a glare that dared the younger man to move.

Dena didn't know what to do. Never in all her years of being a senator's daughter had she had to handle a situation quite like this. She was scared. What if he broke confidentiality? She was angry. And though she knew she shouldn't be, she was a little ashamed.

But she had to do something. She didn't want to just stand around. Her eyes fell on her discarded wine and she realized she was half-dressed.

"I'm going to put some clothes on."

Jeff nodded, never moving his eyes from Ron.

She reentered the living room seconds before someone knocked on the door. Everything felt so surreal, like she was watching a movie. She crossed the floor, looked out the peephole, and let Daniel, Julie, Nathaniel, and Abby in.

Julie gave her a hug. "You okay?"

She nodded.

Daniel had a look of disgust on his face. She thought it was directed at Ron until he spoke. "Shit, Dena, I'm so sorry."

"You? Whatever for?"

He ran a hand through his hair. "I feel responsible. If it weren't for me, this would have never happened."

"Don't blame yourself," she said, trying to reassure him. "I don't blame you."

"First Sasha and now you." He shook his head and glanced at

Jeff, and she realized he was disgusted with himself. "We have to redo the entire mentor program. We're doing something wrong."

"This isn't the time, but yes, I agree," Jeff said.

"Did you call the police?" Nathaniel asked, and Ron turned green.

"No," Dena said. "I don't want them involved. The group can deal with it."

"I think that's a really bad decision," Nathaniel said.

"It's mine to make." She looked at where Jeff still towered over Ron. It didn't appear either was paying her any attention.

"Piece of shit, threatening women," Jeff said. "Dominants protect and treasure submissives; they don't try to scare the hell out of them." He cocked his head at Ron. "Were you at the party Dena and I were supposed to demo at?"

The fear deepened in Ron's eyes. "Y-yes."

"So you know what happened?"

"Vaguely."

"Did you know she was late because of your call? Did you hear me punish her?" Jeff put a hand on either side of the chair and got in Ron's face. "Were you *glad?*"

Ron didn't say anything.

"Dena, go get my toy bag out of the truck."

Dena felt rooted to the floor. *What is he thinking?*

"Uh, Jeff?" Daniel asked.

"I figure he deserves at least what I gave Dena."

"I agree with you in theory," Nathaniel said. "But perhaps now isn't the best time?"

"You're probably right," Jeff said, and at that moment, Dena knew he'd had no intention of taking a strap to the younger man.

"I want you to remember one thing, Ron. I owe you thirty lashes. I will pay up."

Or maybe he just didn't intend to do it that particular night.

Ron left two hours later.

"I don't think he'll be causing any more problems," Jeff said, closing the door behind him.

"After the talk we gave him?" Nathaniel asked. "Not if he's smart."

The three men had taken Ron into her guest room. "To talk," Daniel had said. She wasn't sure what the men told him, but he'd scurried out of her apartment as soon as they were finished.

"I only wish Cole had been here instead of in meetings in New York," Daniel said, and there was still a trace of guilt when he spoke. "He can be one scary bastard when he wants to be."

Dena hated that Daniel felt guilty. It wasn't anything he'd done or hadn't done. No one had suspected Ron had been the one harassing her. The whole thing made her want to cry or throw something. Probably, she'd feel better if she did both.

"Sometime later this week or next, we need to sit down and decide what we're going to about the mentor program," Jeff said. "But right now I think Dena needs some rest."

The men spoke quietly near the door, while Julie and Abby hugged her and promised to call the next day. She was so thankful to have such supportive friends.

When everyone left, Jeff turned to her. "Are you okay?"

She took one look at him and burst into tears, sobs shaking her body.

"Dena." Jeff crossed the room, swept her into his arms, and carried her to the couch, where he put her in his lap and let her cry until there weren't any tears left. All the while he rubbed her back, whispering things she couldn't hear, but just the sound of his voice and the feel of his arms around her made her feel better.

"Stay with me tonight?" she asked, looking up at him with wet eyes.

He wiped her cheek with his thumb. "I'm not about to leave you alone."

"I'm just . . . I can't . . . I *played* with him." She felt betrayed, and worse—she felt dirty. She buried her head in Jeff's chest. "I just want to crawl into bed and pretend nothing happened."

"He better stay far away from you. If I ever see him again . . ." His threat hung in the air.

"Would you really take your leather strap to him?"

"That's the least I'll do." He stroked her hair. "Are you hungry? Thirsty?"

She shook her head, not wanting to move from Jeff's arms, but a yawn escaped before she could stop it.

"Bed it is," he said.

He carried her to the bedroom even though she protested that she could walk just fine. He said he simply wanted to hold her and she'd just have to deal with it.

After putting her in the middle of the bed, he told her to stay put and then rummaged through her drawers, looking for pajamas, she supposed. Suddenly, everything caught up with her and she felt exhausted. She watched him for a few minutes until her eyelids grew heavy.

"Sleep naked," she heard herself say. "Do it."

Jeff mumbled something, but she couldn't hear, so she started taking her clothes off. Within seconds, his hands were on hers. She couldn't tell if he was trying to stop her or if he was helping. Eventually, she just stayed still. It was Jeff; she was safe.

The last thing she remembered before sleep overtook her was the security of his arms around her and his heart beating strongly in her ear.

Chapter Sixteen

Present day

She woke gradually the next morning, taking time to grow aware of her surroundings before she opened her eyes. She was warm, wrapped in her soft sheets and downy comforter. Bentley hadn't crawled into bed yet, so it couldn't be that late. The room was still mostly dark, she noted, opening one eye. She shifted slightly and bumped into hard muscle. Hard *male* muscle.

Jeff pressed a kiss to the nape of her neck. "Good morning."

She remembered falling asleep wrapped in Jeff's arms, but he had never been one to hang out in bed once he woke up. "Good morning," she said, twisting her body to face him and realizing at that moment that she was naked.

His eyes swept over her. "I'll say."

"Umm, why am I naked?"

"I tried to find you something to sleep in last night, but you started taking your clothes off. I decided it wasn't a battle I wanted to fight, so I helped."

She bet he did.

"Don't look at me like that," he said. "You'll notice I'm not naked. And for the record, it was damn hard keeping my clothes on."

She decided to cut him some slack. He normally did sleep naked, and holding a nude woman all night would be trying for any man. "Thanks for staying."

"I told you last night I wasn't going to leave."

"I meant for not leaving this morning."

"I didn't want you to wake up alone," he said softly. "After last night, I wasn't sure how you'd feel this morning. I didn't want you to be scared."

She started to say something, but her stomach rumbled. He grinned at her, his disheveled hair falling across his forehead.

"How about I make us breakfast?" he asked.

"There's nothing here to make. I've been with Nathaniel and Abby."

"You don't have anything?"

"Cereal and almond milk."

He propped up on an elbow and looked down at her. "You are never again to make snide comments about my coffee. Cereal and almond milk? Seriously?"

"We all can't be gourmet chefs on the side like you."

"How do you milk an almond?"

"How do you what?" Her brain obviously wasn't working at full power yet.

He reached under the covers and slapped her butt. "You get dressed. I'll get the cereal and milk. We'll eat."

It was only a playful slap, but his touch sent a spark of desire throughout her body. She suddenly wished she'd turned breakfast down and suggested they remain in bed. "And after we eat?" she whispered.

He'd already sat up and moved to get out of bed. At her question, he turned and looked over his shoulder. "We'll see."

Two words. That's all he'd said. Two *tiny* words even. Yet those two small words echoed in her head during breakfast. *We'll see.* They were back in Delaware, her father had been dealt with, his father's business had been tied up, and they had agreed to start over.

There was nothing holding them back.

Fifteen minutes later, she looked across the table to where he sat eating as if it were any other day. As if he ate at her kitchen table regularly. God, he was such a *man*. He caught her staring at him and winked.

Fucking winked.

She crossed her legs and uncrossed them. Crossed them back the other way.

"Are you okay?" he asked, spoon halfway to his mouth.

"Yes. Fine." She took a bite of her cereal to prove it.

"I was thinking about last night," he said, and her heart sped up. He put his spoon down. "How the evening would have gone if we hadn't been interrupted."

"Me too."

"Then I suggest you hurry up and finish eating. We have unfinished business to take care of."

Her appetite was gone. Without a word, she pushed back from the table, walked to where he sat, and held out her hand.

"Be sure," he said.

"I am," she replied, and she knew truer words had never been spoken.

He took her hand and led her down the hall. He turned to face her once he reached the middle of the bedroom. "Before we go any further, I have to make sure you know." He lifted a hand to her throat and gently curled his fingers around it. "If I take you again, there's no going back. You'll be mine."

His touch felt warm and protective, but she hated the glimmer of doubt in his eyes. Hated that her past actions had put it there. If she had to, she would spend every day, every night erasing those doubts. "And you're mine," she whispered.

The devilish grin she loved so much, the one he so rarely shared with anyone, teased the corners of his mouth. "Got that right."

She placed her hand over the one he still had around her neck. "There's no place for doubts here today."

"And no room for guilt," he softly commanded. "Or apologies."

He knew her so well. Knew her struggles and strengths. "I need to say one thing." At his nod, she continued. "When you took your collar back, I said one day you'd beg me to wear it again—"

"Dena."

She shushed him by placing a finger at his mouth. "I don't need you to beg. Just knowing you want me back is enough."

"I'm all prepared to beg."

"I like it better when I'm the one begging." She grinned. "Sir."

His eyes grew dark. "Like I said once before, when I have you beg, it won't be about that."

It stung just a bit that he didn't call her "Angel," but she decided not to dwell on it. Technically, they weren't in a scene and she wasn't wearing his collar. There would come a time when he'd use the name again regularly. She was certain.

She ran a hand down his chest. "Do you plan to make me beg for something else this morning?"

"I have lots of plans for you. Of course, they all involve you being naked." He unbuttoned the top of her shirt. "Let me fix that."

She closed her eyes to better concentrate on the feel of his hands on her again. His touch was sure and warm and made her entire body quake with need. The brush of his fingers against her while he worked on her shirt made every nerve she had tingle. No one else had the power to make her feel so much with such a small touch.

He made quick work of the buttons, and when he finished, he dropped his head to place a kiss on her shoulder before slipping the shirt from her body. Then his hands were back on her, teasing her nipples with his thumbs.

"Your body was made for mine," he whispered coarsely in her ear. "The way we fit together." He unhooked her bra and tossed it aside. "Watch," he said, cupping her breasts. "See how perfectly you fit in my hands."

She pushed her chest out, giving him more room, all the while delighting in the rough feel of his touch.

"I used to think we were too different to be good together." He moved behind her and pressed her naked back against his chest. "Now I see it's those differences that make us so right."

He was caressing her upper body while he talked, and she

tried her best to listen to him. It was just so difficult when his hands felt so amazingly good. "How so? How do our differences make us right?"

His lips nibbled their way across the nape of her neck. "You're a submissive and I'm a Dominant, right?"

"Mmm." She tilted her head to give him better access.

"Two completely different beings, but they fit together only because they're opposite." He undid the button on her jeans and unzipped them. "Should I keep going?"

"Please." His erection pressed against her butt, and she wiggled to get closer, pushing her jeans and panties down in the process. "Don't stop."

"Turn around. Look at me."

She did, and as she watched, he slowly stripped his shirt off and stepped out of his jeans. He looked magnificent naked. Always had. His toned abs, strong arms, and sculpted calves spoke of a man who worked hard. The hint of a knowing smile on his face told her he knew exactly what to do with his body to make her feel good. Her gaze dipped lower. She licked her lips, remembering his taste.

"Another example," he said, stroking himself. "The sight of you standing there makes me so hard." He reached out and trailed a finger along her waist. "Whereas you"—the finger slipped between her legs and traced her wetness—"are soft."

She shifted her leg, inviting him to go deeper. "Want you."

"Wait." He took a step back from her. "Get on the bed. On your back."

She smiled. Even when they weren't in a scene, he couldn't help taking control during sex. That didn't mean she couldn't tease him a little.

Once she got on top of the bed, she lifted an eyebrow. "Like this?" She parted her legs. "Or like this?" She closed them again.

He walked toward her looking exactly like a tiger on the prowl, or more aptly, one who wanted to play with his prey. "Keep them open."

His gaze was so intense and filled with desire, she didn't want to disobey him. Without further argument or teasing, she let her knees fall so her legs were spread. He gave a low growl and joined her on the bed, near her feet.

Taking her left leg in his hands, he kissed the inside of her knee. "Every part of you was made for me. Made for me to kiss, bite, lick, and love."

She buried her fingers in his hair. "When do I get to kiss, bite, lick, and love you?"

"Later." He kissed and nibbled his way up her thigh. With a heavy sigh, he laid his cheek against her upper leg. "You can't leave me again, Angel. I need you."

Angel.

Her heart skipped a beat, and tears formed at the corners of her eyes. She tugged at his shoulders until he moved and covered her body with his. Holding his face, she made sure he was looking at her when she spoke. "I'm not going anywhere you aren't." It was difficult to talk with the lump in her throat. "I've lived without you long enough to know I don't want to do it again."

"I love you," he whispered.

Tears slipped from her eyes. "I've always loved you. Always will."

Their lips touched softly. Just barely brushing. She shivered under him, delighted to be with him like this again. For so long she'd thought it would never happen. And to hear him say those words. She trembled again.

"Are you cold?" he asked, misjudging her shiver.

"No." She held tight to him. "Just blissfully happy."

He kissed her again, not as soft this time. His mouth grew demanding, and she opened herself up for him. She'd missed his taste. The feel of him over her, his weight pressing into her.

She ran her nails across his back as his kiss grew more and more urgent. He moved his knee so it pressed between her legs. Her body throbbed with the need to have him claim her.

He broke away from the kiss, breathing heavily. "I need to be inside you. Now."

She lifted her hips in invitation. "Please."

He shook his head. "I wanted to take my time. Enjoy your body. Tease you for hours."

"Later. There's plenty of time for that later."

He pushed up on his hands, and she saw his body tremble. "I don't think I can be gentle."

"I've never been a fan of gentle." She dug her nails into his upper arm. "Take me. Use me hard."

He studied her face as if judging the truth of her words. He must have found what he was looking for because, without a word, he slipped a hand between their bodies and pushed two fingers inside her.

"Yes." She answered his unasked question with a half moan. "I'm ready for you."

His penetration was hard and fast, and she clung to him as he pounded into her over and over. He'd been correct. There was nothing gentle in his use of her. It was almost punishing, and she relished it. With each thrust, she felt her guilt falling away until it disappeared completely.

She opened her eyes and found him watching her as he moved in and out of her body. She lifted a hand to cup his face and whispered, "Leave it."

Leave the past, all of our mistakes, our should-have-beens, and our what-ifs. Leave them behind so that only you and I remain. And we are forever changed, but never broken.

"Leave it," she repeated.

His body stiffened and he came with a yell. He thrust once more deep inside her, and her own climax followed.

Though he was still breathing heavily, he wrapped his arms around her, rolled them to their sides, and kissed her with an intensity that took what little breath she had away.

Chapter Seventeen

Three weeks later

No one dared try to tell them they were moving too fast. The way Dena saw it, they'd been moving too slowly and they had to make up for lost time. Though she regretted the years spent apart, they both agreed they were stronger as a result of them.

Tonight, though similar in many ways to that night so many years before, was different. She walked outside to where he waited under the maple trees in his backyard. Strings of lights were wrapped around the branches and provided just enough light for her to see him.

They'd thought about inviting a few people to join them tonight. But after discussing it, they opted to keep this special moment private. Experiencing the way Jeff was looking at her, Dena was pleased with their choice. What they were doing and feeling was too intimate, and she wanted to keep it between the two of them.

She knelt down at his feet on the soft plaid blanket he'd spread out, unable to suppress the sigh of contentment she found at doing so. He reached out and pulled his fingers through her hair. She closed her eyes. His touch was so gentle, so reverent. Again he stroked her hair, but then his hand slipped under her chin and lifted her head.

His dark eyes seemed darker than normal, and they were filled with the intensity of emotion she knew he felt at that moment. "I love you, Angel."

Tears stung her eyes. No matter how often he said it, it always struck her body to the innermost depths. She parted her lips to tell him how much she loved him, but he stopped her by placing a finger over her mouth.

"Not yet. Stand up for a minute, please."

She stood up, unsure of his intentions.

He took her hands in his. "When I collared you six years ago, I did it because I wanted to claim you as my submissive. I don't want that this time."

Her heart, already pounding, picked up speed. *What?*

"I want more," he said simply. "I want more than your body. I want your sharp mind, your passionate soul, and your beautiful heart. I want all of you, and I'll give you all of me in return. Though, admittedly, I'm getting the better deal. I know the way I'm going about this is a bit unorthodox, but Dena, Angel." He took something out of his pocket and dropped to one knee. "Marry me?"

The something was a gorgeous diamond solitaire. She didn't even have to think. The answer slipped effortlessly from her. "Yes."

He stood up, slid the ring on her finger, and leaned forward to kiss her. She wrapped her arms around him and kissed him back, suppressing a giggle. Only Jeff would propose during a collaring ceremony. She was his. Her arms tightened around him. *His.*

Almost.

He pulled back. "I have something else I want to offer you." He bent down and opened a box at the corner of the blanket. A thinly braided black leather collar was in his hands when he made it back to her. Something in the collar glinted in the moonlight. She looked closer and saw silver entwined with the leather.

"To remind us both," he said, running his finger along the metal.

"Remind us both of what?"

"To treasure what we have and for that reminder to bind us together forever."

She couldn't believe how perfect the collar was. "I love it."

"If you agree to wear this, it won't be like last time. My collar is as binding as the ring I just gave you. I want you to wear it always."

"Nothing would make me happier."

He nodded. "Then take the dress off and kneel before me, please."

He'd told her to come outside wearing something she could easily remove. She'd remembered Julie and Daniel's collaring ceremony and had known she wanted to wear a white dress like Julie's. She loved its simplicity and what it symbolized. Even more, she loved standing in front of Jeff and taking it off.

His eyes were hungry as he watched her draw the dress over her head and then kneel in front of him.

"I wish to claim you as mine," he said, once she'd settled. "To be your Master."

Though she knelt at his feet, she looked up as she answered. "I want to be yours. To wear the mark of your control."

"Be certain of what you ask for, Angel." There was a warning in his voice, but she couldn't determine what it related to.

"I am, Sir."

He didn't question her again. He simply took the collar and placed it around her neck. With the soft click of the lock, Dena felt her world settle into place.

"You are mine," he said, his voice heavy with emotion.

"Yes." Silent tears ran down her face. "Thank you, Master. Thank you."

"Show your Master your appreciation."

She bent to kiss his feet, wetting them first with her tears before her lips could brush their tops.

"Yours," she whispered against the right.

"Forever," she promised the left.

The evening air held just a teasing touch of the cooler weather to come with autumn. For the long minutes after she resumed kneeling, Jeff simply stood and watched her, and she grew increasingly aware of the colder temperature. Her tears cooled against her skin and her nipples pebbled. Even still, she felt the warmth of his love and protection.

"I think I could stand here and look at you all night," he finally said. "Simply stand and delight in seeing you wear my collar once again."

"Maybe we should try that someday, Master."

He growled. "Say it again."

"Master," she repeated, knowing what he wanted to hear.

"Again."

"Master."

He pulled her to her feet and, without saying anything, crushed his lips against hers in a demanding kiss. She leaned in to his embrace, thrilled by the possessiveness in his touch. He was rough and hard and demanding and she loved and craved every second of it.

When he pulled back, they were both panting.

"I decided against candles tonight," he said.

"I look forward to experiencing what you have planned."

He seemed decidedly devious when he spoke again. "Go stand between those two trees."

Looking at the spot he indicated, she wondered if she'd spoken too quickly. He'd obviously been busy earlier, because ropes hung from the branches, ready for his use. She stood in place while he came up behind her and slowly and efficiently cuffed her wrists and ankles, effectively binding her spread-eagle between the trees.

"How do you feel, Angel?"

She pulled experimentally against the rope. There wasn't much give. "Like we should have done candles, Master."

He chuckled and dipped a finger between her legs. "But your body betrays you. You're excited about this."

It was true, so she didn't see the point in saying otherwise.

"Your earlier statement—what was it? You want to wear the mark of my control." He moved so he stood in her line of vision, making certain she saw him as he removed a pocketknife and cut a small switch from a nearby tree. He sliced it through the air a few times and then struck his palm with it. "The group play party is tomorrow night. You'll no doubt still be wearing some of my marks. What's your safe word, Angel?"

"Wings." She didn't feel aroused anymore, but she tried to relax anyway.

"Why do you look so frightened? I haven't done anything yet."

"I just . . . You've never . . ."

"Look at me." He held her under her chin so she had no choice. "What did I say I was doing with the wax play, the time I first collared you?"

The calmness she found in his eyes helped ease her anxiety. "Proving you're the best."

"And in the years since then, do you think I've grown better or worse?"

"Better, Master."

"And my feelings toward you, are they stronger or weaker?"

"Stronger, Master."

"Anything you'd like to say?"

"I'm sorry I doubted you."

"Apology accepted. Now, on a scale of one to ten, with one being mildly frightened and ten being scared shitless, what number are you?"

"Three, Master."

"I can live with that." He let go of her chin and moved behind her.

He started with gentle taps of the switch along her upper thighs, interspersed with gentle passes of his fingers between her legs. Gradually, he increased the taps so they became like little licks of electricity dancing along her legs and buttocks. Still he kept stroking her, sliding fingers in and out of her and teasing her clit.

"What number, Angel?"

"Mmmm . . . Negative ten, Master." She tried to rock her hips, but he'd bound her too tightly.

"Very nice. Perhaps I should actually start now?"

Her eyes flew open. "Master?"

The switch whistled through the air and landed with a sharp line of pain on her right butt cheek. Before she could say anything, his hand was back between her legs, stroking the fire within her again.

"Oh, yes," he said. "That'll leave a nice mark. That was one. I'm going to give you ten. You are not allowed to come until I've finished all ten. If you do, I'll add ten more."

She figured there was little chance of *that* happening. "Yes, Master."

But by number four, she discovered she'd vastly underestimated him. Between his fingers, the delicious pain, and the wicked things he whispered in her ear, she was dangerously close to coming.

"Please, Master, let me come," she nearly shouted, trying to stand on her toes.

"Poor Angel. You have six more before you can come."

Number five landed precariously close to her pussy, and she moaned as his expert hands transformed the pain to pleasure.

"I'm trying to decide," he said, "if I want to fuck your pussy or your ass."

Numbers six and seven fell on her sweet spot, right where her ass met her thigh.

"I love sinking into your pussy, but it's been a long time since I've had your ass. It's so tight, the way it clutches my dick. What do you think?"

Number eight hit right above the back of her knee, and once more he circled her clit. She bit the inside of her cheek to keep from coming.

"Angel, I asked a question." Three fingers pushed inside her pussy.

"I don't care, Master, please."

"I didn't bring any lube, and I'm not going back inside to get it." There was a rustle of clothes, and she knew he was naked. "Two more and then I ride you hard and make us both happy."

Nine and ten were quick and hard, but she barely knew they were over before the head of his cock was driving into her. With one swift thrust, he buried his length inside. He reached above her head and pulled loose the quick-release knots so she fell back into him.

He held her steady, one arm around her chest while the other held her hips in place. And though she couldn't move, he worked himself in and out, taking them both to the edge. His thrusts were relentless, and when he dropped a hand to rub her clit, she let herself go.

He gave a grunt of satisfaction. "Love the feel of your release when I'm buried deep inside you." He circled his hips, grinding against her in a way that allowed him to hit new spots. "I want you to come again."

Somehow he moved faster and deeper, and within seconds, she was coming again. This time he followed, holding still and releasing inside her with a grunt of complete pleasure.

He held on to her, not letting her go because her feet were still bound. "Hold on to me," he whispered. "Lean on me."

She let herself relax against him, and after she assured him she was good, he let go of her just long enough to unbind her ankles. With his customary gentle strength, he lifted her in his arms and carried her to the blanket.

For a time they stayed in each other's arms, watching the stars come out and speaking in whispers. They spoke of their future, their hopes, and their dreams.

And when it was fully dark, she leaned closer, placed his hand on her belly, and whispered a secret.

Epilogue

"Mr. West," my admin, Sara, said when I picked up the ringing phone. "Mr. Parks is here to see you."

"Send him in," I said, standing up to meet him. I'd been awfully curious as to why Jeff wanted to see me when he'd called the day before to schedule a meeting.

As the door opened, I crossed the floor to shake Jeff's hand. "Come on in. It's good to see you. What brings you into the city?" I waved toward a small sitting area. "Have a seat."

"Thanks." Jeff sat down. "Dena wanted to do some shopping."

"Sounds like another woman I know. Speaking of Abby, she told me your news. Congratulations."

He smiled, and I noticed how different he looked. Nothing like the guy I'd first met, with his always-stern expression. He looked happy now.

"Thanks," he said. "We're trying to settle on a date." He leaned forward. "I know you're busy, and I'm sure you want to know why I'm here."

"I was surprised when I got your call."

"It's about the group. I know you and Abby are joining when you move, and the senior members would like for you to take an active role as soon as possible."

"What kind of role?"

"You know what happened with Dena?" At my nod, he continued. "She's not the first submissive to be mistreated by a Dominant in the group."

I had heard murmurings the few times we'd been with the Delaware group. I knew a friend of Julie's had been badly whipped. "Sounds like there's a problem."

"There is, and we'd like for you to help us. I'm here on the group's behalf to ask you to take on the responsibility of restructuring the group, especially the mentor program."

"That's no small task."

"I know, but we think you're what the group needs: an experienced Master with an outsider's perspective."

"Can I say I'll think about it and let you know?"

"Absolutely."

"If I agree, I'll be working with Abby. You need a submissive's input, too."

"Of course."

Abby and I were still working through the details of our newly extended playtime. Working with the Delaware group might be mutually beneficial. I thought back to a conversation Abby and I had had recently, during which she'd admitted how much she'd enjoyed the demo we did in Delaware. Since then, I'd been looking for ways to push her. This might be just what we both needed.

A way to expand all our limits.

Read on for a sneak peek
at the next seductive book in Tara Sue Me's
Submissive Series

THE Exhibitionist

Coming soon from Headline Eternal.

The smell of lust filled the room. In fact, the sexual tension was so high, I would bet most of the women present longed to be in the place of the lovely redhead. Currently standing in front of Cole Johnson, the Partners in Play group's newest senior Dominant, the petite woman trembled slightly. Although she was fully clothed, she displayed a vulnerability I was all too familiar with.

"Daniel told me she's been having difficulties focusing," my husband and Dominant, Nathaniel, said. We were at a play party being held at a private residence. He stood behind me, and though we were somewhat removed from the group, he still whispered. "He said he hopes the session with Cole will help."

"With everyone watching?" I asked. "That seems unlikely."

"I guess we'll see."

We couldn't hear Cole's voice, he spoke too softly. The submissive's gaze drifted from him to the crowd watching. Bad move.

Quick as a lightning strike, Cole grabbed her chin and forced her to meet his eyes.

"On me," he said, the threat in his voice noticeable before it dropped back down to a whisper.

"Perhaps he believes if she can focus while in the middle of a crowd, she can focus during anything," Nathaniel said.

There was probably some truth to that. The submissive certainly didn't appear to be tempted to look our way again. Then again, Cole had placed his hands on her shoulders and started a slow stroke up and down her arms. All the while, he kept his eyes locked on hers. I doubted there were many women who would be able to think about anything else if he was looking at them like that.

After a few minutes, he stepped back and spoke to her again. "As far as you're concerned, you and I are the only people in this room. Understand?"

She answered with a softly spoken, "Yes, Sir."

"Louder," he said. "Own your words."

"Yes, Sir," she repeated, this time with more confidence.

"You are to keep your eyes on mine the entire time we're together unless I tell you to do otherwise."

"Yes, Sir."

"What's your safe word?" Cole asked.

"Red, Sir."

"Thank you. Take your shirt off."

Her gaze briefly flickered to the floor.

"That's one, sub," Cole said, and she sucked in a breath. "Tell me what you did."

"I looked at the floor, Sir."

"And what were you supposed to do?"

"Keep my eyes on yours."

Cole nodded. "Take your shirt off the proper way."

This time, she kept her focus on him while she unbuttoned and slid the shirt off her shoulders. It fluttered to the ground.

"Very nice," Cole said. "Now, remove your bra."

I wasn't a Dominant by any stretch, but I'd been an active submissive for long enough to know and recognize hesitation. Hell, I'd done it often enough myself, but I always learned something new when I was an observer. It was certainly interesting seeing things from a different prospective.

Cole took a step toward her. "On the checklist you filled out, how do you have *public nudity* listed?"

"As *won't object*, Sir."

"And how else am I to interpret your hesitation as anything other than objecting?"

"I don't know, Sir."

"That's because there is no other way. That's two. Now, remove the bra."

She quickly reached behind her back to unsnap her bra, but my own focus was suddenly shifted to my husband's two hands, which were unbuttoning my shirt.

His voice was rough in my ear while his fingers stroked my breasts. "You like watching, don't you?"

"Especially with you teasing me like that with your hands, Master."

"You like teasing?" he asked.

I realized what I'd said and how he'd probably interpret my words. "Uh, well . . ."

He chuckled. "Too late. I'm going to thoroughly enjoy teasing you tonight, but for right now, watch Master Johnson."

In front of us, Cole had bound his submissive for the night with her arms above her head. Two identical floggers sat on top of a bag off to the side of where they were standing. Florentine flogging, I assumed he'd be demonstrating with those.

Cole went right into the scene with both floggers, warming up the submissive with light and easy strokes. Interesting. Whenever Nathaniel used two floggers, he'd start by warming me up with a single one first. But the technique appeared to be working. The submissive's expression transformed into a look of complete bliss, and by the time Cole started putting more power behind his swing, she was in subspace.

I was transfixed by the sight of them. It appeared almost like a choreographed dance, the way his arms moved in time with her side-to-side sway.

"Very nice," Cole told her. "I'm going to bring you down. No climax for you tonight since you didn't follow directions at the beginning of the scene."

She started to protest, but he cut her off. "Unless you want me to demo how to properly discipline with two floggers, you'll keep that comment to yourself."

She wisely didn't say anything else, and Cole's movements grew slower and slower.

I jumped when Nathaniel slipped a hand down my skirt.

"Someone liked watching," he said.

I pressed back against him and wiggled my butt across his erection. "Yes, Master."

"I'm going to flog that wiggly ass. Let's go to the garage."

The garage was set aside for public play and filled with all sorts of fun toys. Plus there were always people observing the play scenes. It would be our first time being in the garage, and I smiled at the thought of finally being a participant.

I walked in front of him, nodding and smiling at the people we passed on our way. The party had been going on for about an hour and a half, so the house was filled to capacity. I feared the garage would be too crowded and have no room to play, but I was happy to see there was a free whipping post in a far corner.

I looked to Nathaniel for instructions, and he nodded toward the free area. "On your knees in front of the post."

I crossed the floor and knelt down while I waited. I closed my eyes to focus myself on serving him. I thoroughly enjoyed playing in front of others, but I never wanted my focus to drift from where it was supposed to be.

"So you like it when I tease you?" he asked.

"Most of the time, Master."

"Whereas I, on the other hand, always enjoy teasing you." He took a few steps and stood behind me. "And I love to hear you beg. So tonight, I'm going to start a scene, and we're going to finish it at home. How does that sound?"

"Like a long ride home, Master."

He laughed. "And if you don't want it to be an even longer night, you'll behave."

"Yes, Master."

"Stand up and face the post."

I rose to my feet and turned to the post, imagining how I looked to the crowd as I did and positioning myself to please Nathaniel.

He ran his hands up my back and situated my arms so they were above my head. "You would enjoy this better if you were naked, wouldn't you?" he asked.

"Most things involving you are better if I'm naked, Master."

He gave my ass a slap. "Someone feels a little sassy tonight, doesn't she?"

"Maybe just a little," I wiggled my butt, hoping he'd spank it again.

But he didn't, instead he moved my hands to two grips on on the post. "Don't let go and no speaking unless I ask a question."

He hadn't brought his toy bag with him, so I couldn't imagine what he was going to do.

"I'm going to lift your skirt," he said. "Are you wearing anything under it?"

He was the one who had picked out my outfit before we left. He knew the only thing under the skirt was me.

"No, Master."

"Everyone's going to see your ass. The only thing better would be if everyone saw me spank you."

I tried not to think about how much that thought turned me on. He said he was going to tease me, which probably meant he wasn't going to let me climax at the party.

He drew my skirt above my waist, and I expected him to continue his upward trail, but instead his fingers slipped behind me and he pinched my butt. I bit the inside of my cheek to keep from making a noise.

"You're being so good," he said, keeping one hand on my ass and shifting the other to stroke my breast.

I relaxed against the post, enjoying the feel of his hands on me, the experience made more erotic by the accompanying sound track of sighs, whimpers, and moans from other couples in the garage. Nathaniel's hands finally made their way between my legs, and I held my breath, anticipating his touch right where I needed it and reminding myself that no matter how good it felt, I could not make a noise.

"I'm going to finger-fuck you." Nathaniel's warm breath kissed my ear. "You can't make a noise, and you can't come. Do either of the two, and I won't let you come for two weeks."

I wasn't about to let that happen. I took a deep breath and started reciting German in my head, my tried-and-true way of delaying orgasm.

"Are you doing your German, Abigail?" he said, moving his fingers lightly over my clit and making me rise up on my toes. "Are you?"

"Yes, Master."

"Do you think the German alphabet is going to keep your mind off the fact that I have my fingers inside you?"

"No, Master. Not entirely. Just enough. . . ." I arched against him as his fingers found that spot inside me that felt so good. "Just enough to help me . . . be good."

"There's a man in the far corner. He's in the shadows, so I can't make out who he is. He's watching us."

I sucked in a breath and almost let out a moan before I remembered I couldn't make a sound. *Fuck.* When I knew I was being watched, my skin broke out in delicious shivers, and I became a puddle at Nathaniel's feet.

"I know you like that. I know it gets you off." His fingers moved faster. Deeper. "Too bad he won't be able to watch you come."

He stroked over and over, and my release built within me. I started conjugating German verbs. Translated the preamble to the Constitution into German. Anything. Just when I thought my body was going to fall apart all over him, he slowed his movements.

He slipped his fingers out and straightened my skirt. "Are you okay?"

"Yes, Master."

"You can let go of the straps and stand up."

I straightened and turned. He watched me with his intense green gaze.

"You did very well, Abigail," he said, and I felt my heart flutter at his praise. "I'm going to have to think of a suitable reward."

He dropped his head and gave me a soft kiss, but his lips didn't linger. Pulling back, he brought his finger to my mouth. Without being told, I sucked it inside and licked, tasting myself and cleaning him.

When I finished, he kissed me again. "Very nice, Abigail."

I sighed and Nathaniel tightened his arms around me. The pounding need to have him inside me was still there. Yet it was tempered by the knowledge that he would reward me once we were home. Or, more to the point, when we were back at the hotel we were staying in for the weekend.

A few months ago when we had been in Wilmington, Delaware, for a conference that Nathaniel was speaking at, we fell in love with the area and the people. According to him, the tax rate was wonderful, so we decided to buy a place. Initially, we'd looked at the coast, but we soon discovered that most of our time was spent in Wilmington, and it only made sense to buy there.

I loved our new house. It was from early in the last century and filled with character. But more than that, it would be the first place we'd live in as a family that Nathaniel and I had bought together. He'd inherited our Hamptons estate from his parents, and our New York City penthouse he'd bought when he was still a bachelor. I owned a chalet in Switzerland, which he had given me as a wedding present, but we only ever visited there. I was excited to have a space that was "ours."

Wilmington, Delaware, was also where the Partners in Play BDSM group was. One of the group's core Doms, Jeff Parks, had rescued me one night from a raunchy nightclub I'd made the mistake of going to with a friend and without Nathaniel. Another Dom, Daniel Covington, was a colleague of Nathaniel's. That was how we'd met the group. In the last few months, I'd become friends with both of their submissives. Dena was now engaged to Jeff, and Julie had moved in with Daniel a few months ago.

A phone call from Jeff a week ago had led to our visit tonight. Jeff wanted Nathaniel to attend because there had been trouble within the group lately. Namely with two relatively new Doms.

Nathaniel took my hand, and we left our little corner of the garage. I was tempted to look around and try to locate the man who had been observing us. Without much thought, I decided not to. Sometimes, the fantasy was better than the real thing.

Nathaniel squeezed my hand. "Would you like something to drink?"

"Yes, Master." And sometimes reality was better than fantasy.

Nathaniel and I made our way into the kitchen, where we greeted a few people. He took a bottle of water from a cooler, and we walked into the living room.

He nodded to the floor, and I sat at his feet while he sat on the couch. We were experimenting with different levels of protocol to see what we liked and what worked for us. Sitting at his feet was something we'd been trying lately, and I was surprised to discover I liked it. In that position, I felt protected and secure.

He opened the bottle and pressed it to my lips.

"Thank you, Master," I said when I'd had my fill.

The door to the room's left opened, and Cole and the red-headed submissive stepped out. He spoke to her softly and stroked her cheek. She left him with a smile on her face and a spring in her step.

Cole was still somewhat of an enigma to me. According to Dena, he'd broken up with his long-term girlfriend several months earlier. He usually traveled for his work, and I gathered the breakup was his reason for coming back to Delaware. He was a journalist and a good one; I'd read some of his articles. I wrote for a national news blog, and since he was a writer, I was interested in getting to know him better.

Cole spotted us and headed our way.

"Master West," he said, shaking Nathaniel's hand.

"Master Johnson."

Cole inclined his head in my direction. "I haven't been formally introduced to your Abby yet."

I wasn't allowed to interact with Doms at a party unless Nathaniel gave me permission, so I remained where I was.

"We must correct that." Nathaniel smiled at me. "Come meet Master Johnson, Abigail."

I moved to my feet and waited to be introduced.

"Master Johnson, this is my Abby." Nathaniel lifted my hand and kissed my knuckles. "She is my everything."

I didn't miss the subtle lift of Cole's eyebrows or Nathaniel's slight nod. Granted permission to touch me, Cole held out his hand.

"Very nice to meet you finally, Abby."

I shook his hand. "The feeling is mutual, Sir."

"I understand you're a writer," he said.

"I just write a blog for WNN, Sir," I said, slightly taken aback that he knew anything about me. It wasn't a secret, of course. It was just that he was a *writer writer*.

"You express yourself through written words. You're a writer."

"And a damn good one," Nathaniel added.

The corner of Cole's mouth lifted in what could only be called a devilish grin. "I know. I've read her blog."

"You have?" I nearly squeaked and then remembered where I was and composed myself. "I mean, you have, Sir?"

He chuckled. "Yes."

I wanted to return the praise. "I'm really enjoying the series of articles you're writing based on your time in India, Sir."

All traces of joviality left his expression and darkness covered his face. I wasn't sure what I had said to upset him, but now I wished I hadn't spoken at all.

"It was a very *unique* experience," he finally said.

"It's a very unique county," I said.

"Yes. There are parts that are breathtakingly beautiful, and I met some incredible people. But I think—" He looked pained. "I think I won't be going back."

I was momentarily stunned since his articles seemed filled with a real love for India, but fortunately I was saved from any long, awkward silences by the appearance of Jeff and Dena.

"There you guys are," Dena said. She was holding hands with Jeff, and they both looked so happy, I couldn't help but smile along with them. I spared a quick look back at Cole, but whatever had upset him was forgotten. The devilish grin had returned.

"What's going on?" Cole asked.

Dena spotted Daniel and Julie in the hallway and waved them over.

"What's happening?" Daniel asked.

"I'm wondering the same thing," Cole said.

Dena looked so excited, I wouldn't have been surprised if she'd started bouncing up and down. "We set a date!" she finally said.

"A date for what?" Cole asked, and Dena's smile temporarily deflated. Nathaniel thumped him on the shoulder. "Just teasing, you guys. Congratulations!"

"I love weddings," I said. "Tell us when it is."

Jeff replied with a date less than two months away.

Dena held up her hands as we all started speaking at once. "I know it's short notice, but it'll be small. We thought about just having the Justice of the Peace do it, but since our collaring ceremony was private, we thought better of it."

Jeff slipped his arm around Dena and kissed her forehead. "I was the one pushing for a private ceremony."

"Thank goodness she didn't go for your idea," Daniel said. "I've been waiting on this day."

"But if she had," Jeff said, "we'd be married already."

"There is that," Daniel said.

Dena had stayed with us at our Hamptons estate recently. Jeff had been out of town, caring for his terminally ill father, and because she'd been getting threats from a stalker, we'd offered for her to stay with us. She was a prosecutor, and her father was a prominent politician, and no one was sure who was threatening her. That was all in the past now, but Dena and I had become good friends during the weeks she'd stayed with us, and I knew exactly how happy she was to be marrying Jeff.

I didn't know Jeff quite as well, but I'd actually met him first, and one of the things I'd picked up on was an underlying sadness about him. There was no sadness now. Only joy and, as he gazed down at the woman who wore both his collar and his engagement ring, love.

It made me a bit nostalgic for the early days of my relationship with Nathaniel, when everything was so new and we couldn't keep our hands off each other. Of course, we still didn't want to, but it was harder to find time to ourselves. I hoped the move to Delaware would mean more time at home for him and allow us to reconnect.

"Angel," Jeff said, "didn't you want to talk to Abby and Julie privately?"

"Yes, as long as it's okay with Masters West and Covington."

"Of course," Daniel said, dropping a kiss on Julie's cheek. "Don't stay away too long. I have a new toy."

The brunette's eyes lit up. "Yes, Master."

"I don't have a new toy," Nathaniel whispered in my ear. "I just want to fuck you."

My knees almost turned to jelly. "Yes, Master."

"Hurry back to me," he said.

I would. I definitely would.

Also available from
New York Times bestselling author

TARA SUE ME

TARA SUE ME

THE
SUBMISSIVE

THE WORLDWIDE PHENOMENON
Before there was **Fifty Shades of Grey**...

Abby King yearns to experience a world of pleasure
beyond her simple life as a librarian—and the brilliant and
handsome CEO Nathaniel West is the key to making her
dark desires a reality. But as Abby falls deep into
Nathaniel's tantalizing world of power and passion, she
fears his heart may be beyond her reach—and that her
own might be beyond saving...

headline
ETERNAL

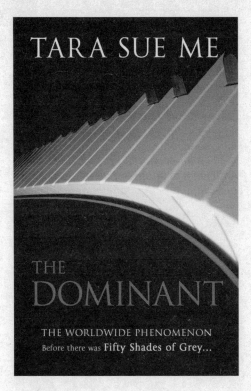

TARA SUE ME

THE
DOMINANT

THE WORLDWIDE PHENOMENON
Before there was **Fifty Shades of Grey**...

Nathaniel West doesn't lose control. But then he meets
Abby King. Her innocence and willingness is intoxicating,
and he's determined to make Abby his. But when
Nathaniel begins falling for Abby on a deeper level, he
realizes that trust must go both ways—and he has secrets
which could bring the foundations of their relationship
crashing down...

headline
ETERNAL

TARA SUE ME

THE
TRAINING

THE WORLDWIDE PHENOMENON
Before there was **Fifty Shades of Grey**...

It started with desire. Now a weekend arrangement
of pleasure has become a passionate romance.
Still, there remains a wall between Nathaniel West and
Abby King. Abby knows the only way to lead Nathaniel
on a path to greater intimacy is to let him deeper into
her world than anyone has ever gone before...

headline
ETERNAL

TARA SUE ME
The Chalet

From the *New York Times* bestseller
A SUBMISSIVE NOVELLA

Submitting her body was only the beginning.
Abby King didn't know true passion until she gave herself to
Nathaniel West, one of New York City's most eligible
bachelors and desired Dominants. Now, on the eve of her
marriage, she realizes all her dreams are coming true.
And with a romantic honeymoon getaway planned at a
secluded Swiss chalet, she's sure Nathaniel will find
even more fantasies to fulfill...

headline
ETERNAL

Abby West has everything she wanted: a family,
a skyrocketing new career, and a sexy, Dominant husband
who fulfills her every need. Only, as her life outside the
bedroom becomes hectic, her Master's sexual requirements
inside become more extreme. As the underlying tension
and desire between them heats up, so does the struggle
to keep everything they value from falling apart...

headline
ETERNAL

TARA SUE ME

FROM THE
NEW YORK TIMES
BESTSELLING AUTHOR
OF THE SUBMISSIVE
TRILOGY

SEDUCED
BY FIRE

Julie Masterson craves a taste of danger. And once she meets the seductive Senior VP of Weston Bank Daniel Covington, she's drawn into a titillating new world of passion. As their sizzling connection heats up, the dangerous side of their liaison rears its ugly head, and Julie must decide if she trusts Daniel enough to surrender completely—or if she should escape before she gets burned...

headline
ETERNAL

headline
ETERNAL

FIND YOUR HEART'S DESIRE...

VISIT OUR WEBSITE: www.headlineeternal.com

FIND US ON FACEBOOK: facebook.com/eternalromance

FOLLOW US ON TWITTER: @eternal_books

EMAIL US: eternalromance@headline.co.uk